ZARA

ZARA

Meredith Steinbach

TRIQUARTERLY BOOKS
NORTHWESTERN UNIVERSITY PRESS

Evanston, Illinois

TriQuarterly Books
Northwestern University Press
Evanston, Illinois 60208-4210

Printed in the United States of America

ISBN 0-8101-5059-X

Library of Congress Cataloging-in-Publication Data

Steinbach, Meredith.
    Zara / Meredith Steinbach. — TriQuarterly
Books/Northwestern University Press ed.
      p. cm.
    ISBN 0-8101-5059-X (alk. paper)
    1. Women physicians—Iowa—Fiction. I. Title.
PS3569.T37546Z3 1996
813'.54—dc20   96-30635
                                      CIP

For Joy

Grateful acknowledgment is made to the following publications in which portions of this novel first appeared, in slightly different form: *Antaeus, Cutbank, Ploughshares, The Pushcart Prize, II: Best of the Small Presses,* and *TriQuarterly.*

I wish to thank the publishers for permission to quote brief passages from the following books: *Human Reproduction, The Core and Content of Obstetrics, Gynecology and Perinatal Medicine,* Ernest W. Page (W.B. Saunders Company); *Cunningham's Manual of Practical Anatomy,* edited by James Cooper Brash (Oxford University Press); and *Life Saving and Water Safety,* The American Red Cross (Doubleday & Company, Inc.).

I would also like to thank The National Endowment for the Arts for its generous assistance during the preparation of this work.

M.S.

ZARA

Zara took the little car, the German one, and drove the long road back to her, round and round the Iowa country roads, the gravel spinning beneath her tires. The land fell softly up and down in little mounds that they called hills. She closed the door. The wind rustled low through the grasses, whining around their roots. She heard it hum like moths behind a summer curtain. She felt it brush against her ankles, tickling at the divide of skin and new black shoe. The pasture lay fifty feet from the family plot, and in the distance she could see the horses running: their flanks would have shone if there had been more sun today.

Once, the horses had startled at the sound of an auto winding its way slowly, belatedly toward her, as the Reverend Grey droned on under the canopy. The minister glanced up past the dark scarf floating beside him: the car was stalling. He began the prayer. The hood was thrown open. Steam rose, and the driver ran across to the fountain where today the daughter would take the same dark green watering can. Long flames rose from the engine as the man, sloshing water from the can, bounded between the tombs at the graveyard's edge. He poured water on the engine. From under the funeral tent, Zara Montgomery watched him drown the engine block; she heard it crack. A smile flickered across the minister's lips.

The sod had been cut that morning, the blade lifted, turned at right angles, the grass rolled like a carpet, replaced over the casket. When even Forster Montgomery had gone home again, when the mourners had fallen asleep, tossing throughout the house in the dark vapors of whiskey, the rain fell like fingers against the window panes. Zara drove out again to her mother's grave. She ran her hands around the edges beyond the slick grassy leaves, beyond'the roots thick like sponge.

Zara could not remember when her mother's outward healing had given way to a deeper wound. Kathryn lay bundled in the blue blanket, almost supine in her chair, listening as her daughter pushed. Wooden wheels pressed against modern earth. Branches clicked against their spokes as Zara wheeled her mother through the dawn to the favorite spot overlooking the cliff, the water, where Kathryn could see, remotely, Chautauqua Park down the beach where she used to sing, where the crowds used to shout and wave their handkerchiefs high over their heads to hear her again. The days had grown shorter; the leaves fell. The weather was crisp, and life was full as the sun rose, struck them obliquely, shifting low through the shrubs and growing rose-colored across the lightly capping sky.

Zara stayed with her one semester and then another, tending to her, carrying her about as her mother grew smaller, lighter, as if she were evaporating on their brief travels from room to room. And as they walked, Zara would press her belly to her mother, and Kathryn would wrap herself around it, coiled, as if a fetus wound about some revelation in the womb.

It was then that Zara thought perhaps this was not her

mother dying here, but that she herself was dying wrapped up in her arms. The little bundle, the babe, the mother-child. "Little one, little one," Zara sang and tucked her mother in and washed her skin and kissed her gently on the ears.

"Once," her mother said, "once we took the train. All night it was bugs and rain and soot. And the conductor crying, 'Feet out of the aisles, feet out of the aisles.' All the way from Oakland with our legs cramped from riding upright. And how we hurried," she said. "We hurried to get to our tent, we hurried to finish our songs, we hurried to catch the next train out. We hurried even when we slept. And, of course, we never did sleep. Not really. We were too tired. Hopping from train to motorcar to train, and when we did get a bed we didn't want it. Bugs again. It's funny," she said. "Traveling all that way for a whoop or two. But we were doing something; the Chautauqua was," Kathryn said. "Don't be a crusader, Zara. If you have to have a cause, make it be yourself."

"But, Mother," Zara said. "Wasn't the Chautauqua route your crusade?"

"I thought my work was important," her mother said. "But maybe I was wrong. It was important to me."

The feathers were piled on the chopping table. Beside the pheasant heads, black eyes lay like polished stones.

"Have you washed your hands?" Mrs. McGehry asked the child. Zara turned her palms for the inspection. At the table, the woman reached into the flesh at the neck of a bird and with one motion pulled the entire skin away, the down intact. She handed Zara the knife. "Now bend the leg back and cut through the joint." She took the girl's hands into her own, guiding the blade into the niche, and the child felt a little pride in being asked to help with this task. Zara cut the other leg herself, hearing Mrs. McGehry say, "Someday you'll be a fine lady. Someday you'll have to know these things." And Zara thought, Mummie is a fine lady, and she doesn't know. Why is that?

Mrs. McGehry poked absently at the whole pellets of corn in the green innards. "This is a fat one," Bridie said. "This one was still preparing to be served up with the sauce."

Mrs. McGehry measured out the milk for the afternoon scones. She poured it into a pool in the center of the flour. Zara's great grandfather had been an apothecary pouring syrups into bottles; Zara had heard her mother speak of this. Zara took the broom with the handle Mrs. McGehry had shortened specially for her. She heard the wooden spoon beating against the great blue bowl. She made the dust fly out the crevices on the back porch. Soon her mother would be galloping the mare over the far hill, soon she would fly up the road under the trees and walk the mare into the stable.

"Your mum will be wanting to hear your piano," Mrs. McGehry called from the kitchen. "Have you practiced?"

"Yesterday, a long time."

"You mean, a little. You'd better make tracks, girl."

In the living room, Zara put the large dictionary on the bench. On the west coast of Ireland, Mrs. McGehry said, if you were a bad sinner, they put you in a wee little boat without oars and set you out to sea to fend for yourself. Zara wondered how bad you would have to be to deserve such a very mean fate.

Kathryn Montgomery wanted to say many things to her daughter asleep behind her on the bed. Selfish words, some of them. Sentimental phrases, too. She would have asked Zara to take her from this room, to carry her as she used to do. Impossible tasks now. There were other things. Zara slept lightly and all Kathryn needed to say was: Zara, I have a pain and I can't sleep. Zara would have opened her blue eyes, blue like her father's, blue as Kathryn Montgomery's were. She would have said, Foxglove, do you want me to rub your back?

Pink flower lotion on skin over bones, stretched very tight. Lotion and fingers to relieve the roaring in her ribs. Instead, Kathryn's pencil moved under the light at her bedside table, slating words in her crossword puzzle book, confining them in small tight squares.

She could not turn from her side by herself nor with help from anyone. Her world was divided into quadrants. Fore and aft, port and starboard. At the edge of her puzzle she wrote with a felt-tipped pen: I am stamped on my sheets like a label. She crossed it out again.

The culprit was the hip. The Hog. Or so she called the tumor rising there. She would have tattooed it with a fine fat swine if that too had not involved the pain. She drew fat features on the sheenless cover of the magazine. A pugnacious snout, the tips of teeth. She gave him legs with which to run. Cloven hooves throughout her body. A word for metastasis: stampede. *Then went the devils out of the man, and entered into the swine: and the herd ran violently down a steep place into the lake, and were choked.*

Kathryn adjusted the lamp. The slender beam picked out the ruffle of white at latticed window, a sailing ship of darkened blue on darker blue and papered wall, the red-black of roses drooping in her milk glass vase. She shined the light behind her toward the ceiling, fixing the table mirror on its painted stand. She tilted it until her daughter's face rose sleeping in the mirror's frame. Zara. Auburn hair tumbling around your oval face. A word for help, six letters: hold me. She put the book aside. Arms.

Doctor Montgomery had gone to the office, and Zara was asleep in the bassinet upstairs when Katie came down in her nightgown. Her little breasts were full.

"I need something to wear," Kathryn said.

"There it is—" Mrs. McGehry pointed to the fresh clothes she had just ironed, crisp as new lettuce from the garden.

Kathryn took off her gown and put on the first dress. "This isn't right," she said. "There's a crease in the collar."

"Where's a crease?" Bridie asked her. Kathryn showed her the faintest of lines. "That wrinkle's been ironed out, Katie."

"I can see it. I can't wear that dress."

"It's on the back," Bridie said.

Kathryn took it off and put on the next one, looking at herself in the mirror. "This one makes me look so bloated."

"Katie," Bridie said, setting the iron up on its end. "You could use a little bloating. Water, fat, take what you can get. You're scrawny as a mosquito."

"Fat," she said.

"Put on the blue one. You always look nice in the blue."

She pulled it on after Mrs. McGehry had watched her rumpling the green cotton in a chair, her face puckered in the mirror.

"You look lovely. Comb your hair, you'll feel better."

"I can't find my comb."

"For goodness sakes, Katie. What's the matter?"

"I can't find anything to wear in this house. Not one thing I look decent in. I look like a hag in everything I own." She threw the blue in the chair. Mrs. McGehry could see it wrinkling without even laying her eyes on it.

"Here, Katie, I'll iron up the flowered one. It's the most beautiful dress you own." Bridie McGehry knew this. Katie could have rivaled anyone in that dress. The purple setting off her eyes like the Persian turquoise she wore at her neck and dangled from her ears. On top of those dresses, she sat down, naked and waiting, fussing with her hair, braiding it up and letting it down. Combing out the waves and then saying it never curled.

Bridie McGehry was careful not to scorch or crease it, even on the interfacing or seams. She said, "There. You couldn't have wanted it better from the Chinese laundry." She watched Kathryn Montgomery pulling it over her head, the folds falling over her shoulders, then drifting onto her breasts and belly.

"Now I've caught my hair. Now I caught my hair on a button."

Mrs. McGehry set her own small hands to unwinding the dark strands from the button. "My Lord, Katie. You are having a bad day."

"What makes this day so different?" Kathryn asked from under the cloth. "Every single day is unbearable for me."

"Why, Katie, the Lord should reach down and slap your face. You have a wonderful husband, a brand new baby, a big house. You don't even have to do your own cooking. You can do whatever you want." Mrs. McGehry zipped her up the side. "Now don't tell me you don't look good in this one. Don't try to tell me that nonsense."

"You don't know what giving up your work means."

"Go down town, Katie. See a movie."

"With whom? Who would go anywhere in this town with me except for Forster? Everyone hates me. They hate me because I sing, because I'm different."

"No one hates you, Katie."

"Then why am I alone every day? Every day I am alone and no one asks for me."

"People ask for you all the time. I go down town and

everyone asks how you are and how's the baby. Mabel Willoughby inquires after you every day when I see her."

"Mabel Willoughby!" she screamed. "Do you think Mabel Willoughby and I have anything in common? Do you think she wants anything more than gossip?" Then Kathryn Montgomery ripped her dress right down the front. The little pearl buttons she had chosen so carefully scattered all over the rug. She kicked the silk dress under the ironing board and ran upstairs. Bridie McGehry shook her head. She runs naked, she thought, right in front of the living-room window, where anyone driving by can see her. Mrs. McGehry heard her sobbing for over an hour.

When Kathryn came down, she put on the first dress, the brown one, leaving the front open. She went upstairs and got the baby. She nursed her on the window seat where the sun fell pink through the stained-glass window spreading like leaves across her hands.

Kathryn had not slept for days now. Her mind made distortions of body parts the cancer hadn't yet affected. Each night she witnessed the loss of every hair, the slow bending of her bones. The week before, she thought her face another victim. "The Hog has gotten loose," she blurted, breaking into tears.

"What's that?" Zara asked, looking up from the book she was reading aloud to her.

"The Hog has done this, too."

"What do you mean?"

"It's my face."

Zara held the mirror for her mother at angle after angle. She held up old photographs: from under the flap of the great canvas tent, her mother stepped squinting into a silver sun. Zara took her mother's makeup from the drawer. She drew with the lipstick around the crest where her mother's lips rose in two soft curves; she filled in the center with the crimson flat of the tube. "Now, be objective, Foxglove."

"I can't," she said. "I don't know how."

"How do you like music camp?" Kathryn asked, taking off her shoes and setting them side by side next to the door. Belted at the waist, her skirt flared below the knees. Seams ran straight down slender legs. "Is it what you expected?" She watched her daughter folding underwear, arranging neat stacks inside the drawer.

"I like it all right," Zara said. The others were swimming now. Michael and her friends were in the pool.

"Only all right? I thought you wanted to come here this summer. I'd hoped you would be enthusiastic, Zara."

"I met a boy," she said, although she had met him before.

"A boy?" Kathryn looked out the window then. "But what about the music?" she asked, waiting for Zara to model the dress she had chosen for the evening concert.

Zara shrugged. The music. She remembered the metronome clicking, her fingers memorizing first scales. "I can hear you humming," her mother said. "Do you want me to hear you?" By the time she was eight, Zara had the mechanics. "Play with feeling," her mother said. Feeling, the child thought. Two hours on the hardwood bench each day and she could not know feeling, only her fingers growing stronger, more articulate.

Kathryn watched her daughter removing the long dress from the closet. "What about the music, Zara?"

"The music is fine," she said. "Everyone plays well."

"And you?"

"I do all right."

"Could you do better?"

"I do fine, Mother."

"You don't need to snap at me. I only asked if you could do better. We could all improve. I wonder if you realize that."

"I practice, I get better."

"I only wondered, Zara."

"You only wondered if I would embarrass you, if I was as good as everyone else."

"Of course you're as good as everyone else. I never doubted you, Zara."

You have always doubted me, Zara thought. She took off her jeans, untied the white, men's shirt where the tails had been knotted at her middle. "I have to shower now," she said, putting on her robe.

So it is Michael O'Dea, Kathryn thought, sitting in the fourth row of wooden chairs. She watched the boy's eyes meeting her daughter's in quick glances as if their bodies were touching. The camp director pointed at individuals with his wand. The orchestra tuned. The notes falling like the random knots in the pine behind the white dresses and shirts, the grand piano and violins, the black claw-footed music stands in what had once been a stable.

One day Kathryn's father had come home early from the bank and ordered the stable boys to bring the mare from the pasture. Kathryn Sheridan sat on top of the fence and watched them put the collar around her horse's neck, straightening the leather straps down its sides, shackling the mare's hind legs so it could not struggle.

She could remember her father laying his tweed coat beside her, rolling his sleeves as he walked. The young boys hanging on, each to a rope. They planted their feet firmly in the grasses, as if they, not the mare, were tethered, waiting to receive the stallion: the black shadow moving against the earth as her father led it through the gate toward them.

"Give us a good one," he said, as the stallion scented the mare and rose up, his hooves glinting like shells in the sun as the mare tried to kick free. The stable boys leaning like the pickets of a fence in strong wind, their heels dragging. The hobbles creaked as the mare shifted. The stallion on top. The mare shaking off attempt after attempt, until "Hell," her father said and took the great pike of the horse in both hands and guided it in. Her father was flushed when he came for his jacket. He was silent.

Zara waited, hands lifted, fingertips on keys while the bow rubbed gently across the strings of Michael's violin. It wouldn't matter who he was. It made no difference how he helped her, or how she needed someone. Kathryn watched, listened to them tuning as the others did, but a crease cut between her eyebrows and ran onto her forehead. Every night when they were young, before Zara's birth, Doctor Montgomery pedaled his bicycle up and down the rutted lane that made a circle in front of the house. Round and round he rode the rusted machine while Kathryn leaned out the upstairs window, the white curtain waving at her side. "Give Monty a little ride, Forster," Kathryn called as the dog yapped along behind him nearly catching its head between the spokes. The housekeeper drew her hands to her hips, crying from the front lawn: "That dog is going to bust his head off. Sever it off right above the collar if you don't watch out."

Doctor Montgomery wrinkled the corners of his eyes and cocked his head to the side. "Now, Bridie," he said. He always said "Now, Bridie." Kathryn Montgomery remembered that. Then he reared up on one wheel and pedaled off, his coat tails whipping under the trees.

Forster stood a medium height then with light brown hair and beard, and his forehead was advancing on his hairline even then. This scarcity of hair had attracted Kathryn to him, that and the erratic way the young man whirled into sudden motion. Doctor Montgomery liked to say he had saved her from a life of meandering with the Chautauqua from rooming house to small-town hotel. "I took her off the railway," he'd say with his arm around her, "and what a struggle I had with that conductor." Then Kathryn would smile up at him and press her fingers gently at his side, thinking behind the azure pleasure of her eyes not of her husband but of the crowds and the sound of her own voice rising in the farewell songs from the railroad platform. She would look a little sad then and he would take it for the melancholic effects of love. "Would you like a little brandy, darling?" he would ask her. "You look tired this evening." At this she would shake her head and smile at her guests, thinking how pleasant it was to have a husband who was concerned and gentle and protective.

Red streaks crept into Kathryn's eyes. "My leg is ruined. And my arm. Now the Hog has started on my nose."

Zara looked at the photograph. "Turn your head," she said. "You're wrong, Foxie."

"It's shrinking. It's twisted out of shape just like my leg. A dreadful chicken leg. And now my face, Zara. Look at it."

Zara took the picture to the window and examined it. She watched her mother a long while. Combing Kathryn's hair, she fluffed it forward, giving it the effect of its former fullness. She stood back and looked again. "All right, Foxie," she said. "It's changed."

Kathryn covered her face with the motionless fingers of the hand she called the Right One Gone Wrong.

"Yes," her daughter said. "It's longer."

Kathryn pulled the mirror toward herself. "Longer?"

"Yes. I think it's gotten rather long now."

Kathryn turned the mirror to its magnifying side and back; she held the tip of her nose down and let it up again. She studied the portrait. Her face went suddenly red with anger. "Zara Montgomery, my nose is not at all longer than it was. You lied to me. You lied and it was horrible. A horrible thing to do to me."

Zara shrugged, tapping her mother gently on the forehead. "How else was I to get you to believe me? Your nose is *not* shorter, Mother." She kissed her on the ear then and went to retrieve the book.

Kathryn fingered the edge of the mirror. "But, Zara—"

"Foxie. There are two things I'm positive have not been affected."

"What?"

"They're your appetite and your nose."

"Oh," her mother said, knowing that, for some reason, even when she would be throwing it all up again, she was, as always, continually hungry.

On the trunk of the automobile, Zara leaned against the warm back window as she watched them pitching the softball back and forth. She could almost see the indentations their fingers made, the crest of their fingernails gone white as they wound up for the pitch. Burnout. That's the way they played it. Too hard for her, they said. Why then did they use the softball? she had asked; and they had not wanted to say that their older brother had taken the baseball and told them to move their game elsewhere.

It was the glove she liked, the leather of it around her hand. Her father's worn catcher's mitt with a bit too little padding in the palm. Yes, you could feel the sting of a real ball through that, but you would have to wait until one boy tired and the other wanted to go on with the game. Until they resorted to you as a partner. Today she was not waiting for them to summon her. It was her father for whom she was waiting. He would come out of the house soon now, carrying his black leather case, his anger transformed into hurry. Zara rolled the cuffs of her dungarees. What did it matter what caused it? They were shouting and the anxiety had filled the house and threatened to blow the top off. She had seen her mother recoil at her father's touch. She'd seen her make a joke of it. "Unhand me, you cad," Kathryn Montgomery said, an edge in her laughter, a chill across the shoulders. She watched her father's face, saw the quick motion of his throat.

Zara put her hand on the doorknob. "Dad, can I go on the house call?"

"Yes," he said, without turning away from his wife.

"I'll wait outside."

"Yes, do that."

The ball flew back and forth smacking against palms. "Yes, Kathryn. I know, Kathryn." The front door slammed, and Zara leapt from her spot on the back of the car into the front seat of the Buick.

"Where are we going?" she asked, watching him shoving the window button. The glass buzzed downward.

"Mary Colley has a belly-ache."

"Mary Colley?"

"I've got aches myself," Forster said. "And they aren't caused by Mary Colley's mother." He looked into the rear-view mirror as if he could still see the house. "To top it off, this damnable hay fever." He crumpled a handkerchief onto the seat between them.

"Mary Colley goes to school with me."

"Is that right?" Forster said.

"She's in her last year. She's up for autumn queen."

"Watch your arm." He reached for the button again. "It's either bake and breathe or explode coolly."

The window rose like a crack in the scenery as the road swerved into the country and straightened, narrow now with hardly any variation. Forster's head turned automatically left then right as they passed the sections of farmland squarely marked when each mile had ended. The corn would be high in a matter of minutes, golden tassels pollinating in every direction. Forster blew his nose. Would the woman never stop needling him? Was it his fault, after all, that she was unhappy? He had not been the only one to want to move to this town, though she seemed to think it had been his decision. Even after twenty years she held that against him. And hadn't she been the one to suggest giving up her performances? Yes, he had wanted it that way, but he had never said it. A few years after that the Chautauqua had gone down anyway. People were no longer interested in tent shows, Shakespeare and Schubert, when they could roll into town in their new automobiles and see a moving picture with sound in it. Yes, after that his wife's voice had meant little or nothing. Forster turned up the lane to the farmhouse in time to see Mary Colley's petticoats being hung out on the line like a row of tinted carnations.

From the corner armchair, Zara sang one of the Haydn songs. Her right eye closed, as her mother tilted the mirror to see her. " 'My mother bids me bind my hair,' " she sang one afternoon.

"So I thought you were going to read," her mother said, "not bring down the house."

It was this, Kathryn thought, watching her daughter sleeping behind her, that made the old women in town nod over their pale print housedresses saying the girl had a quiet wit. It was in this same way Zara had renamed her in her illness. Kathryn, lying in her bright yellow nightgown one afternoon, had looked into the oval mirror to see her daughter coming through the doorway: Zara stopped suddenly. "Oh little foxglove!" Zara cried, spying her. "You look so lovely!" It was this that resurrected them from their gloom. It was Zara.

Kathryn pulled her notebook from beneath the crosswords. In her newly learned left-handed penmanship, she scrawled a list for her daughter:

Rehabilitating Your Mama

Count pills.

Sponge bath with new soap. Skin cream for the bad spots.

When washing hair, avoid tangles—no circular motions. Move cedar chest. Try bigger pitcher. Bigger pan on floor.

Change sheets. Hair hunt: Get strays off sheets or I won't sleep. (You won't either.)

A snack for the Hog. Swineherd craves a chocolate pudding.

Clip toenails.

Teeth—not white enough. New brush, paste, or something.

At night she lay in the bed with Kathryn, one arm slowly circling against the back, the ribs, soothing Kathryn toward an elusive sleepiness, while the other wrapped itself around a pillow pressed to her chest as if it were a man, someone she knew. Each day as she lay there, stroking, her mother's back crept away from her in subtle ways that neither noticed in this form of contentment. Sometimes lying there in this way, Zara would remember things that had happened to her and could not quite know their significance. Driving into the country with her father, Zara had watched him drape his handkerchief out the window and leave it there to dry as they swept up a new paved road. It was like a road he said that his father had helped to build and when they were almost finished all the men had thrown their hats in. Her father had tried to talk to her that day, telling her of things remembered. Then suddenly he had stopped the car.

"Listen," he said: "Do you hear it? It's a cuckoo bird." She had heard it then, the song coming clear across the field, the rise and fall of it back and forth. "Beautiful, isn't it?" he cried. "Can you see the bird? Can you spot it?" He put his hand to his forehead and scanned out over the rows of grain that lay like rails across the pasture. Again they heard the call, slightly out of tune now.

Her father snorted and closed the door. "Blue jay," he said. "Imitation. You have to watch out for that." The handkerchief fluttered at the window like a gesture.

Zara put her head down on the kitchen table. As she wept, she made no sound at all. When Mrs. McGehry came into the kitchen her heart quickened seeing this. She took hold of the table edge. "Zara, whatever is the matter?"

Zara handed her a scrap of paper. So this was the poem Kathryn had been writing all week with Zara excited and waiting to see it. Scrawled in a crippled script, it was as if a bird had scratched it there with its beak:

> *I am writing this poem*
> *I am writing this note.*
> *I am tied to my bed*
> *I have given up hope.*

"Ah God, Zara," Bridie said.

Zara wiped her eyes on a napkin. "Finally Mother has

accepted it," she said, but Bridie McGehry could see Kathryn Montgomery's daughter hadn't.

"You go down to the drugstore," Bridie said. "Go have yourself a soda. I'll sit with your mother."

Bridie went into the laundry room, thankful that the girl had listened to her for once. She heard Zara upstairs saying goodbye to her mother. Mrs. McGehry pressed her hands fondly into the basket. For twenty years she had buried her small yellow-white head in the sweet smell of laundry, letting her feet guide her on the familiar path back to this house. She heard Zara on the stairs. When the girl came down, Mrs. McGehry was more startled than she could remember.

"Mother says she'll be all right she thinks. She'll ring the buzzer if she needs you." Zara had on her winter boots and coat, her gloves and scarf.

Mrs. McGehry set the basket down. "Zara Montgomery, how long has it been since you were out of this house?"

"I don't know," she said.

"My God, girl. It's spring. It's been warm out for close to two months."

"Oh," she said, taking off her mittens. "I didn't know that."

Zara changed her clothes and was gone half an hour before she was back, her arms laden with magazines and lotions for her mother.

Kathryn studied the seed catalogs again, circling in a shaken hand the ones they would order. Feathery Baby's Breath. Blue Stokesia. Giant Primroses. *Primula Polyanthus. Finest of the new hybrids, larger blooms . . . brighter colors! Grape Hyacinths—Prince of Monaco. Fantastic clusters of closely set, dark blue bells on 6 inch spikes! Increase from year to year without care at all.*

Christmas Rose. One of gardening's most thrilling experiences is to walk through the snow and pick these glistening white blossoms.

Kathryn scanned the bedroom with her cone of light. In her notebook she wrote her way around the room. Beginning with the bed she named the objects, the legacy she would leave her daughter.

The soft wool of the blue blanket rose and fell at angles over her body, drifting on her shoulder with the motions of her sleep, the fabric swelling unnaturally where the tumor distorted the hip. In the far corner of the room, Forster Montgomery watched his wife. He straightened his tie and restraightened it, pulling at the knot, running his hands stiffly along its length, over the place where middle age had fattened him.

He heard water running, drumming against the shower walls in the next room, whirling down the drain at his daughter's feet. Through the window the early-morning light shone onto Kathryn's face. Her dark hair was thin now, the fine wisps of it stirring around her temples in the breeze, the rest drawn behind her head in a sort of tail to keep from bothering in her fever. He had offered Kathryn medications, insisting it would ease her pain; but she had refused saying she was saving it for some time when her agony would be more severe. He hardly knew how it could be worse than it was for her now, though he had watched the disease progress: the clusters of tumors throughout her body, spreading from bone to bone in fragile spiderings until each had grown brittle, yet heavier, as if in their weight they were seeking a depth, as if they had already ceased to live.

He felt his gaze go out from him, tracing the tiny ribbon his daughter had fastened around his wife's hair. There were many things Forster could not express now. Each morning when he woke to find himself in the guest room down the hall, he heard his wife and daughter in their private conversations and he felt his sadness grow.

He went to the window now and pulled the curtain toward himself. The light shifted away from her, piercing the opacity of a white plastic pitcher at the side of her bed, on the cedar chest. Something about this glow captured in the center of the jar reminded him of the wood frame house where he had been raised; it reminded him of a stone basin there in Minnesota in that childhood forty years before. He had watched his mother standing over that basin, lathering her blond hair in wintertime, the soap frothing around the basin's edge, spilling onto the cabinet. He remembered the thick white foam at the nape of her neck above the place where the satin chemise had ended.

His mother, too, had died young. Downstairs in the white-painted kitchen of the little house, he and his brothers had set their chairs on abrupt back legs as they listened to the wailings of her labor. When the midwife came down, the bloodied sheets in her arms, and shook her head, he had not understood what it meant to lose someone, to lose a mother. That night he held out nails to his father for the building of the coffins, the small one and the smaller one. He made patterns in the sawdust with his feet, while his father planed the lids.

Now he pulled the blanket up a bit to cover his wife and returned to his place of observation. It comforted him to keep her company, even when she was not awake. He unfolded the newspaper and folded it again. Kathryn had been in her early thirties when pregnant with Zara, their only child. He had grown more and more frightened with her growth, and finally when, walking in her wide straddling pregnant way, she had voiced this fear herself, he had said: Nonsense, Katie, death is far away for you. And, after all his worry, it had been an easy birth. Then he had chided himself: professional men should be beyond that sort of destructive self-indulgence.

Now, he saw her wake up and the color drain suddenly from her face. She was reaching for the pitcher; it was this motion that stopped him in his speech. Katie, I'm here, he should have said, and would have, but now it was too late. Her body doubled on its side. Thin strands of muscle worked along the bone of her arm as she threw green bile from her mouth and nostrils. He would have announced it. The base of the pitcher grew dark with contents. He would have said, Katie.

Perhaps she didn't know he was in the room: he would go to her. He would hold this pitcher for her as he had seen his daughter do. The sounds he daily heard in his work now rose from his wife. But always when she needed help, it was Zara's name he heard: Zara. A tear squeezed out the corner of her eye and rushed down her cheek to where the circle of plastic cut into her face. Perhaps she had seen him watching her. Maybe this pained her. The tear ran down the pitcher at a slant and stopped in its movement like a small snail of innocent condensation. He would stand up and leave her in some privacy, he thought. Katie. But then wouldn't Katie think he had found her repulsive? And if she had not seen him until this sudden departure, then that surely would be her reaction. He clasped his hands together. Slowly, methodically, he wrung his fingers, two against one, one against the other, worrying them as if they were the beads of a rosary.

Her hand was groping on the bed behind her where she kept the stack of towels. It ran along the sheet, the blanket, the bristles of a brush until she found the soft nap of the cloth. She grasped and pulled it toward herself, the towel unfolding as she did this, the bulk of it falling against the place where the blanket rose over her hip. He saw her wince.

She wiped her face. Under her hand, the mirror shifted on its pedestal until a gold rectangle rose from the hallway. "Zara," she called, ready to have the pitcher taken away. There was a lilt in her voice as if this self-sufficiency had in some way pleased her. Feet, a chair moved in the corner. "Zara?" she asked, startled.

"Katie, I'm here." He came around the bed. "Can I help you, Katie?"

Quickly she stretched for the towel, clutching it with one hand, placing it over the mouth of the pitcher. "I didn't know, Forster," she cried.

"You were asleep when I came in. I didn't want to wake you." He stooped beside the bed, his fingers on the handle of the pitcher.

"I thought—"

He set the pitcher down again. "I didn't mean to startle you, Katie." His hand moved along the sheet, his fingers a coverlet for the sudden immovable angles beyond her wrist. "Katie."

She saw his features gone soft with pity, his hand lying upon the bones of the Right One Gone Wrong.

"Oh, Katie, don't cry. I didn't mean to creep up on you." He laid his hand gently on her back. He felt the thin slices of bone like a fence beneath her skin, the ribs with nothing to conceal their tortured trembling.

Her gaze fell against the pitcher. "Didn't mean to creep," she repeated.

"I didn't know what to do, Katie. Here, let me take this out for you."

"I want to be alone," she cried, the Right One Gone Wrong against her breast like a sparrow.

He stood a moment there, the dark blue tie dangling futilely. "Certainly, Katie. I don't want to be here if you don't want me. I just thought to sit here with you awhile would be pleasant for us both."

"Yes," she sobbed. "Wasn't it? Wasn't it pleasant for you?"

"I'm sorry, Katie. I really—"

" Take it. Please take it out," she cried.

Kathryn brushed her teeth quietly using her water glass; she washed with her new soaps. Then she called, "Let's have music, Zara." It would be a fine day: a slice of toast, a poached egg, a piece of bacon. Dishes rattled in their water, silver against plates, plates against sink, while Kathryn made speeches to the day. "Hold me," she said in preparation.

At the piano Zara stopped on her way from the kitchen. She played the Schubert *lieder* her mother had sung on the Chautauqua. She listened fondly to hear her mother shouting out, "Two and, three and." Then as Zara came to the softer parts, the places where her mother would have lowered her voice and whispered pianissimo, she heard her mother's voice rippling in a kind of joy that Zara had never heard.

> *Am Bach viel kleine Blumen steh'n,*
> *aus hellen blauen Augen seh'n,*
> *der Bach der ist des Müllers Freund*
> *und hell blau Liebchens Auge scheint,*
> *d'rum sind es meine Blumen,*
> *d'rum sind es meine Blumen.*

As Zara played, it was as if she were curling on her mother's lap while Kathryn fluttered the pages of Gainsborough, Blake, Madame le Brun. Out the window, she remembered this too now, the plains were passing in the moonlight, for they were on a train going across country. That night her mother had sung to her, as she was singing now, and she thought then that perhaps her mother's voice had parted the huge shafts of grain and let the locomotive through.

Kathryn straightened the sheets around herself and brushed the stray hairs from her face as she heard her daughter on the stairs. Zara's nightgown flowed along the rim of the mirror; her face came into view. "Sit on the bed with me, Zara." Kathryn reached over her shoulder and took her daughter's hand. "Zara," she said. "It's the touching I miss the most. I want to get up and hold you." Now Kathryn stroked the hand. "I can't help it anymore, I have to say it. I want you to pick me up and hold me."

"But, Foxie, I don't know how to do it anymore. I don't know how to do it without hurting you."

"Just once. Please try. I'll tell you what to do."

Zara could see the night when she was a child and a noise had echoed through the house. All night it had gone on. The hollow winging had stirred her mother from sleep and sent the woman pacing through the hallways in her long white nightgown, latching windows as she went. In the morning, her mother cried when she discovered the source: during the night a bird had fallen through the chimney into the dark chamber of the furnace and could not get out. In its frenzy the small yellow bird had beaten itself to death against the walls.

Kathryn told her how to slide her hands beneath the side and pull her onto Zara's lap. That would be the best that they could do, she said. As she watched her daughter's reflection moving behind her on the bed, she reassured her.

"I'm not poking you with my fingernails, am I, Foxie?"

Kathryn shook her head as the sheet fell an inch away and then another. Together they came into the focus of the mirror.

Zara saw in the oval glass her mother's lips open and close. "I'm hurting you," she said.

"No," Kathryn said. "Go on."

Zara nudged her leg beneath the tender side, lowering the tiny woman's frame toward her knee. In her palms, Zara felt a pulse flutter beyond the ribs. "Mother, are you all right?" Her mother's lips parted.

Kathryn's ribs did not crack like normal bones. As logs smolder, then surrender suddenly to ash, her ribs gave way, the flesh folding in on itself around her daughter's hands.

When the bug crawled into her bosom, right there in McNurty's Red Owl, Mrs. McGehry cried out: "OH OH OH! There's a bee in my bonnet and a bug where it oughtn't to be!" White-aproned clerks disposed of their heads in adding machines and red feather dusters as if to say the old woman had not set one diminutive foot into the Owl that warm July afternoon. In haste, wire baskets formed ranks and departed for faraway aisles, while, behind a pyramid of fancy tinned peas, Zara Montgomery crouched, staring up at her governess in disbelief. Bridget McGehry had both hands down the front of her blouse; they fluttered. The little girl covered her face to hear a round of shrieks bursting the air like the pings of a pellet gun she'd once heard echoing from the high mysterious walls of the community dump. "Jesus! Mary! and Joseph!" the old woman cried. Zara felt the tingle as something was flung and then the rush of someone behind it. There was the crunch as Bridget McGehry dispatched the untimely offender; there was the sigh.

Outside the Owl, Bridie hoisted the brown paper bag onto her hip, saying she was sorry to have killed the poor unfortunate beast right there in the frozen-food aisle, but it had chosen the wrong victim, the wrong time and place to commence such a brunch. The child's small auburn head filled with sudden recognition: Certainly death was something that came to you when you were where you oughtn't to be.

Years later, when Zara Montgomery was in her first term at high school, she accompanied her father on a house call into the country. Mary Colley would have died, her father said, if they had not arrived when they did. Where, Zara wondered even then, did help leave off and helplessness begin? And what was that nearly imperceptible whoosh the skin made when the knife went in? Was that life? Or was that death being released?

And now? Something was gone. Someone. How, how had they gotten her mother into the coffin, distorted as her little body had been, twisted into a pretzel on its side? *If necessary the undertaker will break bones to get a body into the coffin.* Fragile legs snapping like the twigs of a wishbone after a holiday feast. Under brightly lighted lamps undertakers performed other tasks, sewing the gums of the dead one together so the mouth would not come open again. Mummie in a box with her lipstick painted on. Red as the lips she wore on Christmas holidays when Mrs. McGehry brought in the goose. Fat trussed goose with the drippings in the pan and parsley sprinkled all around. Dead goose. And her mother sang all day: *Fuchs, du hast die Gans gestohlen,* as she buttoned Zara into the little red dress and helped her to pull the white anklets on with the blue cornflowers embroidered at the top.

Everyone? Zara asked. Yes, her mother said, just like the bee Mrs. McGehry killed in the supermarket, though she hoped most everyone would not have such an humiliating demise. The patent leather shoes tapped around the floor. Hollyday, Hollyday, Zara sang, prickling her fingers against the temperamental festooning around the fireplace.

That Christmas the doll was born: Bonnie Bonita out of a green shiny box with a silver ribbon ripped from the top. And then after she had given it to her, years later, her mother had said to Forster across the dining room table: "If she wants to be a pianist, she'll have to put away those dolls." Bonnie Bonita, barely five years old on the high chair Forster Montgomery had made for her, stared past them all into the refuge of the thick gold yams, her china eyes ready to flutter closed in an after-dinner recline.

"Tomorrow we'll take Bonnie Bonita down to Goodwill Industries where she will do a poor little girl some good."

"Never mind the doll, Katie," Forster Montgomery said. "I've got a notion those are a surgeon's hands. Not a pianist's."

Her mother set the napkin perfunctorily beside the plate. "A surgeon's hands— My foot! The doll goes."

Bonnie Bonita hidden in a box underneath the bed. If someone went to someone else and never returned, then would that someone be dead or would she still then be alive? You give it up to keep it. What did that mean?

Saturdays the girls came over to play Old Maid. Amy VanderVenter proclaimed one day that Zara was a peculiar name. Yes, the other girls agreed, surveying Zara's new cotton dress with its handsome M embroidered on the blouse. They would have liked a name like that, they said. The cards went out across the flower of the Persian rug. And then the hideous gray card would come up and there it would be: the Old Maid in her quintessential hat with the flowers blooming all around the top and everyone would say: Pooh! Pooh! There was the worst name of all. You might as well be dead. Old Maid! Old Maid! they would cry, though secretly Zara thought the little pink cheeks quite quaint beneath the brittle spectacles. She would have liked a hat like that. It was just a game, her mother said, and one was not to worry too much what the other girls called you when it was all in sport. When was it really a game? she wanted to know. And when was it real? At Catechism the boys chased Becky Carter around the church piquing her in cruel ways. "Carter's a little liver pill! Carter's a little liver pill!" they screamed, chasing her around the vestibule until she cried to the teacher before Bible class. Becky Carter's father had been poor.

Michael came up the street; always he would come up the street this way now, his white jacket draped over his left shoulder, his heart a tightening knot around the thought of Zara Montgomery. In the funeral home he had stood beside her looking into the coffin. He, too, had winced when they shut the lid. He wondered whether Zara, standing there in her new dark dress, had seen the slender crescent of blue, almost like a winter moon, staring out from the slightly opened eye, from under the long dark lashes. He was not certain that he had seen it.

Now Zara was in medical school with him, now they went to the cafeteria and then to the library to study before their anatomy lab. Together they read the books, learning how they would dissect the various parts of the body, how they eventually would take ropes and bind up the hands to the feet so that the knees of their individual cadavers would be held apart, so that they might cut into the muscles of even those most private of sectors. Each day, reading together these procedures for the afternoon labs, Michael glanced up to laugh: "Today Smith gets it in the neck," he said when they came to the exploration of those muscles surrounding the cervical spine. But when it was Zara's turn to pull her sheet back in the laboratory to reveal the woman, the skin caving in beneath the ribs, the tiny breasts that once pressed against the lips of men, of babies, she said to herself: This is nobody now. This is a mass of formaldehyde and fibers. This is nobody. Then she bit her lip and began as if she were reading the book, as if she did not see the agony the body had had to endure coming to this place where she would set it on wooden blocks, where she would divide it with a knife. They sat at the table and read books now, the dark odors of the library a comfort to her as she turned each page. *Introduce the handle of the scalpel through the median incision in the aponeurosis and push it forwards and backwards and from side to side to ascertain the different degrees of looseness of the areolar tissue under the different parts of the muscle.* Mrs. X, I did not know you.

There in front of everyone she came over to sit on his lap behind the massive oak table with the college history engraved on its top: Oleson, Anderson, Brown, McCarthy, January, Pierce, Pavandi, Jensen. There, too, was the name of Forster Montgomery. Zara did not have to tell Michael what it was that made her come to him, and he would stroke her hair awhile as he was reading.

Zara sponged her mother's breasts: around the gentle points of them, dipping the cloth into the basin at the bedside, smoothing the soap into a silken froth. She washed between her mother's thighs and then the little feet, between the toes, toweling her mother's body down as she went so Kathryn would not be chilled. Zara placed new bandages on each of the sores and held the bedpan up to the backside of her mother, reading aloud to her as they waited together for this most natural of transactions. Again Zara cleansed her. She trimmed the toenails and slipped a nightgown over Kathryn's shoulders. When her mother was content with the way the hair had been combed back and braided behind her head, when the room had been straightened, Zara drew the covers up around her mother. She went down to the kitchen and baked a cake in a heart-shaped pan. The kitchen was quiet: Mrs. McGehry was muttering in the basement. The snow drifted like a blanket high against the window panes.

Yes, it had been a sentimental valentine. And no, Kathryn had not minded sentimentality now. They cut the little cake on the bedstand and served it up with the silver service. The tea just strong enough and the cake perfectly sculpted on the platter.

"I want you to do me a favor," her mother said.

The daughter nodded. Certainly what her mother wanted now was what Zara herself was wanting.

"Get into the attic and find a dress box in the farthest corner." Kathryn laughed then, delighted with the thought of this new venture. "When you find it take the dress out and put it on."

When Zara came into the room, the wedding dress circled like white icing around her slippers. *Put the cheeks and lips slightly on the stretch by placing tow or cotton wool in the vestibule of the mouth. Stitch the red margins of the lips together. Stretch the eyelids.*

"I guess there isn't much to say," Zara told him, her voice catching like a bit of confusion in the middle of her sentence.

Michael asked her then if she wanted to talk about it, thinking of his own childhood: the convent orphanage where he had spent his first years burying his face in the starched white chests of nuns, feeling their dark robes like maternity folding around him, the long sequence of Catholic foster homes: the Murphys' with the Sacred Heart above the white vinyl of his headboard, the O'Connors' where he had had to sweep out the chicken coop and gather the small, warm eggs each morning before he came to breakfast, the seven Fitzpatrick boys all of whom he had had to fight before they would call him brother. There had been other homes, other separations. He encouraged her then, saying, "Perhaps you feel a little like I did when I would wake up and find someone from my new family sitting on the side of my bed. You don't even have to say it, I would think, as they sputtered some inadequate goodbye. As if I had really mattered to them at all. I felt deserted." His fingers moved at the back of her hair, brushing it away from her face. "It must be very hard for you, Zara."

"She was so unhappy, Michael."

"No one else would have sacrificed all you did for her, Zara. Any other family would have admitted her to a hospital and left her there."

"Mummie didn't want to go anywhere else. She wanted to be at home."

"You were very good to her, Zara."

"It isn't my garden. It's yours," Kathryn cried. "Everything is yours now. It's yours, it's yours. Take it!"

Zara stood beside the bed, her fingernails in her palms, tears in her eyes. "Foxie, don't cry. Please don't cry. It's supposed to be our garden. It isn't yours or mine. It's ours. I got the primroses, I got all of them. And the hyacinth. I got everything you wanted that they had. Everything."

"And what are those?" Kathryn cried. "What are those horrible wormlike things?" Beside the bed the little potted plants drooped around the floor; brightly colored packets of seeds faded against the cedar chest. "What are they, Zara?"

Zara picked up the little green box and held it out to her. "They're moss roses. They'll be very beautiful with the hyacinth. They open in the morning. Don't cry, Foxie. Please don't cry anymore. I won't plant them if you don't want me to. Really I won't. I'll do anything you want me to."

"It's too late," she cried. The Right One Gone Wrong scratched at the packets on the bureau, knocking them to the floor. "It's not mine anymore. I'm not any good anymore and now even my garden is yours."

"Foxie—" Zara reached out to touch her face, but the Right One Gone Wrong sprang out at her.

"Take me to the nursing home." Tears ran down Kathryn's face onto her shoulder like little pellets of rain. The claw of her right hand banged futilely against the telephone, the receiver falling to the floor into the incessant wailing of the dial tone.

"Don't, Foxie. Please don't."

"Call them. Call the nursing home. You don't want to help me anymore."

"I don't want you to go away. I don't want you to go there. I want you to be here with me." Now Zara, too, was crying.

"You want me to die so you can be with boys. You want me dead. You don't want me anymore."

"No," Zara cried. "It isn't true. I want you. I want to be with you, Mummie."

"So what?" she screamed, the claw in the air shaking as if it would clench itself, shaking as if it could say all those things she could not say. "All I wanted was to be able to look into the mirror and see my garden. You've ruined my little garden for me, Zara. Take me to the nursing home; I want to die in the nursing home. I want to go away."

Zara ran from the bedroom weeping. She ran full length into her father. "What have you done?" he shouted. "Why is your mother crying?"

"She never wants to help me anymore," Kathryn cried to Forster. "She wants me to die. She wants me to die, Forster."

He grasped this moment; now he could be of use to his wife. He rushed into the narrow hallway. "I take care of a hundred patients in one day and you can't take care of your own mother? You make her feel like this? What good are you anyway?"

That night Zara did not come home. All night she walked along the streets staring at the trees, the starless sky, a light in a window. In the morning, she went home. Her mother said nothing about the garden or the day before. They continued.

All the older girls wore saddle shoes to school with the toes scuffed properly and the fur of their anklets brushed with a rattail comb, but at church they held their heads straight up, trying not to look at their new high heels bursting like foreign nodules under their feet. They did not play Steal the Bacon in the pews with Zara and her friends. Once Amy VanderVenter had seen one of the high-school boys take a ponytail and crush it in his hands. At this incredible report all the first-grade girls had squealed, "No, no," grabbing onto the little sprouts behind each other's heads. At school on the way to her swimming class, Zara saw the older girls leaning against their lockers, their arms full of books so large she didn't know how they carried them. She heard the way their voices changed when they talked to boys. Did age itself give you knowledge? she wanted to know. Or was understanding like something in a room you had never noticed before and suddenly inexplicably saw? It would have been nice, Zara's friends confessed, to have the older girls in the same swimming class when everyone took off their clothes.

In the shower, they had seen Angie Miller's little nether

lips sticking out like a rooster's comb. Did Zara look like that to the other girls? No, her peelers were set close inside, and she did not have to worry what the other girls thought. Rooster comb. Outside of town there were farms and land cut up in squares where grain grew out of the night-black soil. Town girls rarely went out there, unless they were going along for the ride, and they didn't get too close to animals if their fathers should decide to stop the car and talk awhile. On the radio an announcer said that a farm woman had been killed trying to rescue her little daughter from a sow. Zara's mother looked up from the book she was reading and said, "Oh my, one mother against another and always the beasts win." What did that mean? And if the mothers opposed one another, then surely wouldn't the daughters do the same someday?

When it was time to be confirmed, Zara sat at the kitchen table, the slight red flush of her first blemish about to begin on her cheek. She looked into her mother's smooth white face. "Oh, go ahead with it," her mother said. "You can join now and decide as you go along." When the minister laid his hands on the top of her head along with the hands of her mother and father, when Zara heard him asking someone to bless her and welcome her into His family, she guessed maybe her mother was right. But why, then, she asked herself, had her mother only gone to church that one time?

Several months before her mother died, Zara had entered the room to find Kathryn in her sickbed watching the television set, watching the palms of hands swaying with the spirituals. And on that final day, Zara had seen clouds shifting across the sky of her mother's eyes as Kathryn spoke to someone else when Zara was the only other person in the room.

Kathryn Montgomery had reached out toward the wall and said to someone: "Are they dead, too?"

Pulling into the lane of the Colley house, the doctor and his young daughter had almost forgotten the disagreement at home. *Incise the peritoneum along the lateral margin of the ascending colon: move the colon and caecum out of the way, and clean the structures that lie immediately behind them.* There they were: Mary Colley's petticoats strung gayly on the line like a row of tinted carnations and the house set white in the knoll as if it were a stage. And in the background were the outbuildings, the old ones and the new, the barn painted red as a late-summer vegetable and behind it: the old home place, abandoned now, its empty windows lined in perfect symmetry to frame the dark green stalks of corn flowing behind it. And there, too, were the willows black and moving against the wire fence that marked the yard.

"Have you got my bag?" Doctor Montgomery asked the daughter who had had it sitting in her lap for the last quarter mile. He didn't need to tell her that she would be seeing someone she knew at school and so this would be a private thing, something not to be discussed at lunch with her friends. He didn't need to say so and he refrained, seeing her leaning toward the windshield in her adolescent dungarees, watching the older girl's underthings kicking up on the line in chorus.

The doctor put a familiar hand on the gate and lifted the metal rod. It scraped across the walk as he closed it after her. He didn't know why he held the little square of fence for her, but now it seemed natural even though he saw her take a skip and quell it as her black-and-white sectioned shoes hurried over the weed-ridden cracks of the sidewalk. *Incise the peritoneum along the lateral margin of the descending colon.*

She watched her father disappear behind the broad cot-

ton dress of Mary Colley's mother into the darkened rectangle that was Mary Colley's room. The door swung shut
and she could hear their voices: the one explaining and the
other questioning and then the small whimpering that
paced back and forth between the sheets in fever.

On the maple end table was Mary's senior photograph:
the perfect small straight nose, the teeth that had needed no
braces, the lips a kiss of congratulation to her perfect skin.
Those eyes painted in the photographer's studio could
hardly be so blue as Mary Colley's were, all the girls had
said that. On the end of the bookshelf a ceramic cat licked
an aqua bowl and beneath it on the second shelf was a
china doll with hair as golden as Mary's. Perhaps Mary
Colley herself had sacrificed such curls for the making of
the wig. *Place a block under the back of the head to raise it
to a convenient angle.*

Once Zara had seen a doll like this in much greater
proportions. Although she had been very young, still she
remembered this: that doll in a long fancy dress with dark
brown hair as lovely as her mother's. Zara had asked her
mother then what "in effigy" meant and why was that life-
sized doll hanging from the tree outside the window? "I
really don't know," her mother said. "I wish I could understand it." A sign swung out from the doll. "Foreigner," it
said.

The door sprang open with the sound of her father asking in whispers why the woman had not told him it was so
bad over the telephone, why she had not called three days
ago. He would have sent the ambulance. "Clear this table.
Zara—"

Helen Colley rushed about the room. "You don't understand," she said. "I faint at the sight of blood, Forster."

"You do what you have to, Helen," he said. "If you have

to faint and leave me to this operation, then I guess you'll faint and that's the way it will be."

Helen Colley pressed the rose-colored towel against her chest. "It isn't just me. Harold faints, too, at the sight of blood. I would have brought Mary in myself if Harold hadn't been away with the car, Forster." Helen Colley begged that she might be allowed to sit outside on the step until it was all over. She would sit outside until Forster Montgomery and his fourteen-year-old daughter had opened and closed the belly of her daughter.

"You will do no such thing, Helen," Forster Montgomery said to Mary Colley's mother, laying out instruments on a dish towel. "You will go in there and bathe your daughter in alcohol; you will collect white towels and put them here and boil a large kettle of water with all these things in it. Then, Helen, if I don't think of anything else, you can go to your room and faint. Those few things, Helen, and then you can faint." Helen Colley nodded her large way into the back bedroom, a basin in her hands.

Zara hardly knew when the preparations ended and the operation began, when Mary Colley, this year's Autumn Queen, was suddenly lying on the table crying first one moment and asleep the next with a few fine curls of yellow hair springing out from her pelvis. It was just as her father had said: Helen Colley had been laid out in her own bedroom with a cloth on her forehead and they were left alone to this operation.

Doctor Montgomery removed the ethered handkerchief from Mary's face and told his daughter how to hold the clamps and lower the weights over the side of the table. She sponged the incision as he separated the layers and moved aside the long white coils of intestine, searching down what he explained was the anterior taenia coli to find the appendix, long wormlike organ without a purpose. Her father took the infested eel in his hand and cut it loose, holding it then into the sunlight. His fingers ran along its slick surface feeling for perforations. He dropped it into its new receptacle. Zara watched the eel; the red, the yellow-white and brown, winding upon itself in the bowl of Helen Colley's heirloom teacup.

"Now we stitch our way out," her father said. "And then you count the instruments." Zara looked at the abnormal length of this appendix, the open wound. "Count them once and then again and then the third time." She counted.

That night in the den Forster Montgomery handed his daughter his suturing needles and a piece of yellow fruit. "Jab," he said, piercing the skin of the banana. "Then pull through steadily." He sat beside her demonstrating the knots he had used that afternoon. "You know," he said, his hands in motion, the overhead light shining on his bald spot, "the most important knot I ever learned was when my father taught me in his store to tie a one-handed bow on a package."

Her father had never once said that he was proud of her. She had expected it that day; but he had said nothing. Now she was determined; she would make him proud. When Zara had finished stitching the fruit from end to end and was tying knots along its skin, she heard her mother on the stairway. Together she and her father looked up to see the brightly colored kimono descending, her mother's dark hair waving like youth over her shoulders.

"Listen—" Kathryn said. "I bought you a record."

"You did?" Zara manipulated the thread with her left hand.

"Yes," her mother said, smiling eagerly. "Do you want me to teach you a dance?" she asked. "I learned it from the television."

Zara looked up from the needle, the suture, and said, "Not now, Mother." Kathryn went upstairs, her head down, her fingers running dejectedly along the railing. Always Zara would regret that she had not danced that one time with her mother. *With the aid of saw, chisel, and bone-forceps, remove the roof of the orbit and also the thick cranial wall above the orbital opening.*

No, Zara was thinking every day now, I was not good enough. The fact that her mother was no longer alive was evidence of her failure. The garden incident was another smaller one. A change had occurred in Zara Montgomery during the time she was caring for her mother. Every time Kathryn made a request it became Zara's own desire until slowly it was as if Zara herself knew always what her mother wanted. And those times when she did not know? They were both reminded of her helplessness. In self-defense and in compassion, Zara gave her will up to her mother; and as they grew closer, easing themselves into a perfectly painted pastel of love and devotion, they approached that moment they both denied: their separation.

When her mother did die, Zara knew it was true: she had failed her in some insidious way. She had not done enough to ease the pain, to lift the spirits; she had not been able to infuse Kathryn with strength. She had been selfish with her own identity. Or had she? Hadn't she given up everything for her mother? No, here she was: Zara Montgomery, hideously alive and her mother was dead. She had failed. Had she? Perhaps her mother had planned to die that way in Zara's arms; but if she had, then wasn't that an act of cruelty on Kathryn's part? Or was it an act of love? Zara did not know. She knew only that she had lost her identity in this woman and the woman had left her. Part of Montgomery had disappeared. She turned now to

Michael O'Dea for comfort although she could not bring herself to explain those special circumstances that delivered her now to him and to her grieving. And if she had been able to tell him everything, which she could not and would not ever do, she had no hope that he would understand her.

"Zara," Michael said, seeing the tears starting from her eyes. "Let's go outside and sit on the steps awhile." She shuffled her papers together and they went out. On the bench he put his arm around her. "Do you resent her, Zara?"

"I loved her."

"You could love someone and still resent them."

"Don't you see?" she cried, falling into his arms. "Don't you see? She's dead and I'm alive."

"Stop now," Michael said, pulling her away from his chest.

"I don't know who I am."

"Stop," he said. "You're going to buck up now and do your work. That's all you have. That's all anybody has. You're the best surgeon in the class. Even Oleson says so."

"I never thought she would die, Michael." She turned her eyes on him. "I mean, I knew she would but every day I knew more and more that she just couldn't."

"You will stop now. You will give up this self-indulgence. Do you hear me?"

"Yes," she said.

"Will you?"

"Yes," she said, looking up at him, her eyes wide between hope and sorrow.

"I love you," he said. "That should mean something. You have your work. And you have me. That should mean something to you, Zara."

"Yes," she said, her eyes going out across the flat green

grass and up the lane of maples along the sidewalk. "It does."

"Good," he said, mistaking the distance in her voice for resignation. "Now we'll go back in and study. It wouldn't be very good now, would it, if we went into lab and mistook the jugular for the trachea?"

"No," she said, feeling his arm tighten around her in encouragement. And so they sat in the library for the rest of the morning, trying to make up for the time they'd lost to emotion, Zara attempting to bind her thoughts to the words in front of her without thinking of Mrs. X, without thinking of her mother. Michael glanced up in silence to see her palms spread face up under the study table as if she expected something to land, to place its fragile self there. "Zara," he said. "Study."

Michael was in Seattle when Zara was caring for her mother; and the few friends she had seldom called, fearing the dead, the dying, the mourners even before anything had transpired. One day, though, her girl friend had called from another state to ask how Zara was. When the telephone rang, somehow her mother had managed to pick up the receiver. Kathryn, overcome with pride at having answered the phone by herself, had heard the voice: "You must be Zara's grandmother. I didn't know you were coming to stay. How is poor Kathryn getting along?" Foxie, Foxie, I didn't know that even your voice was slipping away. *Turn the head well over to the side, and explore the superficial fascia.*

Michael O'Dea had one of the dissecting tables at the far side of the room. Michael O'Dea whose face shone brightly out at her from across the bodies and stainless-steel tables. Michael O'Dea whose face was almost pretty with a soft gold freckling on his ivory skin. And always it had been Michael O'Dea, his green eyes looking down from his great height. Michael O'Dea, a Catholic orphan in a pre-dominantly Protestant town. And her mother had said once, "I don't want you going around with that Catholic boy. We had Catholics in our family once, generations ago. This family, I hope, has given up that nonsense."

It was with Michael O'Dea she had first made love at the edge of the tennis court in the far reaches of her own back yard, the night before he went away to school. Eighteen and he was there putting his fingers into her to prepare the way. "Am I hurting you?" he asked; and she had lied see-ing his shoulders white and wide above her. And when he came and she had bitten into her lip with pain, his head jerked back. "Mother of God," he said, pressing her face against the soft hairs of his chest, against a silver medal. And she had bled, bled and bled until she thought she might not stop. Michael O'Dea took his shirt from the top of the tennis net to wipe her and she felt then the little buttons of the collar cold against her thighs like sudden raindrops.

"All right, Montgomery," Oleson said.

She drew the scalpel, slitting the chest in an inch-long incision where the anesthetic had been given, where the needles had numbed only the surface flesh. She took the hard plastic tube in her fist and drew all her strength back. Both hands came down, thrusting the tube through the chest wall into the lung. "God! God! My God!" the patient screamed. "My God!" The tube sucked fluid; the lung cleared.

"Good work, Montgomery," Oleson said. He patted her on the back. "You're a chip off the old man for sure. I've seen people with twice your strength have to go at it twice."

She didn't know why they had done it. The woman was going to die anyway. Multiple myeloma. And what if the lung was collapsed, what if both of them had deflated? It might have been an easier way out. Oleson left the room, followed by the nurse, the X-ray technician, the orderly, Dr. Grossman behind them. She was the last one out. She leaned down beside the gray hairs curling around the ear. Little pearl ear, can you hear me? "I love you. I love you," she said. The eyes opened, they closed. They opened, they closed.

Oh! the steps behind the public bathhouse were alive that day. Wild cacophonous flurry of canopies and parasols. Artists in their gypsy scarves and paint-spattered jeans. The potters' wares: a stone to hold the breakfast cream, a platter glazed: the blue sweeps up from the horizon and overtakes the brown, the mauve will hold the meat. Silver rings and collars, beads and polished stones swing out on brown silk cords along the banks of Lake Marian. The painters, too, were out today. Green landscapes lie against a lush green hill. Against an oak a wheel still turns, bicycle ajar. Serendipitous wheel discovers light. Casts the future on the ground, crisp shadow spokes of inconceivable doom. On the lake, canoes pass like panoramic time: abstract melancholy arrows there. Bathers sun, draw in their long hot limbs for oil. They stretch up the granite blocks of the bathhouse stairs toward the noise, toward lemonade, toward a rush of children from the past. A russet hound, irretrievable beast, flies after the pure white fur of Mrs. Willoughby's cat, undeniable pink dot beneath the feline tail. The artists barter, the artists sun themselves, the artists smile. A silver ear bounces against Zara Montgomery's waist; sand shifts in her shoes. The stethoscope droops against her front. Fluorescent lights replace the sun; she enters the emergency room.

"We might have gotten neurosurgery down here if you'd

radioed in. Bartlet, the pig, takes an eternity to answer his page." Marilyn Kleinliebelink's secretarial chair swung toward the phone. "Oh, Dr. Montgomery," she said, calling her Doctor though it would be two months before she was one. "When you're ready, Grossman's been screaming for help in number four." Zara walked into the lounge and shook the sand out of her shoes. The door was open and she could see the ambulance driver leaning against the door of the secretary's cubicle. He drained coffee from a styrofoam cup as Marilyn Kleinliebelink answered the phone. Someone was half-dead in number two and still that someone was moaning.

"Page neurosurgery for Bartlet again," Kleinliebelink said to the page operator. "Tell him not to call back. Tell him to get his ass down to the emergency room quick."

The curly black hair of Dr. Grossman wound tight above his stethoscope. "Marilyn." He unplugged his ears. The ballpoint tip went back and forth in her hand.

"Here it is," she said. The sheaf of papers flipped into his hand.

"Give renal a call as soon as you can do it."

"Transplant?" The number was already dialed. Zara tied her shoes. Marilyn was an excellent secretary, although sometimes Marilyn thought she knew medicine, which she did not know.

"Tell them we've got two good ones they can plug into one of their people," Grossman said. "I'd give the kid in room two three minutes before he's ready to spit the kidney beans." Zara poured herself a cup of coffee in the lounge, watching Grossman writing on the patient's chart; she heard him sigh. A few minutes and she'd be ready to begin. She gathered her energy; she was early.

"Did you sign this time?" Marilyn asked Dr. Grossman.

"I signed. I signed."

"You're going to lose this kid. Is that right? Want me to call the morgue?"

"C-spine fractured. Can't put the tongs in, hardly any skull left on the poor boy."

The light flashed on line three. "Dr. Grossman—it's Bartlet on three."

The head of Grossman went up and down. "Charles, you got thirty seconds to save our boy from renal transplant. What are you doing on the phone?"

As Dave Grossman went out, two members of the transplant team sauntered in. They sat down. "Hey, Marilyn," the tall one said. "You been dancing too much at night? You look dreadful."

"Get out of here," she said, throwing back her wedge of yellow hair to smile. "You bunch of vultures get your rubber soles off my chairs."

"Hey now, everybody knows you and that punk orderly stole these chairs from us."

"They're the best. Move your feet."

"We brought you a little present from the artists' market today." The tall one reached across the counter and plunked a ceramic skull in the outbox. A rose sprang from its eye.

"What the hell is that?" she asked, continuing to log information on the patients' list.

"Paperweight. Like it?"

"Gads," she said. "All you white coats are alike."

"I didn't make it, Marilyn," the tall one said. "I just bought it, along with Tom here's advice. It's too derivative for me."

Tom tipped his chair against the wall and smiled. "Ever hear of Georgia O'Keeffe?"

"Never," she said. "And don't tell me. There goes the hotline again."

The red phone rang out in its peculiar harsh cry. "Want to listen?" she asked and flipped the switch. The voice went out around the room: "This is County Ambulance, Emergency. We're on the interstate and we're running hot."

Marilyn covered the receiver. "Must be some new squirrel out there; he thinks he's cute." She picked up her pen. "What the hell does that mean, County?" she said into the red disk.

"Auto accident. Four to you. Two to the morgue. We've got skull fractures, fracture-fractures, and blood. You've got ten minutes till we come peeling through your front door."

"Thanks a lot, County," Marilyn said. "Now give me the names this time, Bozo, and any other information you've got." She took it down, hung up the phone and punched the names, addresses, the dates of birth onto identification plates.

"Want to hear our plan for the spring picnic, Marilyn?" Tom crossed his feet on her chair. "We're going to drum up a little business for the team."

"Vultures," she said. "What are you going to do?"

"We, the members of your family transplant team, are going to sponsor a motorcycle race. What do you think of that? We're sure to get a set of beans. We'll make them sign before they enter the race."

"You're disgusting," she said. She turned on the intercom and called back to number eight. "Dr. Grossman, we've got a big crunch coming in. Four skulls. Want me to call Bartlet again?"

Transplant poured themselves another round of coffee and looked at the registration sheet. "Have you located the kid's parents yet? We want them to sign soon as the kid dies."

"While you're at it, why don't you ask them why they

didn't get the kid a helmet to go with his hot motorbike?" Marilyn picked up the phone again. She called X-ray, neurosurgery, orthotrauma. The requisitions for the lab work were already prepared and signed.

When the second cervical fracture came in, Zara Montgomery helped to drill the holes in the man's skull. They set the tongs into them, the metal pincers gripping tight the newly shaved head. Now the body would not shift, the neck would be straight. No sudden movement would sever the spinal cord. The orderly wheeled him out. "How do you like your new hat?" he asked the patient, spinning the cart through the door. Hardly had the accident victims been sent to intensive care when word came in that the drowning had occurred. They were bringing in the victim's girlfriend and the woman who had saved her. Later the second woman would say that she had seen the boy go down but she hadn't been able to save them both.

Zara remembered only the minuscule thread of skin that grew strangely from the side of her grandmother's throat, a sort of mole, her mother said. Grandmother Sheridan had come to visit them only once, and during that time her mother had not sung or hummed or smiled. Years later when Kathryn was dreaming each night of her mother, this grandmother who had come from England when Zara was five, Zara had asked her mother why that sadness had occurred. "She resented my success," Kathryn said, studying her daughter in the mirror. "But after you were born and I stopped singing on the Chautauqua, she decided it was all right to love me. I was a mother then. I was what I was meant to be; I had my place in her view of the world."

Every night her mother dreamed of Grandmother Sheridan buried in her own country, fortunate, Kathryn said, not to die in a foreign land. *Fuchs, du hast die Gans ges-tohlen, Gib sie wieder hier.* Kathryn was British but she had studied German for her songs. *Schwanengesang.* Songs, Kathryn said, about the imaginations of the heart. When she was fifteen, Kathryn had run away from home; she had come to America to sing these songs. Speaking about it from her deathbed, her eyes filled with tears. "Once," she said, "I sang on the same stage with Madame Schumann-Heink. She was very old then. And do you know what she said to me? She said I was great, really great, and I should never give it up."

"Why did you, Foxie?" Zara asked, smoothing cream on her mother's skin.

"I don't know," Kathryn said. "I just don't know."

After Kathryn died, Mrs. McGehry insisted that they wait outside for Forster and the ambulance to arrive. She steered Zara out along the grass to sit on the wicker settee where it tipped at the lot line into the weeds. She said, "Now, now. Your mother's better off dead. Poor thing. She's out of pain for the first time in her life."

"I've been trying to get her friends all afternoon," Marilyn said. "Everyone is still at the flea market, I think."

Zara looked through the drawer. "Have you called her mother?"

"She says she doesn't want her mother to know."

"Her mother will hear it on the news anyway. Call the woman; I'll talk to her. Where's the children's pressure cuff?"

Marilyn pulled the cuff from behind a stack of papers and shrugged.

"Thanks," Zara said and went into the far examining room. When it was time to leave for the day, the two young women were still there, standing in the corridor, waiting for a cab. In the operating-room greens the orderly had given them to replace their soaking clothes, they were nearly the same size there, looking at one another: the woman who had saved the one, the woman who had lost her boyfriend and had been pulled onto the shore. They looked into one another's eyes; they talked about loss.

"I'm leaving now," Zara said to them. "I'll share the cab with you if you want."

The woman who had dived into the water looked relieved; she had never met Jeanne Hollings before this day. "Thanks," she said. "I have an exam tomorrow, otherwise I'd go with Jeanne."

"I talked to her mother. She's going to meet her at her apartment."

Jeanne's brown hair tipped as if to protest.

"You shouldn't be alone tonight. Your lungs could fill."

"All right," she said. On the floor of the cab, water beaded up on the inside of the plastic bag with her clothes. Zara put her hand on the green cotton knee as they went past the lake. The water was dotted with tiny boats, the shore congested with people; tent flaps and pennants wallowed in the summer air. From each boat a long pole dipped and pulled back again. Under the water would be the grappling hooks.

"A lousy day to be driving a cab," the driver said, unaware of the day's misfortunes. "I'd like to be out there right now with all those fishermen. Like to see if I could catch the big one." The woman paled.

Zara reached over the back of the driver's seat and tapped him on the shoulder. "We're having a private conversation. Could you keep your observations to yourself?"

"Certainly, lady," he said. "Just commenting on the weather."

"Keep them to yourself, all right? Just drive."

"Sure thing, lady. I ain't here to cause you aggravation.

Just pick them up and drop them off: that's enough for me."

Jeanne's eyes had filled with tears. "You can call me tonight if you want," Zara said. "I'll be at home." Rarely had she extended herself beyond the hospital. She handed her a Kleenex. "You're a painter?" she asked, attempting to steer her toward other thoughts.

Jeanne nodded.

"I'd like to see your work someday if you want to show it to me."

"Thank you." She sat up straighter now. The cab was rounding the corner toward the house where she lived. It was an old house; a row of mailboxes lined the front. Under the sweep of maple trees, a woman leaned her flowered house dress into the side of an Oldsmobile.

"Is that your mother?"

"I wish she didn't have to be here. I didn't want her to be upset."

"It's better this way. She'll be less upset than the other way. Do you have my phone number now?"

Jeanne's brown hair went up and down. "My mother will have some money. Can you wait?" Her head went down. "Even my glasses fell into the lake." The cab stopped in front of the house.

"Don't worry about the money." Zara reached over her and opened the door. "Call me if you need me. Even if you just want to talk, okay?"

The long hair was dry, a ribbon of it falling across one eye as she stepped from the car, pulling the plastic bag from the floor.

"Call me tonight if you want." Zara knew she would not see her again.

"Thank you for helping me."

The door closed and Zara leaned toward the driver.

"Could you wait a minute please?" She watched her walking toward the woman. She watched them: mother and daughter talking a long while on the sidewalk. An arm went up around a shoulder, an arm closed around a waist.

"Want to go now, lady?" the driver asked.

The sun went round the trees. "Do you know where the Montgomery place is?" The sun fell in shadowed webs across the car.

"Everybody knows where that is." The car moved down the street.

The stale smell of cigarettes had not yet gone out of her mother's room, the bath brush lay in a pile of magazines. That morning Zara had found her mother's nightgown still unwashed lying behind the bed. Zara took a corrugated box from the closet. She held her mother's nightgown to her face. Cigarettes, coffee, the special soaps, lotion, sweat. The gown folded itself and she placed it in a plastic bag and then the box, wrapping yards of strapping tape around it. Someday she would take it from a drawer and strip away the tape; someday she would sense again something of her mother. She sat on the bed, the small box in her lap, looking out the window across the terraces onto the lake. What was the difference between memory and real experience? Between holding and loss? *Place a block under the head.* Now she and her father were alone.

Zara had put on her bright yellow shorts one morning. Her thin adolescent legs sprang down the staircase and she heard her mother speak. "Look at those whitecaps, Forster," she said. "You'll go over in a minute."

"Oh, Mother," Zara said. "You're scared to go out any day. Aren't you?" She rummaged in the drawer looking for her suntan oil. Perhaps other days the water had been this white, although Zara could not remember it in the two years she had been going along with her father. If her mother had been able to swim, then she would not have said that.

"Don't say I didn't—"

"I know, Mother." Zara slammed the door, following her father out.

Forster untied the boat, saying, "Well, crew, have you got your bailing bucket?" The boat was a small one and together they had painted it blue, a blue so light you could barely tell it from the waves if you saw it from the shore and the sail was wrapped around the boom.

The boat heeled toward port, and Zara thrilled to see her father's face set in a sort of solitary determination. The wind whipped her russet hair behind her, and the dock moved off along the shore in a frenzy of water. Zara and her father were only a half mile out and Zara was hooting with excitement.

"How's this for the little sailor?" Forster shouted into the hot August wind.

"I wish Mother weren't such a sissy sometimes," Zara called.

"Your mother's no coward, Zara. Someday you'll understand that."

"What do you mean?" Zara moved suddenly then so she could hear. Without thinking she shifted from starboard to port. She felt the boom switch over her, barely grazing the top of her head. When her eyes opened under the blue-green water, she could see the mast upside down, the sail beside it like a fin. The centerboard scraped along her back as she kicked to the top. Far away the house, the dock, her room, she thought, a doll's house where her mother played. Waves rolled in and out along the upturned belly of the boat; in the froth, clumps of facial tissue rose and plummeted. She clung to the hull of the boat searching for her father in the waves. Daddy, she called against the wind. Daddy, Daddy, she called, thinking: I am thirteen now, I am thirteen. Zara is thirteen now. Where is her Daddy?

She felt his hand on her arm before she saw him pulling himself onto the boat, spitting water out of his mouth in a stream of consternation. "I've told you before, Zara. Never make a sudden move like that."

Her father dove beneath the boat then. Once, twice, unleashing the sail while she waited each time for the summer-browned shoulders, the blue eyes and certain brown face that was her father. Together they threw their bellies over the boat, taking hold of the far rim and pulling their combined weights back against it. The boat tilted, its weight perpendicular in the water, the two of them balanced upright as if they were standing on this broad wave, uncertain which way life would turn for them, unable to know where circumstance might lead. The boat yielded and they sank back treading rapidly to keep afloat so they might not miss the sight of the mast lifting itself into the sky.

"Get that centerboard," he commanded.

She swam for it, dipping the points of her hands into the warm surface waters, watching the white wooden fish rising and falling away from her. Her legs kicked out behind and she lunged for it. She brought it back to him. There her father sat, up to his waist with water in the center of the boat, bailing with the rubber bucket. The pail dipped in and out of the afternoon sky floating around him. "All right." He motioned her into the boat. "Go slowly." She pulled herself in.

"We could have drowned, couldn't we?"

"Bail," her father yelled, rowing toward the shore. "Keep bailing."

When finally they drew alongside the dock, they got out and waded the boat onto the strand, took down the mast, and turned over the little blue victim. Against the shoreline an orange dress was fluttering. The arm of a stranger cranked round and round a small black machine in front of her head, its shiny eye pointed in their direction.

"What the hell?" Forster asked, lifting one end of the sail onto his shoulder. "Christ," he said, staring at the movie camera. "There you have it—the compassion of the female."

Several years after that, Kathryn Montgomery was persuaded to come along when a neighbor offered them a ride in his motorboat. In her life jacket, Kathryn sat small and paralyzed between them, watching the wake fan out behind them as if it were some great disturbance in their lives. Then the motorboat slowed, there was a splash, and behind them at the end of a long nylon rope, wobbling back and forth like some twin-feathered hands of wild applause, were the skis and Forster trying to adjust them on his feet. Again and again the boat made its noise and circled to leave the rope behind while futilely her father tried to get out of the water.

When Forster finally conceded and pulled himself into the boat again, Kathryn spoke, tightening the lifebelt around herself, "By God, Forster, it can't be that difficult." Never would Zara forget her own exhilaration when, still dressed in the red pedal pushers and white blouse, the life jacket tightly secured around her, Kathryn shivered with fright and jumped into the water. The boat's engine roared forward and Kathryn rose to the plane that was Lake Marian. "Hurray!" Zara shouted. "Hurray!" Kathryn did not let go of the tow bar until the boat circled and dropped her at the other side of the lake.

Now Zara took the box with her mother's nightgown into the attic and packed it into a metal trunk. In the kitchen, Zara cried, Foxie, Foxie. Every morning the sun fell through the window of her bedroom and she woke to feel its rays. Violent and disturbing, they submerged her.

She pulled herself from the bed; and looking into the mirror, she saw the hollow beneath each eye, the skin drawn tight against her bones. The shadows grew, dark as that emptiness that filled her. She clung to this void now, thinking that at least no one, no one could take that from her, wishing someone would.

Now she stood before the kitchen drawer, studying Mrs. McGehry's cutlery: the knife for cutting cakes and loaves, the small sharp ones for paring, vegetable knives, the great wide cleaver. *Make a transverse incision through the entire thickness.* The knife cut through the light falling from the fixture above her, her hands knotted around the wooden handle. She would have to do nothing. Soon the blade would turn of itself. Relieve this sickness. *Make a median incision from the forehead to the point of the chin, and a horizontal incision from the angle of the mouth to the posterior borders of the mandible.*

"DON'T BE STUPID!" A voice, harsh, abrupt, stabbed at her from the corner of the doorway. It pivoted. She watched the brown cardigan retreat into the den, into silence, his hands fisted at his sides, his collar starched like indifference on his shoulders.

Mummie is dead, and you say: Don't be stupid? She looked at the blade. Somewhere someone had fastened to it this wooden handle. Don't be stupid? The handle pounded her thigh. *Don't.* Just, undeniable bludgeon. *Be.* The flash of steel skimmed through the air while the handle plunged. *Stupid.*

If anyone saw this bruise, Oh, she would say. If Michael O'Dea should ask in his small apartment above the hardware store what on earth had happened to her leg, "Oh," she would say, "I fell over a chair. Wasn't that stupid?" She pounded her leg. Misery grew, became tangible, manifested.

The long bottom drawer had been taken out of the dresser. The saw ground back and forth as they made the insert. Zara watched them: the two men in their gray-green overalls, the long black scarves around their necks. The saw went back and forth. "But she won't fit if you shorten it. Mummie can't fit in there." The saw went back and forth.

"There," the taller of the two said. "That will do it. Bring her over here, Cappy."

"All right, all right," the gray one said. "Don't be rushing me." He picked the corpse up from the table and laid her abruptly in the drawer.

"A good day's work well done," the tall one said. "Just seal her up and we'll be off to supper."

Zara reached into the drawer. She touched her mother's collar.

"I told you, lady, she'd fit just fine. Now didn't I? You have to trust old Charlie."

"Leave her alone, for Christ's sakes," the tall man said to the gray one. "Can't you see the little girl wants to pay her last respects?"

They went then and the broom went back and forth where they had left the pile of sawdust. Clouds of dirt puffed around the room.

Zara pushed the hair up around her mother's face. They said the hair would go on growing: growing until it filled the drawer to cushion the little bones that had been a mother. "Foxie—" In the chest of drawers the blue eyes opened. "Foxie!" Zara cried. "You're alive!"

"Well, what did you think?" her mother asked. "Get me out of here."

Zara picked her up then and carried her to the little chair, the rocker. Her mother rocked back and forth. Clouds of dust rose from the floor boards.

Und wenn dich alles das nicht weckt,
so werde durch den Ton der Minne zärtlich aufgeneckt!
O dann erwachst du schon, O dann erwachst du schon!
Wie oft sie dich an's Fenster trieb
das weiss sie, d'rum steh' auf,
und habe deinen Sänger lieb,
du süsse Maid, steh' auf,
und habe deinen Sänger lieb,
du süsse Maid, steh' auf, steh' auf,
du süsse Maid, steh' auf, steh' auf,
steh' auf, du süsse Maid, steh' auf!

Michael O'Dea put his arm around her, waking Zara in the afternoon where she had fallen asleep in his bed. "Bad dream?"

"It had a good ending. It's usually the waking up that's bad."

"Oh, I know," he said. "You'd rather be in bed with some other guy. I'm a disgusting sight to wake up to."

"Oh, Michael," she said, reaching across the blankets for him. "That's not true." *Open the eyelids and draw the eye forwards with the forceps.*

He kissed her breast through the sheet and for a moment she felt the sadness go out of her like so much stuffing. He left the room. Now he would be making coffee as he always did before they studied. She heard him open the cupboard. Beside the bed lay one of Michael's books. She opened it to where the matchstick marked his readings.

The page turned. *The Lord is with thee; blessed art thou among women.*

Everywhere she turned she saw her mother on the street: the sway of a skirt, the slight limp of a stranger, a head turned suddenly at the bus stop, her own reflection beyond the green velvet dresses in a window, a piece of paper blown against a fence. Everywhere she expected what she could not find: woman, mother-child, Kathryn. This evening only the horses moved in the meadow. At the grave she set her palm onto the sod. Their tails flicked up in annoyance and one by one their heads turned to look up at the daughter lying full length upon the grave as twilight pressed its light through the fence. Unanimously they tossed their chestnut manes back to hear her weeping, they stamped the ground. "You told me to do it. You told me," she cried. "You knew I couldn't hold you."

That night the rain came in torrents, the tent flaps shaking all around us, the beams and lines swaying in the wind. It could be a bad night for everyone, I said; I was only sixteen. Until this sudden downpour, the day had been hot and getting hotter. Up and down the aisles all afternoon you could hear the programs trying to beat out the heat and the talk of tornadoes and freak cyclone incidents. Families lifted out of their beds by the wind and laid down dead, side by side in the street. Pieces of straw driven straight into the sides of trees. By evening there was a crazy yellow light in the sky, and then the rain.

"We're going on with it, Katie," Roderick said.

"Yes," we said, looking out through the end of the tent at the jaundiced sky. Already the crowd was uneasy, shuffling back and forth rather than taking their seats.

I had on my blue dress. I ripped the hem out as I rushed onto the stage. "Schubert with lightning," I shouted. Right in the middle of my first song, Roderick shook his fist at me. I never sang so loud in my life. Good evening, Nebraska, I shouted. Did you hear me? A sea of white handkerchiefs rose into the lamplight for the Chautauqua salute. It was like looking out onto rough water or rows of grain with tassels in the thousands gone white and moving in the wind. The next I knew we were in the ditch and it was as if, by the sound, a train were coming through. I looked up and the tent burst out suddenly like a balloon and at the center, through the top, one of the big poles came reeling into the air. It flew straight up and plunged down again into the earth, stuck like a mast. Canvas flew around it in shreds. Get down, someone yelled. Get down. Roderick Dawson put his arm over my face.

Tails flicked into the shadows as instinct carried the horses away over the convoluted meadow. "Why have you left me?" she wailed. "Why did you do it?" Against a stream of headlights from the highway, home they flew over the green circumstance of grasses, around the corner of the barn toward the solace of their evening feeding. Their ears turned back against their heads: "Why have you left me?"

They were nearly finished with the bodies now. Formaldehyde permeated the room. Though her eyes barely stung now from the vapor, a chill passed over her each day before she had even entered the lab. Here were the cadavers, their knees drawn up on every table, legs spread wide apart, genitals exposed. Ropes bound hands to feet in lithotomy position. Thirty bodies: seventeen breasts among them, a few long rubber scars, all that was left from the mastectomies; three hundred toes, nails gone yellow with preservative, a miracle that none had been lost; fingers—two hundred ninety-nine—carelessness among the living, perhaps a lawn-mower, a grain dryer, an accident involving cars, the quick splash of glass and blood, the appendage lying in the dark alongside the road where no one had thought to bring it along, where no one had been able to find it lying there among the creeping jenny and the milkweed, the gravel, the blood; twenty-six vermiform appendices, four clean white gashes down the abdomen, scars a surgeon swore would shine in the laboratory dark if the lights were turned out and the moon through the windows were bright enough, one appendix that came out now too late to aid the swollen belly, to stop the gangrenous growth from overtaking the bowels, the breath; aortal strictures, a mass of yellow fiber in the liver, yellow face; massive brain hemorrhages; slashed wrists, tendons severed, hands dangling beneath the rope; bodies; precious loves, flesh, corpse.

Zara wiped the blade of her scalpel with a cloth. *Run incisions round the anus and the pudendal cleft separately.* Mrs. X had borne children, many of them. *Join them by a median cut and make another median cut from the anus to the coccyx.* The blade slit the skin. She thought of diagrams. Mrs. X: stick figure feels no pain. If it were not for the tattoo on the bottom of her foot that said she was the property of this hospital, Mrs. X, too, would be lying in a box. Perhaps it had been that fear that made her volunteer herself for this. Mutilation, rot. What did it all mean? What difference did it make to Mrs. X whether she were carved on a butcher's block to train young doctors in the whereabouts of ligament and bone, of cortex and nerve, or whether she were laid out in her new silk dress to decay slowly in her own hidden fumes?

The long white coat of Professor Adler brushed beside her. He stared between the cadaver's thighs. "Class," he said. "Class. Here we have an example of one of the finest dissections I have ever seen."

Before them lay the ribbons of flesh flayed in agony and precision. Zara Montgomery stood back to let them appraise her work, to let them say how fine Mrs. X looked lying on her back this warm spring day. In boxes everywhere, the under lips of mothers dissolved beneath their Sunday clothes, gave way to parasitic crawling things. Beloved cunt: I have washed you, dried you, come out of you, been you. Where was reverence now?

It would not be long until the term would be over. And when the last cut had been made, perhaps she would say: I no longer intend to be a physician, to deal with death every moment of every futile day. Her father would be disappointed; worse than that, he would be disgraced before his colleagues and that would sour him, that would change his love. Perhaps Michael would leave her, too, then. She would be alone. But still she knew that the day she gave this up would be the day a certain relief would come over her. And that would never leave. Perhaps she had known it that first day when she had seen her father holding the appendix up to the sun, the vile red and flaming worm of disease held up to the light as if it had some beauty of its own, as if it could somehow offer meaning to something. And what could her father do with his skill and knowledge? Offer resistance to the force of death, temporarily. Always losing to time, to circumstance, to one's own erroneous ways. What kind of life was that? Buying time for others, telling others there was no time. How could that expand the mind? Give meaning to the meaningless? And when the time came, when your technical knowledge should have been your savior, you, physician and god, could not save your wife, your mother, your husband, your child. You could not save yourself.

Professor Adler laid his hand on her back. "Well done, Montgomery," he said. She could have been a fine physician, she knew that; always she had known that to be true. Someday she would hand her scalpel to her partner. There had to be something more somewhere. "Thank you, Dr. Adler." She drew back the flesh. She would take her degree; she would hold on as long as she could.

Again it was Mrs. McGehry's day off and Forster would stay at the hospital late taking his supper in the cafeteria with the other doctors. After her graduation Zara would not go to the hospital. No longer would she run her tray through the line and see the table of the hierarchy, her father among them, nodding at her in respect as she went to sit with Michael O'Dea and their friends by the great pane of light that looked out upon the hospital grounds. Expectant mothers would be billowing in pairs along the windy admitting drive. Perhaps the explosive red top of an automobile would swing in under the canopy, and a call would come on the dining-room telephone. The last drop of coffee would be downed, and the emergency A team would leave the room seemingly without hurry, still talking about the spleen on four west or a technique that was being disputed in the medical journals.

After this week, if Zara Montgomery were to meet them, their eyes would shift slightly away from her; and the heads would tip in a perfunctory nod, unable to understand how one of their best medical-school graduates could walk out on them and that best of professions, how she could refuse to do her internship or at least establish a general practice. Zara Montgomery took refuge in the thought that other women had left medicine behind. There would be other ways of making contributions.

This day when she would be alone with Michael in the house would be a break in the beginning of her fretting. Soon Michael O'Dea would ring the front door bell, and she would meet him. They would make love, if he were feeling secure enough, and then he would study. She would read perhaps the autobiography of one playwright or another, identifying with all those indecisive moments in the book before the artist's career had actually begun. She drew her bath, wondering what Michael's response to her defection would be. She pushed down the fear that he would no longer want her; she tried to keep it down.

Carefully she dried herself and rubbed the pink, satiny lotion over her shoulders, her breasts, in the crease between them, over the rest of her body. Soon he would be there, and then he would either show that disappointment her father had shown, that lack of understanding, saying, "Zara, I'd expected more tenacity from you of all people," not caring what her reasons were, not listening when she tried to give them. Or he would accept the decision as hers and, therefore, as one thought-out and intelligent. One or the other, those were the alternatives. She put on a T-shirt and jeans, for it was almost summer again. She bent over, brushing her copper hair where it fell, full and thick, nearly to the carpet. The leaves rubbed quietly against the windows, and the lilacs hung their lavish heads as if unable to decide whether to be proud or ashamed.

She heard his step on the front walk and was down the stairs with the front door opened before the bell could be sounded. She did not want to prolong the agony of wondering how he would receive this news. In his white coat still, he towered in the door, the constant red in his cheeks, the green eyes questioning her. She threw her arms around him, and he bent down his head to touch briefly his moustache to her lips. He put his hands on her shoulders. "Where were you this morning? I looked for you on rounds. I thought you might be sick."

"Michael," she said, blurting it out. "I'm quitting the hospital—all of it."

"Medicine?" he gasped. She felt his hands tightening. "Did something happen?"

"Nothing happened. I want to do something else with my life."

"What?" he asked. "What on earth would you do?"

"I don't know yet." She had to turn her face away from him then. Now her voice nearly failed her. "Something less depressing, that's all I know." Perhaps her mother had felt this bitterness in her stomach, this same excitement, when she had given up her career. But her mother had regretted it! *If you have to have a crusade, Zara, make it be yourself*: her mother's voice. "I don't know—but not that, not that anymore, Michael. I can't."

He turned her face up toward his.

"But you're going to take your M.D. in June, aren't you?"

"Yes, I'll do that."

"And you're not going to do your internship."

"No."

"But, Zara— But regrets . . ."

"No, never." They had said of her and her father at the hospital that Montgomery and Montgomery would soon be their top surgical team. They had said that.

Suddenly and inexplicably the tension went out of Michael's face. Zara had never seen his face so smooth. It was almost as if his acceptance came from something inside himself, she thought then, not from any concern about her well-being at all. He said, "Your father and I will make a sufficient contribution to medicine." His long hands moved abruptly then over the front of her shirt.

"Michael—"

"You'll find something, Zee. I know you will." In the living room, he kissed along her eyebrow and then the soft firm orbit of each eyelid, along the flush of her cheekbones and into the hollows beneath them, his teeth at her earlobe then, his breath like a current running down her neck and under the cotton. The planes of his face riding the planes of her body. She wrapped her arms around his back. Why had he not so much as given a protest or asked? He must have seen it in me, she thought, he must have known it all along. We are so close, she said to herself, that maybe it needn't even be said. He pulled at her T-shirt, and her hands took hold of it, too. Yes, they would marry, something told her that now. He understood. But she would do something more with her life. Something. Her arms went up and with them the lower edge of her yellow shirt. It caught beneath one breast. She felt herself fall free, and the shirt was on the floor. She took his head in her hands: the dark, fierce shocks of hair; and when his teeth found her nipples, her hands crushed the fury of hair against her chest. If her face changed when she heard the metal zipper of her jeans ripping slowly down at her front, she did not know it. She only knew the sound of it: something breaking open bit by bit. The jeans slipped down over her hips, down along the curve of her thigh.

Circling her navel, his lips followed, circumscribing the wings of her hipbones. The short broad wedges of his immaculate nails crept slowly down her middle until he was on his knees, his arms around her, his mouth between her thighs, the spring of his eyes upon her. *Fruhling. Fruhling.* Now the future made no difference. Now his eyes closed; the tiny creases at their corners reappeared as he pulled her onto the carpet. His knuckles nudged up and down the insides of her calves. He took her feet, his teeth and the feathery moustache in tender grazing at her soles. He pressed her ankles against the outer crests of her buttocks, the full white flesh of her thighs. His mouth circled. It pressed at her center.

As she reached for his shirt, her leg straightened. Again he took her ankle and pressed it firmly against her buttock; he put her hand around it and tightened it there. He drew the other one up again. Her fingers gripped her own ankles. "You'll stay with me, won't you?" he asked. "You won't leave everything behind?" She turned her head toward the pink light falling from the window through the hall. "I know you'll find something." She heard his buckle fall against the floor, the rasping of his zipper. His shoulders blocked the light, and it began.

She felt the flush rise over her, first the heat at the insides of her thighs, and then the flood in her abdomen, her breasts, her forehead. She felt it behind her eyes. His mouth hard against her mouth, the pulse between her legs bucking up into a tempo she could not contain. Her back rose from the floor, lifting, twisting him, her, nearly into the mahogany table, lifting them until her wailings could have carried them both around the room: up, up over the flowered vases and the shining bottles of the sideboard, over the dark brown sofa, the potted ferns and the marble mantel. Out out the door they would arch over each effulgent terrace of their sighings until, her face buried in the warm constancy of his shoulder, they could descend into the short inarticulate grass of their beginning: the feelings of that moment and the conflicts they could not explain.

The air in the theater was buzzing with the intensity of the overhead lights. Three o'clock in the morning. He knew it was that hour as surely as if he had looked at his wrist-watch or there had been a clock shining out at him from the corner. He turned out the lights and stood a moment watching the illumination from the street flowing in a dim wedge through the open door over the deserted rows of seats. He turned the key in the lock and walked out into the summer night. Under the lamps he stepped absently along, down the main drive of the town: past the darkened shop windows, the lethargic clicking of the traffic signals, the geraniums potted and stalwart in the heat near the base of the community fountain. He heard the incessant whirring of the locusts as it crowded the air, high-pitched and undeniable, as if it had always been circulating, this sound in his veins.

At the edge of the town square he overtook the massive marble figures. They were brutal looking, these sculpted lions, their forepaws slightly raised as if with the slightest provocation they might spring. Often as a boy he had mounted this one on his right, and there he had gripped the structure between his knees and pressed his face against what should have been the warm fur of the mane. His fingers brushed the stone fetlock of the animal. He could not get the thought of what Tom Fitzgerald had said to him out of his mind. Tom Fitzgerald had never been a father to him, after all. Tom Fitzgerald was a bigoted, staid, and aging man.

He turned on his heels and strode toward the string of shops on the other side of the college campus. It was cooler now than during the afternoon, but still it was hot. The temperature blasting up each day. Nearly ninety, the numerals on the bank said. The trees bowed down over the black heat of the pavement as his steps guided him home. Mickey Fiddler, they had called him. That year on the Fitzgerald farm had been the most comfortable time in his life. He had felt a part of their rambunctious rioting. Now it was time to start a family of his own, he thought. He would join one. He would be respectable and cared for in that family. Forster Montgomery and Zara. Forster had those same features he had always admired in Tom Fitzgerald's face: the pale blue irises of the eyes, the way the crow's-feet started up in laughter or concern. Like the eyes of priests they were: pale and soft and irreproachable. They would call him son, and husband, and father. Still it was almost too much to hope that they, too, would not reject him.

"My God! What's that?" Zara Montgomery cried when she opened Michael's apartment door. "What are all these things on you?" Inside a pyramid of pine branches entwined in plastic curios, Michael O'Dea was jerking across the room.

"What do you think it is?" O'Dea asked. "I'm a Christmas tree. Go ahead, examine. Take me home." He waved his feet; first one long green diving fin and then another came out from beneath the fringe.

"It's phenomenal, Michael!" She stared in astonishment

at the red and silver packages studded on the rubber webs. Only barely visible beneath all his boughs was the old sheet to which he'd sewn the greens. "It must have taken you forever to put this together. It's really very—zany."

"That's my Christmas-tree stand." The fins flapped out onto the linoleum. "I was going to paint them white to look like snow, but I didn't have time."

In her everyday shorts and blouse, her copper hair swaying, she studied the toys he had strung so carefully round and round himself. "Look at this little fan!" she cried, on her knees and pushing the lever that made the little blades go around.

"Zara, your costume! Where is it?"

Now she had the fan turning and the mechanical false teeth chattering back in conversation between the branches. "I have one, don't worry. Where did you get all these objects? Look! a rabbit's foot to make you lucky."

"I'm going to look like a fool rigged up like this if you don't have a costume." He scowled, trundling away from her toward his frayed sofa under the window. The phenomenon turned; his eyes were staring down at her. Under the pine needles, a small dark fringe—his moustache. Two green beadlike eyes.

"Come back! It's in the car, I promise. I'll put it on when we get there."

He turned toward the trees outside, the underbelly of a black squirrel mounting the screen on his window. "You do have a costume?" he asked.

She sat back on her heels and saw the animal scrabbling toward him on the mesh. She saw the little train running up his back on a row of popcorn. "Michael, yes. I have a costume. Cross my heart, I have one. Now come back. I'm not finished looking."

"It's in the car?"

"Yes, Michael. It is."

"So it's in the car," he sighed, turning. "Well, I guess it's all right then. I just expected to see it now, that's all."

"What's the matter?" she laughed. "Afraid our socks won't match?"

"Of course not." He craned his neck then, trying to see himself.

He was young. And he was ignorant, Michael Francis had said of himself. Otherwise he would have known. He had been playing with matches while his parents were hooping across the hall. He admitted having done it. He had struck a match to light the candle on the cupcake left from the party that day. Hearing his mother's moans and then the louder one—it was almost a grunt, he said, the kind one might hear coming from behind a rhododendron bush—he had thrust the candle deep into the cake and lit the match. He remembered the candle glowing, illuminating the sugary frosting in a horizontal peculiar light. The curtain, too, had glowed, swinging out from the window against the doorway in the breeze.

As he had crawled into his bed, he heard the moaning again. "Don't you go disturbing us. Don't be a pest," she had said—much as Sister Catherine, the fat nun, always said. The smoke rose as he peeked out to see the doorway rise in flames. Again he looked and there he saw her, his mother running naked through the fire unable to escape, her hair floating out behind her like a copper wick. And behind his mother—two bare broad shoulders barred the far bedroom door from sight. He heard the staircase collapsing before he saw it: he saw both parents drop into his unintentioned trap.

All his compatriots, the orphans, were staring at him now, and on the far beds only one of the idiots was smearing a tongue along the frosted windowpane. Proudly he finished his tale. When the heat had gone up in the room until he could not stand it, he had called out again and again until through the window a giant rubber-booted foot crashed in beside the bed. It was like a cartoon, he said. The boot, the arm, and then the red rectangle far below him.

Fitzgerald halted, his soft blue eyes full on O'Dea's face now. "Jesus," Fitzgerald said. "That's the girl with the red-brown hair down to her flank?"

"She stands about this high—" his fingers flicked the button between his collar bones. When he felt his own hand at his chest it was as if he felt her breath against his sternum pressing in on him. He pushed her image aside. "You know who I mean."

The man stepped back, the hat cocked on the crown of his head. His handkerchief passed around his forehead and under the rim of his hat. Carefully he folded the cloth and put it in his pocket again. "I'll tell you exactly how I feel about it, Mickey. I said the same thing to Johnny last year, and I'll say it to all my boys. Not that you're not one of them. Always I think I've got seven boys and one good influence in the world. You're the influence, naturally. When my boys go out to get married, I'll tell them like I'm telling you now—find yourself a plain girl. A few flaws and it takes the anxiety out of life. Plain but smart. Whatever happened to that Kleinliebelink girl? Now there was a woman who was plain, but not homely certainly, smart but not overbearing. She would appreciate the living you made for her. What do you want to go hitching up with Lake Marian's jewels for, Mickey? You know every low-life dog and junior executive is going to try to latch onto her."

"She's not the insecure type," Michael said edgily. She

isn't that kind, he thought. He watched Fitzgerald take a step back from him.

"Insecure, hell," Fitzgerald said. "And I suppose you're not?" The hat pivoted and proceeded up the row.

"Yes," Michael O'Dea said, his eyes cast down at the dirt unraveling under his feet. "Yes," he said, downhearted and weary. The row was interminable. The hat went on. "I guess I see what you mean."

Tom Fitzgerald was whistling a contemplative tune, the notes falling one after another almost as if they were forming a song. "She like your fiddle?"

"It's hard to find time to play now since I've been in school and working at the theater. But, yes. She likes the violin." He swallowed now as if he could rid himself of the disappointment in his throat. "She plays the piano."

"She's not a Catholic, Mickey."

"No." I don't practice it myself, he thought. What difference does it make?

"Well, there you have it. She likes your music but she'll never understand you. Why don't you come along to dinner. Anne will want to see you. The boys, too."

The farmhouse moved white and peeling upon them as soon as they had rounded the barn. The yard was empty. "The boys must be in to eat already. Kick your feet against the step. Annie hasn't changed. The guy who brings dirt into her house is better off with six feet over his head."

During the months when he was trying to locate the wife of that pilot—he was certain this woman, a lawyer in Quebec, was his mother—he accumulated various sentimental objects. Maps of World War II bombing missions and color photographs of a magenta sun rising against the Philippines. Vast expanses of ocean were placed in yellow matte board where his old medical posters used to hang. He moved his first violin from the wall beside his bed and replaced it with a large mushroomlike photo of Japan.

When the letters he had sent came back opened yet marked in a delicate feminine hand "Addressee Unknown," he was certain he had found her. Still his mother would not acknowledge him! It was another four months until he had a reply to his repeated inquiries. The lawyer had died the year before and willed her estate to the son she had left behind after the war—Terrence O'Connor, living in Omaha as a certified public accountant. Michael O'Dea did not take the war memorabilia and photographs of Terrence O'Connor's father off his walls. He left them up as a reminder of his own stupidity.

Occasionally he wondered why the other boys had not realized that his story was a fraud, why they had not mentioned that he had been there as long as any of them could remember. Willy Howlett was the only one who had been there longer than he.

When the nuns closed the orphanage, most of the other children had been adopted. Again and again he had told the story of the fire to his foster families, hoping if he told it well enough they might take pity on him and adopt him. When the parents were upset by this and sent him away after a few months or a year, Michael O'Dea blamed himself. It must be his looks, he thought, that made people turn against him. He grew more and more self-conscious. He thought himself to be grotesque. He was certain others knew he watched himself.

"A friend of mine stole that rabbit's foot from Father McKinsey."

"What was a priest doing with something like that?"

"Blessing the Host, of course. *Domine, non sum dignus, ut intres sub tectum meum.* . . . Ever since I got the foot,

Father McKinsey and I've been very tidy agnostics." The twigs went up around his face.

"I can tell that," she said smiling at the holy cards, the nativity characters strung all over his body. "Even the sheep and Joseph. What happened to your friend, the one who filched the lucky charm?"

"He's doing penance at Fort Madison."

"Oh—he's not."

"You're right, he isn't," Michael sighed. "He might as well be. He's got six kids and for that he sells Prudential."

"He should have kept the foot."

O'Dea stooped then so Zara could see the blue-and-green tin globe on the top of his head. "Go ahead, give it a whirl." Around it went, spilling out a tune about traveling. And then he was telling her how he had acquired the thirteen tiny picture frames and the miniature squirt-gun camera, how he had collected nearly all his decorations in grab bags at the orphanage or as hand-me-downs in foster homes. Some, he admitted shyly, he had stolen from the hardware store. He laughed then saying that though his life of crime had been a short one he had enjoyed the rewards.

"Look!" she cried then, as she found clinging to his branches the purple dice he had kept tied to his rear-view mirror in the days before his '57 Chevy gave out. Here collided the Kewpie dolls in pink feathered hats and a pair of red wax lips she remembered buying for him at McNurty's during recess. At his waist the toy bathtub with silver spigots was hung so carefully that it held a little water in it. She counted twenty-six baseball cards—all of Nellie Fox—and one piece of thin rectangular bubble gum with six multicolored bathtub ducklings biting into it. There were forty-eight American flags on him and one for the Confederates, two crèche images of the Baby Jesus tied to a plastic ghost, and a picture of a nun. Here, too, drooped the Mouseketeer ears that had been chewed by some stray cat or puppy, the picture of Annette Funicello in her autographed angora sweater, and a plastic stick-on screen for the television. On his shoulder, a Beatle wig and a pair of 3-D glasses rode a rubber nose. When Michael shifted his weight, she found the hula hoop wedged into all the rest of it, and hanging from that smooth green plastic was a little bow and at the end of it the tiny tan shoes on their pink shoelaces. On each of his battered airplane models was a Kleenex parachute. Here, too, the miniature Corvette hubcaps, a double-exposed picture postcard of Janis Joplin kissing Elvis, a plastic silver bullet . . .

"My silver bullet!" she cried. "Michael! How long have you had it?" She would have known it anywhere.

Sometimes at night in his apartment he would draw the bath water and sit there, legs crossed, a small candle flickering on the shelf beside the tub. He felt the water moving over him, over the soft brown fronds of hair up and down the length of his body. He felt gentle, real, at peace with himself then. Only one other thing gave him that sense of comfort, of integration. When he played his violin, he felt serene, drawing the bow across the strings, sometimes with slow and mellow intention, sometimes with great rapidity. The tempo made no difference. Others might be in the room or playing along with him; yet he was alone, absorbed in what he thought himself to actually be: a rich yet subtle composition that was now too often nonexistent. He had no time for music now. Other people had become an impingement to him.

Considering those persons in his life, he felt a slight yet almost tangible hostility. Why did he have none of those things others took for granted? Parents, siblings, holiday gifts, a prepaid college education. And if the worthy were rewarded in this life, as the nuns had often told him, then, he thought, certainly he must be the lowest, most despicable worm in the world.

At the Fitzgerald household, he had even chosen his own birth date. The sixteenth of February. Chosen because none of the other children celebrated during that month and it was far enough away from Christmas not to be anticlimactic and close enough to Valentine's to make the others sentimental.

He laughed to himself the day Marilyn Kleinliebelink tried to size him up using this false information. "Yes," she said, "that's exactly what you are, Mike." She was reading from her book of charts and astral evaluations. "Quiet, stern, intelligent, and promiscuous. You fit exactly." He smiled then, for it could have been any other date, for all the nuns had told him. Marilyn had gone on to read her own chart, saying that they were, according to the book, quite suited for one another. He had smiled and she had taken it for a sign of agreement.

Even now he despised his appearance. Oh, how he hated it when women kindled a fire in their faces and said, looking up at him: Oh, Michael. Your eyes. So brilliant, so gorgeous, so green, they said. A hawk could have had such eyes, he thought. Piercing little magnets that drew women to him whom he could not trust, who would never love him for what he was. Worst of all, it was his eyes, he knew, that made men stand apart from him, taking an extra step away that they would not take with other men. Why could he not have had that strong and masculine sense of himself the others had? That stern purpose in his body that allowed for casualness? He thought himself a continual buffoon in the company of others, and when they found him charming and delightfully unusual his greatest fears were confirmed.

"Enough, enough!" he shouted. "Enough excitement. I'm about to roast during this exhibition."

"But did I find them all? I couldn't have, could I?"

"You missed the most important." The Tree glided stiffly away from her toward his small bag of groceries on the table.

"I did? Here it is! A red paper heart."

"No," he said, resolutely. "That was nothing. Look up now." The globe was spinning around above the pine needles and a string of berries.

"An A & W wrapper?"

"You're getting closer, Zenith."

"The globe," she said. "I already got that."

"You're extraordinarily warm now."

"Michael!" Imbedded like a crown in the branches around his forehead, barely visible beneath the ropes of swinging popcorn balls and candy kisses, were the firecrackers. "But, Michael, what if they go off!"

He threw his shoulders back, strutting fancifully toward the door. "You'll wear the traditional black, of course," he laughed haughtily. The summer light was streaking through the trees outside onto the thin black cylinders he had strung around his head. Pennants fluttered, ornaments collided. "Well?" he said.

"Well?! It's frightening, Michael."

"Ha!" he laughed. "Zany, zanier, zaniest," he said. "I'm hungry. Let's go."

Every night in his apartment Michael turned on the fan beside his bed, stripped off his clothes, and lay on top of his coverlet. He had, at the most, five hours to sleep, and then he would wake to the alarm and stand beneath the cold bursts of the shower. He would down a cup of coffee on his way to the hospital, where, if he was lucky, he would catch a glimpse of Zara Montgomery in her crisp white jacket and skirt, her long copper hair braided down her back. Then if she was in the mood, they would walk through the corridors together, making plans for the weekend, steering toward the gathering flock of white at the end of the hall where they would begin their morning rounds.

As he fell asleep he thought he saw again the farmhouse door opening. He saw the eyes look up around the table. "Anne Marie—" Tom shouted toward the kitchen. "You'll never guess what turned up in the corn." A greeting came from behind the kitchen door, and Tom Fitzgerald went on shouting. "Mickey Fiddler's come to visit, and he's going to marry Doc Montgomery's daughter."

"Married?" went up the cry of his foster brothers around the fried chicken and potato salad. Through the frame of the kitchen door, Anne Fitzgerald poked her head out.

"Mickey!" she cried. Michael O'Dea hardly noticed the fullness of her dress, the drawn-back graying of her hair. Directly his gaze sought out the dark astonished oval that her mouth made.

"I'll just stand up with the door open and hang out the side." Post-parade watchers gathered in the street: a Cub Scout troop in caps and badges and neck bandanas, men in Bermuda shorts, halter-topped women.

Zara put his groceries in the front of the station wagon. "You can't do that on the Fourth; the cops will be thick today."

"So? Tie a red flag on me. Let's go."

She hoisted a case of beer from the tailgate and hauled that, too, around to the front seat. She shoved aside the ice chest and in it the pig. "Michael, you *are* a red flag." Now the large summer melons rested on top of the beer, and the crowd edged in for a closer look.

"I know just how I'll hold on." He watched her going

back and forth. "What are you doing moving all these things?"

"Rearranging." She went off and came back again with another load. "Don't worry, I wouldn't leave my honey behind in an unfriendly crowd like this." Now the chatter was rising around him, and he wished that he hadn't decked his face with so many branches.

"Zara, I'm getting uncomfortable," he whispered as the children began to circle him. Zara passed by him again, and he could not be sure that she had heard. There she was filling in the place where he was planning to stand, whistling all the time about a white Christmas. Yellow flashes of neckerchief bobbed in and out of his sight on the street, and then a childish voice was hooting under his limbs: "Hey, guys! Look at the goods this turkey's got on!"

"How's it going, boys?" Michael asked, cocking his head in the direction of the child he could not see for all the branches surrounding him. He caught a glimpse of blue arms waving in a woods and someone screwing up a small face at him. The globe swung around on his head.

"Would you believe this weirdo? Witness these firecrackers."

"Mister. Why you got firecrackers on your head?"

"It's a joke," Michael O'Dea said curtly.

"What's so funny, man?"

"I'm going to a costume party."

"Shut up, Packer," came another voice. "Your old lady probably eats them on the Fourth."

"Does not."

With a good deal of pivoting, he could see them: the small blue scouts rocking on their heels, their hands stuck deep in the pockets of their jeans, elbows careening.

"Fartblossom lights 'em up to blow his airs away."

"Maybe this guy's not a Christmas tree," an even louder voice proclaimed. "Are you, mister?"

"What else is green with branches, stupid?"

"Snot."

Laughter went up all around him. "That was a good one, boys," Michael O'Dea said in all humility. "A good joke on me."

Caps were lifting around him; the faces came into view, their small delinquent eyes frisking his own. Just then he felt a tug at his flank where the holiday cookies he had baked and decorated so carefully were strung. "Cut that out!" Michael O'Dea shouted, swinging about in animation like an ornamental haystack. He tap-danced in his fins.

"Cut that out!" the little boys cried, waving their arms and stamping their feet. He felt another hand in the candy canes.

"Watch yourselves. You're making me angry now."

"Ohh delicious!" they cried, smacking their lips.

The heat was rising from the pavement, the sun pouring down as the boys grew more and more daring. He would tell them a story, he would frighten them away. A story of torture. But how had they done it? What had the old man said to him when he as a child had pocketed that last baseball card? He remembered then. "We do it like the natives does," the proprietor of the dime store said. "We takes the shoplifter to the woods and makes a small cut in the belly —there to draw a small piece of his intestines out. We takes a little twig like a peg and drives it through the gut into a little sapling. A tall stick will do. Then the shoplifter he makes a walk, you see, round and round the tree. Unwinding, you understand?, till he sees the offense he has made against society. That is the unfortunate part of the punishment, little boy. Even the primitives knowed it. By the time he sees what mistakes he done—Boom! Too late. The hand of God done carried him away."

Michael O'Dea felt a slight breeze of relief as he managed each of his halting steps. "See you around, boys. Give my regards to Akela."

The chatter grew louder; it did not recede. He swung around: there they were beside him, behind him, following along. An entire rope of popcorn balls went down. He could see the blue and yellow beanies lined up as if the entire troupe were eating along a trough.

"Stop it!"

"Eat it!" the little boys yelled, munching voraciously.

The orphans had called it Running Away from Home, Michael O'Dea recalled, twitching miserably on the hot black pavement in his pine needles and fins. He tried now to understand the thinking of the nuns at the orphanage. He and the other boys had hidden themselves until it was almost dark, watching the nuns like jackdaws moving through the sunset in search of them. "Come in NOW," the less insightful Sisters had yelled, "or it's a hundred rosaries apiece." The threats rose in increments while the orphanage cooks waited macaroni dinners until eight.

Again and again the orphans shifted their position, hunched over and creeping along the rows of corn, moving farther into the country. "*Libera nos, quaemus, Domine, ab omnibus malis, praeteritis, praesentibus, et futuris,*" they cried in unison until hunger wearied them, until they thought of bread, of macaroni and cheese. They would circle around and beat the nuns back to the dining hall.

No one had ever been able to explain why they had surrendered the moment that miniature, feminine hand appeared between stalk and corn silk. There it was: a hand so small and white it looked like a porcelain earring pinching onto Willy Howlett's ear just as Willy was drawing out the stratagem in the dirt. Perhaps it had been the way the Midget Nun had appeared so suddenly in her miniature black habit, the way she said it, so calmly, yet lighthearted as if she were one of their troop. "All right, lieutenant," she said. "The jig is up. Form ranks." While they had been crawling and plotting their circular motion, the Midget Nun had been walking around them all the time, head held high while she figured out just which ringleader to snuff.

Michael O'Dea backed up in irritation when he heard the voice rising up from the huddle of scouts. "What do you want my magnifier for, Wilson?" the fat boy asked. The child-faces smiled up at him.

"For the firecrackers, stupedo."

"Yeah, fart, let's blow this turkey up."

The group parted and the round one ran for home.

"Ka-boom!" Wilson shouted, flinging his cap straight up.

A small voice was whining now as if it would crawl under Michael O'Dea's coniferous wings: "But you can't, Wilson. Mrs. Steiner won't let you."

Michael O'Dea could hear the low drone of Father Mc-Kinsey explaining it again and again. *There is a wealth of beauty in this prayer said so softly, as if the plea were dying down in the deepest emotion of appeal, to the very bottom of our hearts. Evils crowd about us in this life like a mob bent upon doing damage to our soul. . . .*

"Bombs over Tokyo!" one of the boys cried out.

"But I've never been to the airplane museum and we won't get to go—" came the wail.

"Jiminy crickets, Peewee, will ya please shut up your trap?"

"Aw, Wilson, look what you done. You got the Peewee bawling again."

"It's my only chance to go—" the little voice was stammering.

"Wilson ain't gonna light anybody up."

"I'm going to tell, I'm going to rat on every one of you. It's my only chance."

"For Christ's sakes, Peewee. Can it, will you? Wilson's only playing a joke on Fatty Fartblossom."

The wailing slowed to a series of little burps. "He's not?"

Wilson settled his cap back on his head. "Shit no, infant. Didn't you see that tuba run after his stupid science glass? Here, have a piece of candy and cut that bawling out." Michael O'Dea jerked aside as the candy kiss was plucked.

"Well, kiss my ass," one of them said. Another made a large smacking sound.

"Listen, boys," Michael O'Dea said bound and helpless in his costume. "Why don't you help the lady unload the car instead of keeping me company?"

"What lady?"

He looked up then to see Zara Montgomery striding from the grocery store into the pharmacy. He looked down at them; he said, "Disease."

"What?"

"Disease! Dis-*ease!*" he cried. "You can get disease from strangers and eating substances of unknown quality. You can get disease from me, from anyone. Don't your leaders teach you anything these days? Disease is an abnormal condition of an organism, or part, or Scout, especially as consequence of infection, inherent weakness, or environmental stress. Don't they tell you not to take candy from strangers, get into foreign cars? And what about old ladies? Do you waylay them in the streets? Do you eye each delicate haunch? Disease impairs physiological functioning. In this case consider environmental stress as the etiology, i.e., the ingestion of assorted cookies, candies, popcorn balls, and berries made and coated with undetermined quantities of bacteria, microorganisms, germs."

He tried to bend toward this one with the glasses, this one called Wilson. In each lens he saw trees. "What are you sporting under that fourth blue button on your shirts?

What is under that Webelo patch? Salmonella enteritidis?
Shigellosis paradysenteriae, sonnei, dispar? Endamebiasis,
entamebiasis? Amebic hepatitis or colitis? Paratyphi A and
B? Or! you may have nonbacterial food poisonings! What
have the Cub Scouts been ingesting today? Have you devoured amanita muscaria and phalloides right here on the
corner of Spring Street and Main? Is this your last Fourth
of July parade? Do you have mussel poisoning? Listen up.
You could get a merit badge for less. We'll sew it to your
shrouds. Even the immature or sprouting potato can mean
your tomb. I ask you, are these cranberries sprayed with
salts of arsenic or lead? Were they stored in cadmium bins
before you stuffed them in your mouths? Do you have a
feeling of fullness in your gut? That could be a sign. Do
you feel the need to belch?" All eating had stopped. The
scouts were looking up, wide-eyed, at him. He swung himself around and it was as if he were watching a merry-go-
round of blue and gold.

"Other symptoms and signs may occur, perhaps as late
as thirty-six hours from now. Watch for anorexia, post-
prandial nausea, abdominal distress, acid-base imbalance,
prostration and shock. Do you have a feeling of unnatural
warmth or chills, constipation, hiccoughs, impotence, or
bloody stools? Run home and check, little Webelos. In
cases of botulism, visual disorders may set in. Dysarthria,
dysphagia, nasal regurgitation, too. Are you seeing things
you've never seen before? What? Someone gulped! Difficulty in swallowing often leads to aspiration pneumonia,
Cublets. Think of that. The muscles of the extremities and
trunk weaken prior to death. How do you know what a
snack will cost you on the street? How do you know what
you are eating today? A Cub today, a worm tomorrow—
and a belly-ache in between."

Michael O'Dea paused to catch his breath. They were all

looking up at him. Wilson was the first to speak: "Hey, man," he said. "What are you anyway? Some sort of sixties freak?"

Michael sighed. Zara Montgomery was nowhere in sight. He shifted his weight irritably in the heat and looked toward the pharmacy again. On the corner of Main Street and Spring, the silver edge of a telephone booth slid open. There, he thought as he swung in that direction, was his salvation: a slender blue skirt, blue blouse, and beanie. And there the blond radiance and the den mother's pin, all striding with conviction toward his predicament. He said, "Mrs. Steiner, Mrs. Steiner! I'm Dr. O'Dea."

The young woman looked him up and down.

He nodded toward the boys. "I presume you are responsible for *these*—" he said as the globe gave out an unprofessional squeak on his head.

The woman's face turned up, staring adamantly into the bright lights of his eyes. "Well, you could hardly blame them, could you?" She took in her breath so sharply then he didn't know whether it was a hiss or a low seductive whistle. Slowly she studied him again; she smirked at him. "Jerry, Tommy—come on, boys. Leave the man's little popcorn balls alone."

They scattered up over the curb and turned to face him. Mrs. Steiner stepped forward to converse with a man; and just behind her, like a row of mechanical carnival ducks, a series of solitary middle fingers shot straight up, one by one, saluting his beneficence, commenting on the middle-aged adults who had flocked into their positions around him.

"Zara," he shouted. "I am ready to go. Right now."

She came around the station wagon carrying another crate. "All right," she called to him. "One more box and you can shuffle your needles over here."

His heel went forward, followed by a melodic flap of the toe. The other foot followed. "Thank God."

She pointed proudly to the long narrow space in the back of the car. "It hasn't been easy," she said, wiping her face on a tissue. "I had to get another box when one of the bags gave out, and then to move all this—with Mrs. Mc-Gehry's help it took me an hour to get it packed the first time."

"You mean?" His branches motioned horizontally toward the space she had indicated to him.

"Of course. How else does anyone ship a tree?"

Boyish chants assailed him from the walk as she directed him. "Just lean in over the tailgate and I'll shove you the rest of the way. Or maybe you'd like me to rent a trailer?" She turned him around. "Lie on your side, you've got less surface area that way. Here now, I'll move these ornaments around to the front. You won't squash as much."

"All right. All right. Watch out for my stars."

Among the onlookers, ice cream dripped ostentatiously into the street. "Want some help with the shrub?" someone was snickering. Tongues went around the points of sugar cones as Michael O'Dea guided his black tiara under the roof.

"No," he said irritably. "We do not want help." He could feel the pine needles prickling him, certain now that he was developing a rash.

Zara pushed on his fins. "Thanks just the same," she called happily to the crowd. "Pull up your feet, Michael. I don't want to get your flippers caught in the gate." Zara Montgomery closed the door and then, leaning in through the window, she tickled his foot at the edge of his fin. "Hello, sweetheart."

"Don't!" He jerked his foot.

"Ha," she laughed. "Jingle bell hop."

She started the car and then they were off under the Fourth of July banners. Behind them, a round of applause rose like a little cloud of dirt they had stirred up and were now leaving behind to settle again. "Take your hands off my little balls," she chortled. "Michael, this has got to be one of the best times of my life."

His voice came distorted from the back. "All I have to say is—your costume better be good."

Zara looked into the rear-view mirror as she answered him. His green eyes were staring straight into the bulging eyes of the suckling pig.

"That, too!" Michael the storyteller laughed, pounding his covers ecstatically with his fists. "My parents were hooplolling all night long."

Hoopla! the boys cried out, flinging their pin-striped pillows in the air, bombasting one another off their beds. HOOPLA! HOOPLA! WILD MARIE! Words confiscated their sensibilities. There would be no morning confession. They knew no sin. And in the corner, wide-eyed mongoloids entered the festivities: pillows tore, feathers floated round their heavy heads, stuck fast to their short-cropped hair like diadem.

"Michael—Michael Francis?" From under the clamor, from the cluster of new boys near the door, came a high minimal voice. "What's hoopla, Michael?" Billy McDermott's newly issued pajamas were wadded up around his wrists and cuffs, a small stuffed rabbit squashed between his knees. "Tell again, please. What's hoopla?"

"He doesn't know!" Hands cupped mouths; tongues rushed in a migration of slurpings around the room. HOOPLA! Michael threw his head back, laughing on this winter night, as feathers fell around his face.

In the storm a figure rose, short and solemn and condescending, the red hair roaring above the cracking of the voice: "Bastards! Babies! Bugger all! You haven't got one drift what hoopla's all about." With that Willy Howlett dropped the tight elastic band of his pajama pants and spat on the end of his sprout. Up and down the hand went. Up and down went the eyes of ignorance: a mortal sin was protruding from Willy Howlett's pajama pants. It grew, it grew, until—"Gee whicks," Billy McDermott said—a bolt of white foam shot onto Willy Howlett's pillowcase.

"Gee mollykins," Billy McDermott said, as Willy fell like a rail into his bed.

"Again! Again! Again!" went up the chant.

"Bugger all," Willy said, thrusting the pillow to his feet. A finger pointed in Michael's direction. "Go on."

Michael Francis had barely looked up from the completion of his fevered reverie—it was as if a fire still floated in that room—when Willy Howlett sprang from his bed. "Listen to that!" Willy shouted, flinging open the window. A chorus of Christmas carols floated up from the courtyard of the orphanage. "There's your frigging saviors," Willy cried. "There's your saints with fire trucks." He ripped the spattered pillowcase from its place and thrust his head out the window into the thickly falling snow. "Give this to your Baby Jesus!" he screamed. Smashed against the windows, the orphans watched that night Willy Howlett's soiled pillowcase sauntering down in the midst of thick white flakes onto the townspeople's upturned, singing faces.

Forster Montgomery liked to consider himself a tyrant in his work, an altruist at home. He had that sort of unconscious existence, that unexamined, obscure motivating force that brought down others when they needed him most and begged their pity at the same time. It happened in small ways. His expectations of another were always great, though rarely imposed blatantly. His mouth was severe when he was displeased, while his eyes were deep with hurt and the accusations of his disappointment. The mildest of frowns held him up to others as an example of the proper life.

In his work he knew what he wanted. He was an excellent surgeon and his greatest joy in life was to see the tender flesh of a belly, a joint, a chest exposed to the systematic probings of his knife. The psychology of the human being was to him a confusing matter and thus a secondary thing. As he saw it, his work demanded his rigidity; he could not be troubled with the gyrations of the mind when the life itself was in his hands. It was this philosophy he carried over into his personal life; this was the cause of the disparity he felt. What worked so well for him in the hospital worked against him in his home.

Yet he was not totally without feelings. In the unstressed moments he allowed himself over his morning breakfast flakes and eggs or on Sunday afternoons when he took out one of the boats alone, he reflected over the tender moments he had known. He pondered these and the unhappy occurrences of his life, thinking himself on one hand to be the victim of a most unfortunate fate, while on the other he prided himself on his own self-determination and will. He could not have said how his personal experiences had affected him except in the grossest of generalities; and even then he would have added, hastily, that his troubles with his daughter and his wife, serious as they had been and were even now, had never once interfered with his work.

On a larger scale, he reacted in a similar way. He had compassion for the poor, often speaking with them gently about their plight, but offering little insight of his own, other than the need for determination and self-help on their parts. The world was designed in a certain way; and the individual, in order to succeed, must lean down and grasp himself by his own heels. Years ago he had disengaged himself from the church, seeing it as a form of irresolute social club, and joined the Elks instead, where he could be surrounded by men with thoughts much like his own. It was impossible for Forster Montgomery to understand, even in reflection, another person's or class's point of view. The alien philosophy was to him just that: alien, incomprehensible, and therefore unjustified. If someone were to press that philosophy on him, as occasionally someone attempted to do, he took it not as the expression of another's thought and motivation, but rather as an act of defiance, or jealousy, against himself. Forster Montgomery was at the center of all things in his understanding of a natural order; he reacted, as was easiest for him, to every person, event, or crisis with staid, egocentric sobriety.

His marriage to Kathryn Sheridan had been his sole portal to the artistic world and, he felt, an illuminating one. Even though Katie had had a substantial amount of talent and had been devoted to her work, he thought the decline of the Chautauquas in the Depression years and his wife's subsequent hermitage in his house to have been sheer inevitabilities. Wasn't such an end predictable in a career based on the uncertainty of aesthetic whim?

When his daughter told him, finally, of her own decision to give up medicine for a less depressing, more artistic existence, Forster Montgomery was not hesitant to point out to her the difference in her parents' lives, setting out the young woman's mother in illustration of what might be expected from such an irresponsible choice. He described his own life then, saying that he always knew what to expect each day. His existence was not boring, nor would ever be: the security of having a reliable position, and a respectable one, he said, did not efface the total unpredictability of dealing with human life in the operating room.

When Zara objected adamantly, raising her voice and saying without hesitation that the flaw in her mother's life had not been in having sought to express herself in a highly unpredictable field but rather in having given up that pursuit in order to marry *him*, Forster Montgomery set down his coffee mug with a resolution that could be heard to the top of the house. His wife's marriage to him had not been a mistake; it had been a change of direction from an already declining, frivolous affair with a craze-ridden world.

With that he walked, stone-faced, from the room, cursing the influence of his wife, even now, on this daughter whom he had stringently directed in the technicalities of what he considered to be a man's world. He saw her decision as flightiness, an attribute his colleagues had continually ascribed to women in the field. Having no son to forward in his own desires, he had consistently denied this to them, saying that a human being was a dedicated and skilled physician or was not, regardless of sex. He was humiliated in the wake of her retreat. He felt that he had been in the wrong, something he rarely admitted to anyone, though he might this once have been able to admit his disappointment to Kathryn. He had wanted to admit a great many things to her before she had died, but always Zara was there with her, usurping his time. All together, he guessed, he had felt more resentment toward her than gratitude for caring for Kathryn. He knew it had not been easy for his daughter; however, the girl had had a good endurance for the situation. He could not see why that strength had dissipated now. He was in no way himself at fault, he said to himself.

Now with her subsequent determination to marry a young man about to begin his internship in surgery—a young man whom he had personally considered adopting into his family, primarily for his own gratification—he was both comforted and provoked. If his daughter must give up medicine—as she said she would do, no matter what her circumstances with any man might turn out to be—at least she would have something of security, which was a relief to him. He was getting older now and might someday be needing her help. He did not like to think of her adrift in the world. He loved her, he told himself. And there was his own satisfaction in the belief that she had finally seen a part of what he had been telling her about her mother. It would have been most unwise, he thought, for her to go off on her own.

He looked at this situation now with amazement, thinking how he had longed for a son. Now that his daughter had disappointed him he would take that young man under his medical tutelage, if it were not already too late. Forster Montgomery wished now that he had stood up to his wife and taken the boy when he might have molded him as he had done with his daughter. A great deal of damage had been done to Michael O'Dea. The young man was an inferior physician to his daughter in nearly every way. Often erratic and even emotional in the operating room, Michael O'Dea appeared to have a precarious future ahead of him. Uncomfortably the older doctor set these reservations aside, attributing Michael O'Dea's lack of focus to the past and to those unsettling, though conceivably temporary and quite natural, conditions of youth and the single life.

The wedding reception was all out of order now. Not that there had been much order to the dancing anyway. The reception had fallen to its own protocol: the father of the bride had been carried off after three dances for refusing to relinquish his daughter to her guests; young people had filched whole bottles of champagne from the banquet table and were lounging on white blankets around the east lawn. Under a tree near the ensemble, caterers clustered in red coats and exploded unpredictably into song; and on the grassy incline behind the Montgomery house the groom held children, each by a wrist and foot, and twirled them round and round.

From the corner of the summerhouse, Mrs. McGehry noticed this: Michael O'Dea's black tuxedo spinning on the grass, the stiff pastel petticoats whirling against the bushes like the wings of hummingbirds. "Finally we've spied the groom," she said to her friend from next door, Mabel Willoughby. "Now where's the bride? Where is that Zara Montgomery?"

Zara had spoken with Ed Anderson only once before this dance. She had watched his hair soft and white from the sun fluttering around his temples as they talked, watched him reach up and cup his hand around the long, furred side of his neck as he thought about staying in Lake Marian to do his internship and residency.

She laughed at him now, at the way his shyness had disappeared with her wedding ceremony. "What do you think?" he asked, teasing her as they steered toward the porch where the musicians were. "There's still time to be annulled. Just you and me."

"I'll have to change my clothes," she said.

He laughed again. "That's too bad," he said. "By then I'll be gone."

"Aren't you the impatient one."

"And you're the opposite. Think of it: the rest of your life with O'Dea over there."

"I know. Isn't it the worst? Look. Michael's dancing with Mazy, Dr. Rosatti's old nurse. You know, I've hardly seen him all day. So that's who he's been off with."

The old woman lifted her feet straight up from the knee when she stepped and put them down again. "It makes for a rather jerky waltz, don't you think?"

"It'll probably be what Michael remembers most. Twenty years from now he'll say, 'You remember that old nurse of Rosatti's the day we got married? There was a woman who could waltz.' And of course, I won't remember her at all."

"And what will you remember?" Anderson asked, drawing her close to him.

"Finches," she said. "See them perched up there. They remind me of roses the way their feathers are such a brilliant yellow among the leaves."

For a moment Ed Anderson rested his chin against her hair as they watched them rising in their flight maybe ten at a time, the yellow wings spreading into the air as they rose sweeping from one tree to settle again into the next.

"You're a lovely woman," Anderson said. "I've been wanting to tell you that for a long while."

She looked at him then, his shirt white against skin darkened by a summer of weekends on the tennis courts. She watched him and for a moment she thought: What is that something about Michael that makes him so much more desirable than this man, this Anderson, this anyone? Why is this man's touch more innocent?

The twelve wooden rowboats were just being overturned and made ready for launching when Zara and Michael arrived. Michael danced, his fins flapping along the sand, the bright red and green packages shining on his feet: and, beside him, Zara received friendly kisses on each of her masks and the real face. He thought he had never been so happy as he was then. There they were: all his friends and acquaintances rigged up in fantasies that made them buoyant and gay. The guests bantered back and forth as he offered the remnants of the candy canes and popcorn from his frock. They teased him about his curiosities. "Have you got something there for me, O'Dea?" they asked in their own separate ways.

"Have a candy cane," he said generously. "I'm not Santa Claus, I'm just the tree." Then with an air of confidentiality he motioned over his shoulder toward the pit where Zara was giving instructions about the roasting of the pig. "The prizes go to my friends," he said. "All three of her today."

Zara Montgomery knelt by the wreath of stones, arranging the coals and looking out over the strange population of the beach in her long caftan, a mask of herself over each ear. Once, she remembered as she saw her friends in feathers, capes, wound in string and tinfoil, she had felt freedom. As a child she had constructed a papier-mâché animal: creating it, molding the material in her hands, choosing the colors to define that wild image of her own conceiving, moving the brush carefully, so carefully, in order to make the imagination a reality, an existence. She had felt it again in the making of the masks for this summer costume party she and Michael were giving. Always she had lived with a certainty that she would be found out: she could not discover her own core, and she did not feel strong enough to do those things anymore for which other people admired her. So bright, so intelligent, so beautiful, they said. And what of it? There she had been, feeling like an absurd little chicken, a paper flower bleached and wired together in her doctor's uniform. Her mind was seeking a position of honor in her body; her nature was asking recognition from her mind: that scrutinizing offender.

Surrounded again by the cans of paint and glue, the paper, the yarn, she could say something as she worked. She could express something of her nature. What did it matter whether it was a dream, a terror, a memory? She knew as she completed the two faces and bound them with bits of wire to sit on either side of her own face that she was doing something for herself alone. Always she had seen herself through her parents' eyes: *You can't make a silk purse out of a sow's ear, Katie.* She tried now to remember the name she had given to that papier-mâché animal, just as she had tried to remember it on the day she made the masks. She had stood a long time that afternoon trying to unite remembered words with what she had seen. It was a name taken from an imaginary friend she had invented in a childhood even earlier. She had put away that imaginary companion into the same place where she had repressed her own small dreams when she came to understand that that was what her parents considered them. The imaginary friend and the dreams were not real, they had said. But now a name remained, if one could recall it, if one did not forget it again and again, and then: the spotted neck, the long blue head and craning feathered ears: that was a reality of sorts, that was a picture in the mind placed full-blown and tangible in the world.

On that morning when she completed the painted masks with their connecting auburn wig, she set them on her head. Starting down the stairs, she caught then another view of herself in the circular mirror that had perched so long beside her mother's bed. It was then that the name of the papier-mâché animal came to her. A bit of gibberish out of infancy. "Bonen!" she laughed, staring at the mirror. Standing there in her nightgown, she was a three-headed creature with each pair of eyes looking out independently. It was as if she had created and remembered herself. Up the stairs came Mrs. McGehry then, humming to herself until she spotted Zara on the landing. "Mary Magdalene!" the old woman cried. "You've become a crowd!" And then this morning she had forgotten the masks, had left them on the coffee table. She had had to wait in the automobile as Bridie McGehry rescued them. The old woman had danced down the front steps wearing one life-sized mask over each ear, her yellow-white hair sticking out in short permanented tufts around the edges of her own face and the Montgomery masks.

Michael O'Dea could not keep his eyes away from her. Only when she had her back turned to him was her face concealed. He was amazed at the likeness of the other faces, the one looking exotic and whorish, the other looking as she had when she was a child, impish, yet with an innocence Michael O'Dea thought he saw in all little girls. The masks evoked two entirely different responses from him.

The red-mouthed, eye-shadowed mask made him feel as if he had just pressed his face against bare skin. His thoughts were swept out along the black curve of the eyeliner to the sharp termination at the edge of the mask's hair. He was reminded of a night several years before. The woman's hair had been wound up at the top of her head like a kind of elaborate nest with two rhinestone butterflies pinned on one side. She reached across the table over their drinks. Her dark brown painted nails crushed his lapel, and he felt his chest expand when he heard her speak.

"I want it extravagant," she said. "I don't get a performance at home. I need a performance. Know what I mean?"

"You're an attractive woman," he said. Her eyes were brown as her nails, her cheeks cream-white beneath the rouge.

"I've heard it before." She leaned back, drawing on her cigarette, the smoke circling over her head.

"Your husband's at home then? Or is he working tonight?"

"Work!" she said. "That will be the day. I wait tables and he reads books."

Michael O'Dea took her coat from the chair and stood up, holding it open for her. In his apartment when he took hold of the woman's head and pulled it toward his own, he thought he heard the two winged hairpins smack together in noncommittal relief.

Zara turned in the long turquoise caftan she had put on in the woods. She walked around the makeshift barbecue pit. That other face, the child face: He remembered her sitting at the long table at the Montgomery house in that white leotard and frilly short skirt, her pale blue ballet slippers muddied from playing catch with him outside.

"Pass your little guest the sweet potatoes, Zara," Kathryn Montgomery said.

Michael O'Dea was sitting up straight. In his small shoe

he was poking his toe nervously in and out a hole in his sock.

"So you're leaving the Murphys' soon?" Forster said to him.

"Yes, sir."

"And have you found a new situation for yourself?"

"Father McKinsey is working on it, sir."

Forster Montgomery looked up toward his wife. "I suppose you'll be wanting a home with lots of other children around," he said to Michael. "Is that right?"

Zara was bringing a small bite of steak up daintily to her mouth.

"Oh, no, sir. One sister would be good—" He fingered the edge of the tablecloth. "Or a brother, but I like sisters best."

"Maybe you'd like a home with a little more space in it? To romp around in, I mean." The doctor's eyes went back and forth between the boy's face and his wife's.

Kathryn laid down her fork. "Forster," she said. "Why don't you tell us that amusing little story about the chicken pox and the horse."

Sunlight glinted off a piece of aluminum foil as Zara stooped to place the wrapped ears of corn in the pit. Michael O'Dea looked at her a long while then. There was something in that face, the face responsible for the making of the masks. There were things in that person he could not understand. What was it? he asked himself as he distributed the candies from his coat. Why had she made the masks? There was a sharp spear to the core of him he could not dislodge. He thought then that he knew what it was. She had worn those masks because she was taunting him; she was making a fool of him and leading him on in the very same act.

Zara came over to him now, the caftan billowing out

around her as she walked. She was like a beautiful piece of bronze statuary that you could not help reaching out and touching with your palms. Or if you were like Willy Howlett had been you took out your Swiss army knife and cut the smallest sliver from its cheek. He felt her hand reaching in along the branches for his hand; and reluctantly he took it.

She smiled up at him; and, as she did, he saw the profiles of his weakness all around her face. Will she never stop? he thought. She smiled up at him; she smiled up at him. His eyes could not leave hers. Seeing his eyes beneath the clutter of his strange conceit, she smiled at him. "Your lights are flashing," she had said.

Throughout the afternoon, others danced with and kissed the bride, chatting, making small conversations which she barely heard. Michael O'Dea had disappeared entirely from the wedding festivities, though in quietly looking for him she had seen his car still parked in front of the house. She remembered walking home from class several months before she had given up medicine. She had seen Michael through the window of the neighborhood grocery. The bell rang as she opened the door into the flat smell of bananas, fruit, cardboard boxes covered with dust. She watched Michael passing by the tissues and paper products unaware of her presence in the store. He leaned toward the glass cabinet where the fishes lay. His brown hair fell handsomely in strands from the top of his head, his hair clipped close at the nape of his neck. He pushed his trench coat back and out to one side as he explored his pockets for change.

Standing there inside the door of the grocery, she remembered his worn flannel shirt, unbuttoned and whipping out at his side in a similar way. The fishing rod bent, and the sail billowed out as she guided the craft along the shallows of Lake Marian. And if they were not in the sailboat but were rowing instead, then he would call for her, yelling for the net, which she would bring and hold just as he told her so that his fish would swim into its own trappings. The fish, already with the hook in its jaw, the weight in its throat, would swim of its own volition into its only choice. The butcher removed thick slabs of fish as she started toward him then and stopped, thinking perhaps this hurt him some way to buy fish when he took such pride in catching them himself. The storekeeper was stacking filets on thin white papers at the top of the scales when she went out.

She walked around the block to give him time to make his purchase, and when she came upon him again he was striding up the hill several blocks ahead with the white package in his hand. "Michael. Michael O'Dea," she called. "Have you forgotten something?" Her legs rose and fell, the material of her skirt sliding against them. She grew conscious of the motion of her arms. Watching him turn, she thought: How absurd I must look running after him like this. How awkward.

Michael O'Dea felt something catch in the center of him and start up again as he heard her voice behind him unexpected and innocent. He saw her hair out full behind her as she ran, the narrow pleats of her skirt lifting and falling from the small belt at her waist, the material gathered below her breasts where two small ovals of perspiration were spreading. "Need a ride home?" he shouted, offering his back to her, his arms and the package held out from his sides. He felt her gripping his shoulders as she volleyed herself onto his back, her legs wrapping around his waist as he grabbed onto her knees.

She reached down to take the package from where it

rested in his hand against her leg. "I was afraid you hadn't heard me."

"It's easy to hear what you want," he said, bending his knees and hoisting her higher onto his hipbones as they came to the crest of the hill. Down the street the mailman turned from opening the postbox with his key and looked at them.

"Are you sure you won't hurt yourself carrying me all this way?"

"Do I look like a weakling?" he asked. "Do I?"

He had carried her like this one other time when they had been drinking all evening in the tavern. She had kicked her shoes under the pool table and danced with him in the corner until Old Lars pried them away from the jukebox, helped them on with their jackets, and thrust them out the door shouting, "I like it when the lovers drink but we gots to keep the schedule." Every few yards she sat down on the curb to rest until Michael made her get onto his back and carried her stumbling through the darkened town singing out at the top of his lungs, "BEAUTIFUL! BEAUTIFUL! BEAUTIFUL!" His bellow as they ran was punctuated by the sound of slamming windows. The leaves had been silver and spidered with water against her face. She remembered the mist and could not attribute it either to weather or drinking.

She caught a glimpse of him now across the clearing, talking with Anderson by the lake. Anderson stretched his arm across Michael's shoulder as they walked along the beach.

"Feeling a little deserted, are you?" Zara turned to see her father tapping her partner and realized that she had not spoken a word to the guest with whom she had been dancing.

"I'm sorry," she said. "I—"

"That's only natural," the young man said. "A bride should be distracted. I'll try again later."

Forster Montgomery kissed his daughter on the cheek. "So you're having your little reveries, are you, Zara?"

"I don't even know the man's name."

"Don't fuss about it. He's one of the new people in Wilmington's practice. You'll see him again. He wants to impress people."

Over his shoulder she could see the shy, skinny limbs of the town's elderly, gesturing toward her. "Give us a little dance with your girl," they called, but in Michael's absence her father steered her in his slow waltzing pattern deliberately toward more amicable guests.

"I'll do no such thing," he said, squeezing Zara's hand and in it the hem of her veil as she held it up. "How many times does an old man dance with his daughter anyway?"

"And on the day of her wedding."

"Yes, that's right."

They pivoted then. The guests were shifting across the lawn through the summer heat in their long sheer dresses. A young man unbuttoned his coat, took the wide-brimmed ladies' hat he was holding, and sailed it onto the grass, the pink ribbons trailing.

"They're getting rather wound up over there, Dad." She leaned closer to him, speaking over the music.

"Too much champagne. They'll be heading toward the bushes soon."

"No," she said, "the older set, I mean." The old men had begun to chant her name for the fourth time that day, keeping beat with their canes. On a folding chair Judge Henderson clapped his long white hands.

"I'm afraid the insurrection has begun again."

"Let them come," Forster said. Branches bowed under

small, firm weights. "Your mother had a veil not quite like this one. It fell down around her face and swooped behind her several yards. When she danced, she wrapped it around her several times and tied it at her waist. She said something about ritual not getting in the way."

Forster Montgomery stood at the edge of the banquet table in a state of acute embarrassment. His son-in-law was nowhere to be found. He heard the wind rustling in the pines over Zara's wedding dance, over Zara in her mother's wedding gown. It lifted the white veil from his daughter's hair, swept it back and around to the side. It was to him as if his wife and daughter were one in the same and she were upstairs at the window in her room. It was as if he were walking up the drive and she stood at the window waving at him, the curtain sucked around and out through the open window against the side of the house. He raised his hand—running it through the side of his hair.

Zara excused herself, making her way toward the house. She had drunk too much champagne; she knew that as the blur of kisses went by her. Guests were gathered in the hall, leaning against the bathroom doorway. Then there was no one, and she was holding onto the rail, going up the stairs, the skirt and train a white frenzy around her. She held it up, kicking the petticoats aside as she ascended. On the landing she let it down again looking into the mirror. She pulled back her orange hair, looking at the way the wine had flooded her. "Burnt sienna," she laughed weakly. "Pretty, pretty. Humiliating day in my life." The hair fell around her and she went up again and into the guest room.

There, too, the bathroom was closed. She tapped a question on the door and sat down to wait on the bed. Her flat white shoes went sailing, plummeted. "You're too short in those," Mrs. McGehry had said. "Why, you're so short, nobody might even see you."

"Zari—that you?" Ellen Whitney's drunken voice came out.

"Whitney!" Zara Montgomery cried out in relief at the sound of her friend's voice.

The door opened, and Ellen Whitney came careening out in her fine linen pants, her jacket flung over her blue satin shoulder, her dark hair braided elegantly at the back of her head. "If I'd known you were going to serve so much liquor," she laughed, "I'd have brought my porta-potty."

"Port of call, protocol, portmanteau," Zara smiled, reeling.

"Is the bride in distress?" Ellen Whitney asked, watching Zara veering toward the smaller room.

"Well—" she said uncertainly. "Ask me in a moment." With difficulty they exchanged places in the passageway; the door closed between them. "Wait!" But Ellen Whitney had already opened the door again and disengaged the wedding gown.

"Go on," Ellen Whitney said. "I'll wait for you." She put the lace scallop in Zara's hand and closed the door behind her.

The room was too small. She hoisted up the skirts in back and they all came rushing forward. Down came the little tea towels off the rack. By the time she'd settled herself, the soap dish had floated off the edge of the tub and collapsed onto the drain. Nervously she bounced her knees up and down—all the irritating petticoats scouring everything. Nothing seemed right to her that day. Zara Montgomery reached across to the sink and turned the water on. She stuck her finger under the stream and up went her eyes until she could see almost inside herself, until she was relieved. And then her face was in her hands. Why is it all so unusual? she cried. So unusual and it isn't supposed to be like this!

When finally she had arranged all the layers of her skirts again—each layer she pressed lovingly against herself, her mother's skirts—It isn't supposed to be like this! she cried. She ran cold water into the basin; she dampened a wash-cloth and ran it gently around her pale face. "Away with all of them!" she cried out loud. She folded the cloth in half and hung it there in its perfect place, and then the small white towels were swinging beside it again. When she opened the door to the bedroom, Ellen Whitney stood beside the mahogany table. The dark eyes turned up from a gold-framed photograph; the eyebrows rose. She set it down.

"Why don't you rest one minute here?" Ellen steadied herself at the table edge.

"Every twiddling one of them is asking me," Zara said, nearly in tears again.

"He will not take flight! No birds on the bus. I will break his arm."

"You drunk, too, Ellen?" Zara collapsed into the arm-chair beside the bed. "Have need of a bath. Throw the dress in the fireplace." Irritably she brushed at the veil, and then she looked down at the pretty thing. She stroked it across her lap, until finally she had taken up her glass again and pushed the rim of it against her bottom teeth.

"I think you *should* have a bath." Ellen thrust her glass up in salute. "A quick little dip—a cool one. It's your wed-ding, after all, and Michael seems to be taking care of himself. The guy will return." Ellen leaned her long body against the wall, examining her glass. "Too much atmo-spheric pressure. Coffee? Unless you want more cham-pagne." Their eyes met. "Do you want a bath?"

"Yes, but—"

"Well then?" Ellen disappeared and then the long row of buttons at the back of Zara's dress were undone. "I'll be right back. Coffee. Going-away outfit."

Zara slumped in the chair. "What's that?"

"Where is it?"

"Just maybe I will wear something else," Zara said. "The bride wore black, and how they all did dance, eh?"

"Start changing now—you'll never be out of here."

"That's right." Zara told her where to find it and Ellen left. The dress flew off her, and then the slips, the underwear and necklace, the blue garters that Mrs. McGehry had insisted that she wear. Blue garters with the small pink buds arranged neatly along a shaft of the sweetest green, the pure stockings stretching out of them. When Ellen Whitney opened the door again, Zara lay face down on the bed, the coverlet up to the nape of her neck, the crown of the veil like a skull cap still on her head.

"Are you all right?"

Up from the pillow came the head. Ellen Whitney asked it again.

"I'm so glad it's you, Ellen. I'm too drunk to talk to anybody else."

"Me too." Ellen Whitney fell straight over onto the end of the bed. "I admit it. I had another wee sniff of the hooch on the way up here. Is that Niagara Falls?" Ellen Whitney asked. For a long moment they listened to it cascading. "You're not going to Niagara Falls, are you?"

"Washington. Niagara flute?"

"Water," Ellen Whitney said.

"Water!" Zara jumped from the bed, nearly naked.

"Take off the veil!" Ellen called. She raised herself up and carried the coffee tray into the bathroom then. "Told that Michael you were going to change."

"Well," she huffed. "I didn't know we'd invited him. No scoundrels, I told Mrs. McGehry. And she invited *him*."

Ellen Whitney patted her on the shoulder and handed her the washcloth.

"Bon voyage! Bon voyage!" Zara shouted, holding up her hand as she sank into the suds.

"Derry down . . . derry down . . ." Ellen Whitney sang. "I will break an urn over your stern." Ellen steered the silver pot toward the teacups. "Or I'll just pour? Filled the whole blasted tankard right at the banquet table under rampant eyes. Rampant eyes of the good McGehry."

"Pour, pour!" Zara cried out, splashing the suds up over herself.

"The cry of the lower classes!" Ellen Whitney laughed, sitting down on the cover of the toilet.

"Oh, Ellen—you had such sad little dresses."

Ellen Whitney laughed again and shakily they toasted. "To all of us—" Ellen Whitney said, teetering on her perch. "To you, to me, to Sally Welke, to the weird Van Horn, to our lost Debbie Foster—"

"To whom 'nothing happened,' " Zara said sadly.

"Wherever we are, however."

The cups touched and the room went around. Zara set her coffee in the corner. She shifted and the waves went up around her. She took up the washcloth and sudsed her feet. "Little toes—" she said. "Married."

They all turned to see Michael O'Dea lunging up the shore, his silver globe shaking violently as he ran. "He can't sit down," Zara informed them. "It's for his own good."

"Limited movement. Lower limbs," O'Dea heard someone cry. Feather capes, aluminum foil, and leaves rushed after him. "Embalm the boy," someone shouted. "One hundred cc's of chenin blanc! Roll a joint!" the orders rang out.

"Malpractice! Malpractice!" he cried, flat-footed and

running, curiously elated, throwing diversionary candies into his wake.

"You've made a mistake," the Chicken panted, lumbering close behind him.

The Chicken was almost upon him when Michael O'Dea felt the package fly from his foot. "My present!" he cried out as if he had lost a moment in his life, as if he could bend quickly to retrieve it again. He was attempting to scoop it onto his fin when he saw the Chicken and the Runcible Spoon in a peculiar flight pattern aimed for his knees. He felt the globe tottering first on the top of his head; and then he was skidding through sand.

"My word!" the Spoon announced, rolling to her side with her arms outstretched and riddled with pine needles.

"You'll have to resuscitate me," O'Dea declared. "I'll die. I'll swoon."

The Spoon stood up to address the White Hare:

"They roused him with muffins—they roused him with ice—
They roused him with mustard and cress—
They roused him with jam and judicious advice—
They set him conundrums to guess."

"Your consent, O'Dea?" the Surgeon Bean asked.

"Trees are dumb," the Tree said, shaking his head back and forth. He sealed his lips.

"Patient has consented to the operation. Trim the damned thing up."

"I do not consent," Michael O'Dea declared as his limbs fell from his thighs.

At his feet the Nun was kneeling in the sand, pouring pebbles over him. "I can't give you the last rites," she said. "But I can pronounce you dead."

Zara Montgomery removed the red wax lips from above

his knee and attached them to his chest. "I wouldn't worry too much. The survival rate for this procedure is extraordinarily high. Isn't that right?"

The Chicken waved his knife in the air. "I am advising the patient to look for inner strength."

"That's exactly the method," the Spoon said to the Burly Brown Bear, beginning a waltz in the sand.

Michael O'Dea's long, skinny legs swam out from under his Christmas-tree shirt. "I've been truncated!" he cried looking down.

"On the contrary," Zara Montgomery said, lighting a cigarette. "Now you can sit—in a boat." She went to put the cigarette in his mouth. "Dear dear. We'll have to call the plastic surgeons now. I can't locate this man's lips at all."

"She can't find his lips," the Baboon repeated. "Call the grafters now."

"She can't find his lips. She can't find his mouth," the Spoon cried out, doing a dance in the sand.

"Don't you dare—" Michael O'Dea warned.

Michael O'Dea stood up. "If you'll excuse the patient, the patient will take a leak." The applause went up as he stepped into the row of scrub pines by the ridge, and then they heard him curse. One branch, two, an explosion of trinkets flew into the air.

"What's he doing?" they cried. "Shedding the rest of his skin?"

"O'Dea—" the Chicken called out. "Is everything all right back there?"

They heard him swearing again, and the globe went flying, too.

"I know what it is," the Pirate shouted. "Ever try to pee without using your hands?"

"Shhh," someone insisted. "Be quiet now."

It was then that they heard it: the sound of water against a rock.

"Crescendo!" they cried. "A success!"

They had just scattered up and down the strand choosing their boats when Michael O'Dea strode toward them out of the bushes, stark naked and proud in his tan. Slowly their amusement turned to laughter as he passed by each one, for there flying from his backside was the red, white, and blue of the upturned flag.

Michael moved his fingers tentatively along the back of the pale yellow dress. With great excitement he had helped her in choosing it nearly two months before. "Well, here you are," she said suddenly, astonished to see him, taken aback by his nervousness, the pale cheeks and ruffled hair. Why, his eyes are almost blue—with fear, she thought, seeing the lake reflected in them. She gripped his hand, feeling his breath come down through her hair. "I got worried you might have skipped town."

He looked down at her. "Why would you say a thing like that?"

"They wanted to play the wedding dance, but the groom had disappeared."

"I had to be by myself."

"I didn't mean to put you on the defensive. It was just chat, that's all."

"Chat," he murmured. "Just chat."

Over Michael's shoulder Zara watched her father moving dejectedly through the crowd. "Who gives this woman?" the minister had asked, and the answer had not been "Her mother and I" but "I do." Her father in his black coat with the slim lapels. He lifted his hand and waved to her. She saw his lips moving, but the crowd closed around him again. Zara's hand settled onto Michael's coat as they danced. "Are you having a good time?" she asked. "Yes. Are you?"

"People seem to be having a good time. Did you see the old men badgering Father?"

"Here. This is for your crowd." He kissed her abruptly then and heard the hoot go up among them. He felt his shoulders broaden under the eyes of the guests. "You're beautiful," he said, holding her slightly away from him while they waltzed. Zara turned her face up toward his, but he was paying no attention now.

> " 'It is this, it is this—' 'We have had that before,'
> The Bellman indignantly said.
> And the Baker replied, 'Let me say it once more.
> It is this, it is this that I dread.' "

The Chicken with the Rabbit, the Pirate and the Runcible Spoon, the Pear with King Kong, the Poet and the green String Bean: they were all waltzing now to the chant of the Spoon:

> "I engage with the Snark—every night after dark—
> In a dreamy, delirious fight;
> And I serve it with greens in those shadowy scenes,
> And I use it for striking a light:
>
> But if ever I meet with a Boojum, that day,
> In a moment (of this I am sure),
> I shall softly and suddenly vanish away—
> And the notion I cannot endure."

"No, Michael." She touched his arm sympathetically. "You're the beautiful one." He felt as if in desperation she had wrung herself against him then. He detached her fingers from his hands. Away, he turned. Away from her, him, them. He would not continue it. Through the crowds he pressed, rushing past their fallen smiles. The music had stopped as one by one they nudged each other. The violinist's bow hung between music stand and instrument. He had come to the back of the house now, the walk running like a decision between back door and drive. He turned toward where she stood white-lipped among the silent others. Her eyes shone like two milky saucers in her head.

To advance, retreat. To retreat, advance. He had lost his life and found it at once. Back and forth, here and there, he sped on the little walk among the walnut trees. *Away!* He beat his infant fists against his impressionable head.

It is an early-autumn Sunday evening. Still warm, and Michael has not made love to her since August. Each night he sleeps as he sleeps tonight, facing the window with his knees drawn up away from her. This lack of attention is not, he says, because he doesn't want her; it is, he says, because he can't.

In the dark she bends her body around him, listening to the yellow leaves curling against the window screen. His buttocks are warm against her thighs and pelvis. Her face rests between his shoulder blades, the cotton cloth of his pajamas fluttering against her mouth each time she breathes. She puts her arm around him; he clutches her fingertips while he sleeps. Together they have grown self-conscious. They worry together and separately. She asks herself: What changes passion to impotence? What changes it back again?

Wednesday evening at the theater he invited two strangers to their house for dinner. She told him she wasn't interested in anyone else.

"Stop thinking about yourself," Michael said. "You have to think about me now. Think about me."

I think about him all the time. I remember the year right after we were married when we were in Seattle. I remember the day when we were tacking back and forth across the channel, late for dinner. We were waiting for the man in his red hat to raise the bridge over Hood Canal. In the beginning Michael had dropped anchor every time we came in sight of him, whether we had passage through the bridge or not. "It's the Hood Canal Lust," he said.

I wondered then if the bridgemaster would be disappointed to see our boat in motion, no longer floating captainless while we went below into the cabin. I watched the cars from the Winslow ferry snake over the span and into the forested hills.

"It's times like this I want to chop down that mast," he said, scowling at the speck of red in the arched stone tower.

"I'll get you a canoe for Christmas."

"You do and you'll paddle it." Michael wrapped a piece of rope around his hand.

"I like the waiting just fine," I said. "You're the man in the rush."

"Dr. Di Cori will be holding dinner again."

"He knows how long it takes us to get there," I said. "Why don't you read if you can't enjoy me or the scenery?"

"Next time, we drive." His fingers tensed, released, gripped the tiller again, turning white against the grain of the wood.

"Fine. *You* drive. I've had better company."

"Take the tiller." He went below to get his book. "Listen to this," he said, reading from one of his medical texts. "Teratoma—"

"I don't want to hear about those tumors again."

"You do this one. It's just gruesome enough. This tumor starts in the ovary all by itself. When they remove it, guess what they find. Teeth. Spontaneous generation of cells. They've found full sets of teeth in women's ovaries. And hair."

I've got teeth in my belly, too, I thought. Look what

happens to a woman without sex in her life. Perhaps I would ask Dr. Di Cori about Michael's problem. Di Cori was not a young man, but he took an interest in the interns that was uncommon among the staff at the medical college.

"Why don't you tell Norman about it?"

"I'm sure Dr. Di Cori knows all about teratomas, Zara."

"Michael, I'm talking about—"

"That's just what I want, Dr. Di Cori taking me into the conference room each morning to say, 'Well, Dr. O'Dea, did you get it up?'"

I reached for his hand, but he moved it away, running it along the wire of the backstay.

"It couldn't hurt to consult someone, Michael. I don't like us being so nasty to each other."

"I already did, Zara."

I waited.

"I will not see a psychiatrist."

In a waterfront tavern three weeks later, Michael confided in someone else. After five margaritas, he told the whole bar. We had been sitting together in the corner, Michael touching my hair. As I went into the bathroom, I saw him stand up, pushing his way to the front. When I closed the door, Michael began shouting: "Hey there, you drunken anemics! Listen up!" The room fell into silence. I cowered. I ran the water so no one would come in. "I'll give you a guess how long it's been since old Doc here could get it up." When I came to fetch him off the top of the bar, they were all offering to accompany me home.

In the car I cried, humiliated.

"How do you think I feel?" he said.

One could do all those things one had always wanted to do, Zara thought, sitting in the kitchen of her father's home, looking at the ceramic flowers on the teapot. But, and she poured herself another cup of tea now, she hardly knew what she wanted to do with this day. All those things she had wanted to act upon or create or observe had been repressed for so long in medical school that it had become work in itself to think of them.

She had come down to the kitchen in hopes that Mrs. McGehry would abandon whatever she was doing for the sake of chatter. But who knew where she was now? Perhaps she had gone outside to dispose of the garbage. Yes, it was garbage day. It was Monday. She looked out the window and saw Mrs. McGehry leaning over the fence in animated conversation with Mabel Willoughby. Mrs. McGehry pointed along the leaf-strewn ground, then toward the rose garden. She was speaking. Where was that ballyhooing young man Wolfe they had hired to mulch the roses? Zara sat down again at the table. Yes, that was what Mrs. McGehry was sure to be saying.

She stirred the spoon around in her tea mug. If during the day one has nothing but a still house, she thought; if during the evening one's husband were more and more depressed. And here her thought trailed off. She was watching the leaves outside brushing against the screen. The leaves were red as lips, so red they seemed suffused with something secret and sweet. She had tried to go away from her mother, first in giving up the grueling hours of practice at the paino; and then, after Kathryn's death, she had taken up instead her father's medical interests. All the way through medical school—and then she had tried to leave her own depression by quitting that. She had attempted to leave Lake Marian when she had married; but Michael would have none of that. Here she was again living in the same house.

In the den her pen went back and forth.

MOVING MICHAEL

Restring his violin, learn accompaniment. Once we did play music together. I might write the music myself?

Write something with Michael as the hero. Take M. to see himself.

I will sleep in the guest room! Absence and the heart . . . Show no desire whatsoever. Get the pressure off him. (When necessary, I could masturbate—maybe— during the day. I could take care of myself.)

I will definitely cut my hair like the actress M. likes so much. I will dress like her. Wear vests with my blue jeans.

Buy M. some new clothes? Change his self-image?

Be absorbed in my own reading. Do as he does.

Move us both to another bedroom. Fresh start, redecorate.

Talk M. into taking a vacation—with, without me. Somewhere exotic. Homey? Rugged? A change of pace.

Go to a marriage counselor—even if M. won't go. He won't. Advice is mandatory!

Ask Father McKinsey to talk to Michael.

Jealousy as catalyst—Find a lover (??) That is the worst idea yet.

Go back into medicine—for his sake. Maybe he needs someone to share that with him. (?)

Tell him I want a baby/ Tell him I don't ever want a baby, ever.

Put on a little weight.

Read something soothing to him before we go to bed, or when he comes home from work. Or both. Something light, not romantic. But he wouldn't listen!

And! I will never again ask him where he's been, when he's coming home, what he has done at the hospital. Nothing about surgery, about his patients, people at the hospital, his experiences, nothing.

Every day something new and special for him—little gifts, exciting conversation.

"Let me hold you," Michael would say when we got into bed. Still he said these things. "Let me touch you." When I was ready for him, fear gnawed him like an animal, devoured his confidence from the inside out. "Not tonight," he said abruptly. He didn't need to say these words.

"You're tired," I said the first few times. "Get some sleep." I said it nervously, embarrassed for us both.

"Don't worry," I told him whenever he mentioned it. "Everything will be all right before you know it." But there is no end. Every action, every item of apparel becomes a lure or some form of denial. Everything I say spins carefully away from this.

When we were home again, in Lake Marian, I questioned my own body and my mind, wondering if this could be my fault. I grew tired with this worry. Even the man at the soda fountain commented on my state. He set my lime phosphate on the counter and looked at me. "Hey, you don't look so plucky tonight." He wiped his hands on his stained white apron. "In the afternoon you should lie down with your feet up and savor your sleep. Elevating your paddies keeps the swelling out of those ankles, puts the blood in your brain."

"Thanks. I'll try that." I took a newspaper from the rack and pretended to read.

"You've got wear and tear marks under your eyes. Bad circulation, exhaustion contribute to that."

The blond boy who sits at the far end of the counter each night reading his French looked over at me and winked.

When her father asked them to live with him at the lake rather than buying their own house in Seattle, Michael was determined to accept.

"Are you sure?" she asked. "You could finish your residency here. We could stay and buy our own house. You could start your own practice."

"No," he said. "Someday the house will be ours anyway. And your father needs company."

She liked each morning to watch them going off to the clinic together, coming home again to work outside: her father in the garden, hoeing and stooping over weeds, digging furrows around them, twisting them meticulously from the soil, careful not to leave any roots behind; Michael climbing ladders and painting window trims while her father stood below, directing. At night the two men sat in the den at opposite ends of the horsehair sofa, drinking brandy and listening to the waves. "To catch a walleyed pike the right way," her father said one evening after dinner, "you must have caught one before. The eyes are the secret. Catch your first one with some ordinary bait, remove its eyes, and you've got it made."

She remembered her father holding the eye of the pike, hooking the small black ellipse with a quick jab as if he were suturing a wound. "You have to be careful not to puncture the pupil," he said, "or the silver will run out."

"Those eyes are like ornaments on the bottom, Michael." He studied Michael's face. He filled his glass again. "The other perch go wild."

When she was small, she had asked him once what happened to the fish, the ones without eyes.

"Oh, those." His fishing line whined as he reeled the slack out of it. "I swear it doesn't hurt the fish, Zara," he said.

Father felt this tension now between Michael and me, I was sure. He grew uncomfortable, afraid that we would end our marriage and leave him alone again. Every time Michael and I took the boat out, Father moved in his round, aging way down to the dock in time to ask, "Think you'll catch your wild-eyed phantom today?"

"The only wild-eyed phantom I've had anything to do with this summer," Michael said the last time with a discernible note of bitterness, "is your daughter." Then he pushed off from the landing and began to fume, "Won't he ever stop asking about that goddamned fish?"

"We're going to have a good time," I had told Mrs. McGehry that morning, interrupting her ironing to help me get ready. "Put in the good china," I said, "and the linen napkins. I'll get dressed."

Now I laid out a tablecloth in the sand beneath a scrub pine. While Michael rummaged in his bait box, I set the apricots in a flowered bowl. I arranged the salmon we smoked last winter next to a row of wheat bread on a plate. "Let's not cook right now," I said. "Not in this heat."

Michael cut a branch from one of the trees and twisted it into the sand. He threw out a line and put the rod in the fork of the stick. "That's fine with me. Is that all there is to eat?"

"No, there's more. Do you want more?"

"No. That's enough for me." He pulled the wine in from where I had weighted it among the rocks in the water. It was a little after one o'clock when we finished it. The line wavered a bit as the bait bobbed against the embankment. Michael was going to sleep.

The first time—he told me this—when he felt it creep up from his groin he said to himself: Now you are a man. That is something that is yours. Then he had taken his adolescent self in his hand and thought about a woman's pain until the friction sent runners, like roots through soil, flushing around his buttocks and between his legs. He said my name even then. But, before he could clean himself, it would fall away. Always it happened that way, and he would think: the pain was not enough this time. Never is the pain in my imagination enough to make it real. And when there were actual women, he thought it was like feeling your way through the dark into a curtained doorway, pushing the material aside to find yourself finally there, empty and alone.

I am a misfit till the end, he said before we had even graduated from secondary school. If you have no parents, who are you after all? An irritating little splinter in the sides of men, he said. Always they are thinking, this boy could have been something I have sown. The men give you shirts with the frayed elbows patched in by their women, with grease spotted like catastrophes over the chest. Those women soothe their men, he said, by darning and stitching rags. Because they feel it—through their men. The guilt is what they please. It creeps like a surfeit through this town, a worm through pulp and core. And always they are fattening it. Always the women are doing for their men whatever seems to alleviate the worm. But it only fattens it and makes it thick until the men are saying: Why do you always give away what we need? What won't you give to that scavenger around the corner without a father, with no name of his own?

When Michael came home late one evening, "Ha," Zara laughed self-consciously, presenting him with the numerous pastries she had made under Mrs. McGehry's critical eye. "Look what I've made for you," she said, holding out the platter, the warm smell of it drifting around them both, drifting in from the kitchen where the oven was still warm to the touch. She had taken the large blue bowl that day and cut the butter in with the flour just as Bridie had told her.

Already he had opened his surgical text; already he refused to look up to see them. "I'm not opposed, if it makes you happy. Are you happy?"

She sat down on the edge of the leather chair. "I thought you liked croissants. You always want them when we go out."

He nodded, and she looked at them curling on the plate. "I liked doing it," she said. "I've always liked that sort of thing—baking, I mean. Not the meat and vegetables. Would you like to try one? Mrs. McGehry says they're the absolute plum without the pit. It actually surprised her, that I could do such a thing, I think."

"Oh, all right," he said. And his hand came out toward the plate after he had turned his page.

"I'm only playing at this, but I do enjoy it." He nodded again, reading along as he licked the butter from his fingertips. "Today I've been working on some scenery, some little puppets. Maybe they're silly. I don't know. A lot of people would think they're silly, but I enjoyed it. That counts for something, doesn't it? I think it counts for something—to me, I mean. It's funny," she said. "I came to the part where I was almost finished, and I was compelled to come down to make you a little pastry. I thought we might talk a few minutes before you started to read, or we wouldn't even have to talk, if you don't want. We could just look at each other for a second, couldn't we, before you go back to working at your books. I made a little tea."

"Yes?" His head went back and forth.

She looked out the window as he took a bite of the next. "Another hour and I might have finished." She set the empty plate down on the coffee table. "Would you like to see what I've done, Michael? I've been waiting all day to show you." She kissed him on the ear.

"Not right now, Zara. I'm sorry." Slowly his hand came up and brushed. He kneaded peevishly at his earlobe as if a fly had touched him there. "Zara," he said, "do you realize that when your father started out in medicine there was no cure for Hodgkin's? Or polio!" He looked straight into her face.

"There isn't a cure for polio even now, Michael, only a prevention. As for Hodgkin's—"

"Say!" he said, snapping the book shut on the table. "Are there any more of those biscuits?"

"In the kitchen." She watched him sauntering into the other room, the tails of his new apricot-colored shirt hanging down over his corduroys. His new sport coat was hanging on the back of his chair in the dining room where her father would be sure to see it. She had seen the label. He reappeared in the doorway with the plate replenished. "Michael, you really should be more careful with those statements."

"What statements?" he asked, his mouth nearly full with croissant.

"Insinuating that there's a cure for polio and something more than that for Hodgkin's. Things like that. If Father had been home, he'd have been lecturing you for hours. To say nothing of what would have happened at the hospital if you'd made such a comment."

"Oh, get off it," he said. "I'm not at the hospital, and your father isn't here yet. It certainly makes no difference to you, does it? I was just rambling." The book was open across his knees.

"Would you say it's all right for a physician to 'ramble' in front of a layperson, Michael?"

"You're not a layperson. For Christ's sake, Zara, you've got your medical degree. If you would just do your internship and then—"

"Those are precisely my points. First and second. Both

of them. You can't afford—" They heard the front door close then; and they could see in the foyer mirror Forster Montgomery's brown suede-trimmed cardigan and the light blue knit shirt with the alligator snapping on his pocket. He was sorting through his mail.

"Good, good evening!" he shouted. "Do I smell croissants?" She could see him picking out the medical journals. During dinner he would stack them by his plate and point out just which articles were worth reading. At opposite ends of the table the two men would sit each evening with Zara as intermediary listening to them say: Zara, would you hand this down to Michael? To your father? And if there were any really difficult points to consider, her father would turn to her; the little tic in Michael's jaw would start up again.

"Croissants! Croissants!" Forster was saying now quite cheerfully. "Looks like an interesting article here, Michael, on cardiac by-pass." Michael sat forward on the edge of the chair to receive the magazine, but her father crossed in front of him, sat down, and opened it himself. "How was your day, Zara?"

"Good," she said, extending the platter.

"Did I hear you mention polio?" her father asked. "Now there's a discovery a man can actually remember. If he's old enough." He looked over his reading glasses at Michael. "That was something to make a guy emotional. I suppose you remember something of the actual epidemic, do you? What were you discussing?"

"Oh, it was nothing," Michael said quickly. "We'd only just mentioned it." Her father was looking directly at him, and Michael shifted not uncomfortably. "Actually we were trying to categorize those diseases, you see, Forster, which have a prevention and no cure as opposed to those with a cure and no prevention."

The older man's brow creased. "That seems a fruitless enterprise." His hand hovered over the plate. "That's a downright cockeyed notion. I don't suppose you know that?"

"Have a croissant, Daddy." She pointed at it, and eventually he turned his gaze from Michael O'Dea's hardened face.

"Hope no one minds if I elect this choice one," Forster said, holding the largest one aloft.

Michael looked up at it. "Oh no—" he said eagerly. "By all means, help yourself."

It was one of those rare days when they both woke up smiling. Early this morning they had been dreaming their separate dreams; and, by chance, they had both dreamed happily. Zara nestled into his side, her face pressed up over his shoulder and into the firm projection of his jaw. He smiled, half asleep, his eyes barely open, his subconscious still snug in the dream: Standing on shore, a fishing line stretched out in a light breeze, he watched the bobber going under. A large fish was already on the stringer. In his dream, Zara Montgomery held it up. "Look at this fish!" she cried. "Look at this good one!" Up and down the sand came the applause of childhood friends. White hands like fish flew out of the black sleeves of nuns and slapped together.

He pulled her close to him, reveling in the warmth of them together beneath the covers. He felt her hand go up and brush back his hair at the side of his forehead. Delicately, delicately the fingers moved, warm and comforting. He watched the bobber floating on the water.

"Oh!" she said suddenly, starting bolt upright.

His eyes sprang open. "What is it?"

"Today is the day I promised myself some clothes for the puppets I'm making."

"Zara," he sighed, amused and relieved. "Puppet clothes?"

"Yes," she said. "Ellen Whitney's told me about a used-clothing shop that's just been started. And they have fabric. Odd things—old fox-fur collars, pendants. I can reconstruct them for my new project. I might even buy myself a dress."

He didn't know how it was a person became so excited over such a trivial excursion, but today for some reason his mood had lifted and it amused him. Only recently had he developed that idiosyncrasy: thinking that any excitement about the little things—food, clothes, literature, movies—in anyone other than himself was childish. He preferred spontaneity to come from himself; otherwise it surprised him. It made him uncomfortable.

"Yes," she said. "And it's not just material. Beautiful antique furniture. I want to find something, I'm not sure what, to go in my study."

"You already have a desk and chair. What is it you'll be looking for?" He stroked the uneven knobs of her spine as she sat staring out the window. Her hair was like a great copper flame, he was thinking as he often did. It waved over his fingers. He imagined it short and curly.

With a shrug her hands flashed into the sunlight streaming through the window. "Who knows? But today I'll find something. I know it. Maybe something in cherry." Her smile turned full upon him.

"That would be good," he said, twisting a strand of her hair in and out of his fingers: orange cords. "I hope you have a terrific time. As for me—"

"Oh, come with me!" she cried. "Oh, won't you?" And then she reached out and touched his shoulders.

"I don't know," he said pulling away.

And it was as if a stone had fallen into her throat. She had taken to hesitating before saying or doing anything around him; but today it had burst out! It should have been more important! She had made herself vulnerable for a trip to a dress shop. Already she felt the disappointment: the constriction in her throat and then the jolt to her stomach, the humiliation at her own loneliness trembling in her jaw. "You don't want to come, do you?"

She heard her voice gone weak; she heard it go on straying without her. "I guess I should have—" she said. "Oh, I don't know why I thought you'd be interested." It went meeker still. "I just imagined it that way, I'm sorry. I've trespassed on your day off. I don't know why I always do this. I'm just a little trespasser, Michael." Firmly he had disengaged himself from her; he had rolled away to sit on the edge of the bed. He was turned away.

"I've no wishes for dresses," he said. He thought now of fishing on this day off from the hospital, especially since he'd had the dream. Today he would catch the walleye.

She would have pressed her fingers into the ivory, freckled skin of his back—so lightly, so affectionately—if he had not turned it so abruptly toward her. He did not even turn his head to speak. It had become a custom, speaking to the back of him. He would expect her to fill up the silence he had caused. But she would not, she told herself; and she would not let this remind her of all the times he had clasped his warm hands around her wrists and thrust her away. She removed herself from the bed and assembled her clothing. No, she would not let him make nothing of her excitement, no matter how small it was to him. But already it was less! She would not in the future give him her ideas, which he would dissect and cast aside—perhaps they *were* as silly or inadequate as he made them out to be. It didn't matter. She would not point out books she thought he might enjoy; he would not read them unless some other friend had suggested them to him. Nor would she try to play their songs for him on the piano, or suggest places to dine, theater, concerts he would not attend unless he had thought of it himself. She felt a little stronger. And not a word! she told herself, about the times when they had actually enjoyed themselves. Always he would recall them differently, unpleasantly always; and she could not then be sure of herself. She would keep her memories; she would have that much.

He looked around at her as she dressed in the silence at the other corner of the room. She had pulled her sweater on. "So you're mad at me?" he said with accusation.

"Not mad."

"Well, what, then?"

"Tired," she said.

"Oh well, that I understand."

She took the hairbrush from the bureau and stroked her hair. "I envisioned you coming with me today, that's all. I can go by myself and have a good time."

"I could go along," he said without enthusiasm. "If you want me to go. I guess I could manage that."

"You probably wouldn't enjoy yourself. And then I wouldn't either. Let's forget I even brought up the foolishness. It was stupid."

"No," he said, standing up then. "We're going." He pulled on his underwear and his pants. "We'll do this thing. But I'm not going if you're planning to be unhappy the whole time."

"If I'm—"

"Yes. That's right. Let's have a smile for these new dresses, what do you say?" And then he threw her back onto the bed—dead center between the four rosewood bedposts. "No smile—no dresses. What do you say to that?"

She stared up at him, and then his fingers were flying at her stomach. "I'll come along!" he shouted. "What do you think of that?" His fingers made her cry out.

"Don't tickle! Don't tickle anymore!"

"Don't tickle me," he mocked, tickling her. "Don't tickle."

"I'm going to have an accident!" she cried, laughing.

"So have it!" he ordered, but his hands stopped at her warning.

No sooner had he halted than she leapt out of the bed and rushed into the bathroom. He saw her feet poised on her toes, like a child's he thought, her underpants around her ankles. "Do you mean it?" she called. "Do you really want to come with me?"

"Yes," he said. "Even to buy dresses. But this afternoon I'll catch some reluctant old fish."

As he passed by the stockyards and the packing plant, Michael O'Dea thrust back his shoulders and drew deeply on the fetid air. Theresa Walling's house—he had lived there for one year—was just around the corner. If he had turned his head, he would have seen the grass grown waist-high around it, the windows battered out in partial reflections of the wooden stalls and ramps across the street. Twisting a quarter in his pocket, he turned up Whiting Road. Back and forth he twisted the coin, rolling its edge between forefinger and thumb as he approached Marilyn Kleinliebelink's.

On the lawn he could see a crust of bread where it lay with its brown rind sticking quietly out of the zinnias. Michael put his hand on the gate and yelled in through the screen door. "Marilyn," he called in the living room as he passed the vinyl couch and green lamp shades. Beside the telephone—a hospital pen she had taken from the secretarial supplies in the emergency room. "Come out of your lair. It's Michael." He set his bag on the sofa and took off his white jacket.

"Mike!" She opened the bathroom door, and he put his finger on the faint line of ketchup that ran across her terrycloth robe.

"Here I am," he said. "Surprise O'Dea. Raised up from the dead, the maimed and homeless."

"I'm so glad to see you, Mike!" Quickly she pushed the towel up from her forehead.

He could see the water glistening on her calves beneath the yellow housecoat and there behind her the dusty color of azaleas. "Here, Ms. Kleinliebelink." He reached around her into the leaves and broke a blossom from the plant. "I've brought a flower to show how much I love you."

Her voice pattered a scale of laughter, and the towel fell behind them. "Dr. O'Dea," she said. "You are wonderful in a crisis. Even if you aren't exactly what you say. You aren't exactly homeless—"

"Yes," he said. "I know that." Already his hands were at her belt. Her arms around him. He moved his fingers first one, then another under her housecoat and into her, lifting her off the floor, her own weight driving his fingers deeper. The yellow robe hung off her shoulders. Like a wishbone her color spread in waves from her small pink breasts, met, and moved toward her throat, up across her face, toward the tiny beauty mark she called her flaw. In Michael O'Dea's opinion, that dark, wine-red berry added considerably to what would have been a common sort of beauty. When he had released the wet cords of her yellow hair and rolled away from her on the carpet, he saw that he had left a broken row of indentation around the defect on her cheek.

In the kitchen Michael O'Dea listened to the emergency-room secretary completing her toiletries in the bathroom. He fingered a movie magazine on her painted wooden table. Back and forth he flipped the black-and-white pages, looking into the glossy eyes of starlets, the link of arms in every photograph. He had put a matchbook in to hold her place. Now he took it out again. It snapped shut; he watched it close.

"You hungry, Mike?" he heard her ask. Perhaps she had just seen his white pants cuffs protruding beneath the refrigerator door. He had felt that transparent. "I'll make you a sandwich," she said.

"Sure. Peanut butter—"

"On the bottom, I remember. Jelly on the top so you don't get your mouth stuck. And the bread you want toasted. Not dark, not light either."

"It's important," he said.

"I know. I know. Michael, why are you here? Did you have a fight with Zara?"

"Nothing exciting," he said, changing the subject. "I helped the old man with a gall bladder yesterday." Michael patted the rounded semicircles of her jeans as she dropped the toast in.

"Dr. Montgomery's own gall bladder, no doubt."

"Right," he said. "No anesthetic."

Marilyn laughed and stirred the sediment up from the bottom of the preserves. "Did he like it?"

"We couldn't find the thing. Gall we found—but absolutely no bladder."

"Now tell me about the operation, Michael. You don't know what it is to fill out forms and never get the backroom goods."

"Well," he said, pouring himself a glass of milk. "Just below the liver there's a sign that says Keep Right and

Burrow. So Doc Montgomery says *chop,* and I chop a little. Then he says, 'If I were you, Doctor O'Dea, I wouldn't be so hesitant.' So I stick the patient a good one, and six med-students rush in to clamp off one minor vessel. 'Sponge!' everyone shouts until we get to the next signpost."

"Let me guess. That one says—Get the hell out of here."

"Hey," Michael O'Dea said. "Were you that foxy blonde chomping popcorn in the amphitheater?"

Marilyn lit a cigarette, inhaling deeply. "That's me," she said. "Just around every corner. Go on now with the operation."

"So the old man shouts, 'Watch out for that nerve, O'Dea,' and I chop, hack, and spit out blood until some senior resident has to go to the john. Naturally everyone accosts me. 'What's the matter, O'Dea?' they ask. 'Having a little trouble locating the organ?' 'Not me,' I say and snip out whatever seems convenient. Then comes the big reward —I get to sling the prize under the table for the flunkies."

Marilyn put in a second round of toast. "And how do you know, Dr. O'Dea, if it's a success?"

"If the organ comes out from under the table red and flashing, the old man shakes my hand and says, 'My congratulations, Dr. O'Dea,' and the students jump in to suture. If it comes up green or yellow, we all figure the patient had asparagus for breakfast and I've removed the stomach."

"I never knew it was so simple," Marilyn said. "Just like driving through Boston."

"Exactly right," said Michael O'Dea. "And other things just about as boring."

It was a sporty little orange convertible, and in it he would take Zara riding on Sundays after he had finished at the hospital with grand rounds. It had been his idea, and she was relieved to have his company. Like a beetle, the car would skitter through the gravel and the leaves, the license plate its vanguard, the excuse for speed. On the plates, Michael had had imprinted haughtily the two black letters: M.D. Many things had changed about him in their months without sexuality, it seemed to her. On these Sunday afternoons, he wore his new wide striped ties and autumn suits, a scalpel always in his breast pocket. He wore now imported shoes and expensive hand-laundered shirts with the collars starched and the cuffs firmly secured in the old-fashioned way.

He was preoccupied with these cuff links, wearing the same pair with everything. And if no one happened to notice them at a gathering, she would be embarrassed to see him tapping, as if absentmindedly, on their gold encasements. In the centers of that jewelry were two fossils. Skeletons of prehistoric fish, he said they were, though they looked, without trace of fins, more like lizards to her with those diamonds set straight in each eye and one emerald chip at the end of each spine.

"Are you sure they aren't goldfish?" she asked one day as he hunted frantically under the bed for the misplaced one. "I'll bet you've purchased goldfish for yourself, Michael," she laughed, looking under the bureau.

"Of course they're not goldfish," he growled. "Who ever heard of a diamond-studded goldfish. Don't just stand there, help me look, for Christ's sake. Your old man's waiting in the foyer."

"I am looking," she said. "It's hard though to imagine what might be done with goldfish these days. I saw a man in a movie once with goldfish in his plastic heels. A rock star," she said, dusting off something she'd found under the bed.

"Did you find it?"

"It's my earring." She dropped it into the pocket of her robe. "The goldfish were alive," she continued, "and every time the women screamed the camera cut in on the singer's pelvis, then back to the fishes again." She was under the bed now, looking along the edge of the rug. He did not answer; he was pulling out the bureau again and cursing wildly under his breath. The bureau scraped along the wall. "Here now, O'Dea." She crawled out from under the bed with dustkitties all over her. "I've found it for you."

He thrust the stud through the openings in his cuff. "Thank God," he said. "How would it look if your old man and I were late for rounds? Thanks." His lips brushed against her forehead, and she pecked him hurriedly on the cheek. His heels were on the staircase when he turned. "I love you, sweetness," he called. "I love you—no matter what."

From the window she saw the two of them: her husband and her father striding down the walk. Always her father's gray tweed hat had moved down the sidewalk and along the brick drive that way. She laughed—encouraged by what he had said—to see the two hats side by side. For a moment they stopped and the elbow went out and the hand went into the pocket to search for keys. And then Michael O'Dea was handing the keys of his new car to her father. Forster got into the driver's seat as Michael stepped around to the other door. She watched him climb jauntily into the leather seat, gesturing and knotting his tie.

Zara Montgomery threw the window wide open as she heard the engine of the sport car revving up. She heard her father laugh. "Goodbye," she called after them. "Goodbye." Out the window she leaned, calling after them. Together at the end of the drive, they looked up through the autumn leaves at her, waving and smiling. Then the little speedster, bright as blood, slipped away up the road and under the trees.

On a warm late-autumn day Michael pointed out the tree frogs gathered like insects in the hollow of the log. "I've always been fascinated by these." He leaned down, awkward in his coat and tie, his leather shoes on the beach behind the house. He scooped one of the tiny amphibians out of the indentation for his wife.

She felt the small adhesive pads of its feet in her palm. Like a miniature hand, it squatted there, turning colors, lightening toward the shade of her skin. "Michael, do you ever miss living in Seattle?" she asked, watching the little animal. "Sometimes I miss it."

"It was good enough," he said. He put his hands in his pockets and leaned back against the tree. "Clean anyway, but not like this. You remember Di Cori. He used to say that the New Yorkers when they got to that part of the country would sit down right on the sidewalks and kiss their feet. That was Di Cori's theory about the Pacific Northwest: Too much cleanliness led to a narcissistic stance." She laughed a little then; and they looked at the frog. "Twice is enough for Seattle. I would never go back. Besides, I wouldn't want to leave your father in the lurch. He's done a lot for me."

"You know—I even liked the rain," she said. "And we did have some good times there."

"You *would* like the rain," he laughed. "You're such a depressive sort."

"Michael, I'm not!"

"Depressive," he laughed again, holding her wrists to keep her from striking him; but still she held the frog in her hand.

"It's not depressive to like something!" she burst out

angrily. He picked the frog like a spider out of her hand and set it gently on the log. He pressed her blue smock to his chest. "My wife—a beautiful, angry little depressive," he said. And she did not know anymore how to respond. He took her sullen face in his palms and turned it up. "Sometimes you're so remote." His fingers stirred under her chin. "I could comfort you," he said. But it was as if he had missed the point! Surely he was the one—not she!—who needed comforting. His fingers stroked her hair lightly away from her face. There was such tenderness in his voice: "You, Zara, with the fire in your hair." She resigned her cheek to his chest; she flung her arms in relief around his back.

She felt his fingers pressing into her upper arms; and then—just as a spasmodic contraction of a muscle springs one way and then leaps back—he had jockeyed her away from him. He held her at arm's length. "I've told you before," he said. "I've never had much commitment in my life, except to school and medicine. I'm trying, Zee, I am. I'm trying to be good to you."

His hands were in his pockets again, and she knelt nervously down to adjust the strap of her shoe. She pulled the little hook out of the leather circle and returned it to the same place. If she had said that to him, he would have made a joke of it. High and strained, her voice came out: "But, Michael—" For so long she had wanted him to say something, anything, to speak sincerely from what he must feel—something other than rote learned from his studies, superficial talk. Now he spoke; but he backed away. She pulled the band of her sandal tight and reset it again under the edge of her skirt. We are like two dancers who never touch! Two animals who never mate! Your two eyes that never look at me! Through the brief security of her hair, she looked up at him. A pale green light through copper strands, fallen through the impervious needles of pines onto the crisp cuffs of his pants, the knees, the movement of hands in his pockets as they readjusted coins, the front of his shirt where the coat was held back, where the top buttons were undone to display the dark flowering of hair. And his face—hard now, untouchable, intent on love.

"Yes?" he asked.

She rested her face on the fabric of her skirt.

"Why don't you come sit down?" he asked. "You're making me uncomfortable. I have no idea what you're thinking."

She looked up and saw him spreading the thick white blanket on the ground about fifty feet from the beach, among the trees. His gray tweed cap went down as he smoothed the corner out, picked it up, and removed a twig, a stone. He smoothed it out again and sat down. He was looking toward her again: his lean face. He wanted to speak to her. It's all right now, she said to herself. She went to him, she curled beside him; and he put his arm around her. He pulled her close and stroked her hair. He did not pull away this time and she said it again to herself. She reassured herself.

"You wouldn't rather be with someone else—more impressive, better than I am, Zara?" His hand tightened around her arm, and she thought: No; no, this is what I want: the two of us together in this way. The smell of humus around the blanket, the wild scent of him against her, the pressure of his hand. And now his concern: that aperture to how he felt, to what he was, to what they were and might be together. She buried her face in the opening at his collar. "Tell me, Zara."

She kissed him meekly at the side of his throat. Once she would not have been shy. Now it was as if she lived in fear of her dreams, the one dream. "I love you," he said in the dream so very sincerely. She reached out for his hands, and he turned toward the bureau to pull a blanket from the drawer. To wrap us in, she would say to herself. She reached for him; he threw the blanket over her head. When she had the dream, she would lurch up out of the sheets and grab for him. It's all right, he would say patting her head.

"Tell me how you feel, Zara."

"Oh—" she said hoarsely, looking up under the bill of his romantic cap, his eyes directly on her own now. "It's so rare," she said. It was so rare that they looked at one another.

He brushed the backs of his fingers along her cheek. Softly he touched her face, moving his hands along the contours of her neck. "I know," he said. "It is rare what we have, isn't it?"

The whole landscape seemed to soften for her then. She closed her eyes; she could nearly see herself there with him, her red hair laid out against his white shirt, her blue dress. The two of them together were as lovely then for her as the Renoirs she had first seen as a child on her mother's lap. She could almost feel a breath of wind as the buttons of her bodice came undone. She lay back against him until beside them on the stark blanket lay their colored clothing in collision. In his face, the sad, startling eyes that so often went cold with fear. And in each of them her own reflection: her own face grown beautiful as she saw it in his eyes. "We have to keep trying, Zara. It is true, isn't it? You love me, don't you?" Why was it she was disturbed each time he spoke? But his taut belly touched against hers; her fingers sought out the smooth dip of his back, ran along his buttocks and over them. Beyond these, she thought, are his long, slender thighs clothed in their soft black down. Here are the large, cool shoulders, his eyes focused on my own. He did not turn away from her even as she looked into the depths of those pupils, even as she saw him for the first time in months. How small the lips are, how delicate. How gentle the wedge. "You would do something for me, Zara?" How plausible now it all seemed: the two of them together. "We could have a child together. Would you do that?"

So confident was she then in him, in herself, that she confessed her own desire—almost before she had noticed her surprise. "Yes, Michael. I want that, too, for us now. I've always wanted it." What softness was in the air. She could not tell where the hair at the back of his head left off and her hands began. "I do love you, Michael."

The muscles at the backs of his legs tightened, released, and changed. But something is lost, she cried to herself. Something is lost and bewildered in the heart of me. Her palms pressed against his temples as she sought his eyes. "Michael, Michael. Don't—" But his fist had come down. It nearly floats, she thought, as it bashes into the blanket beside my head. And then she was stammering that he should not worry, that he should not now be upset, that they had so much together on that day. But he receded, pulled out of her and cast himself on his belly in the dirt. She saw the dark brown hair bounce up and down in his immense white arms.

The girls no longer sat at separate tables, their fingers pinched like clothespins over their noses as they scooped up mandatory lima beans. Their fingers no longer flew into that perchlike position when boys trooped by. They smoothed their cafeteria napkins over their pleated skirts; they wrote Kiss My Kookies in salt on the junior-high-school table tops. Sometimes Sally Welke sat with Frankie Fortunato, and all the girls were envious. Frankie Fortunato had dark brown hair on his upper lip, or so Zara Montgomery's best friend said. Sally Welke swore she had seen him shave one afternoon when his mother had gone on afternoon errands uptown. Sally Welke had seen dark brown specks in the shaving cream.

Molly Van Horn and Sally Welke and Zara Montgomery had all been at summer music camp together, and they had refused to be split up. They shared a four-person tent and hid the extra cot under a plastic tarp in the woods. Sally Welke claimed to have found Jamie Whitinger, second-chair violin, sleeping there in a red plaid sleeping bag. He said it was an imported bag, made in Scotland, and what was she doing out at night in her nightgown and her tennis shoes? Was she going to the latrine? Oh no, Sally Welke said, shining her flashlight on the sleeping bag; she was just taking a walk to clear out all the noise. Was it true, she wanted to know, that the red plaid bag came all the way from Scotland? Yes, he said, his aunt had brought it home from one of her foreign trips. And was it warm? she wanted to know. It was in this way that Sally Welke talked her way into that Jamie Whitinger's sleeping bag, so Sally Welke said in the hot morning light soaking through the green canvas tent. Molly and Zara huddled over her as she sat strangely forlorn on the bed. *And??* the two of them asked. Sally Welke sighed. It was nice, she said with resignation, but nothing happened.

What do you mean, nothing happened! Molly and Zara cried, rolling their friend onto the grass between the cots. Again and again they pinched her out of her melancholy state, squealing, What do you mean, nothing? You've spent the night in Jamie Whitinger's red plaid sleeping bag—on our bed!

"Oh!" Sally Welke laughed, "I guess I did."

Other rites of passage did and did not occur that night. Debbie Foster, first-chair cello, had come tearing into the tent to get Molly and Zara out. There was a curious stain in

Debbie Foster's underpants—and did they think her time had come, just like it had to Molly and Zara and Sally Welke? The underpants were displayed, the supplies retrieved—the fluffy white pad and the elastic belt, the two shining brass pins. Debbie Foster ripped off her nightshirt; her underpants were already tacked inside out to the center pole of the tent beside the Everly Brothers' photograph. "Be-Bop-A-Lula, I don't mean maybe," Debbie Foster wailed, snapping the elastic band ecstatically as she leapt from bed to bed, rigged for high seas.

At breakfast the next morning Debbie Foster slumped forlornly over her scrambled eggs. "What's the matter?" Molly Van Horn asked with an exaggerated wink. "Got the cramps?"

"Hey, Debs," Zara Montgomery said, swinging her legs over the bench beside her and under the table. "Little Gershwin got the blues?"

"Cut it out," Debbie Foster said. "I got up this morning and guess what?"

"You had a baby?"

Debbie Foster stabbed at her breakfast plate, and at once Molly Van Horn and Zara Montgomery gave each other a kick. "What's the matter?"

"I woke up this morning and nothing happened."

Together the friends leaned forward and turned. "What do you mean, *nothing happened*?" they asked.

"Remember the day I spilled grape Kool-aid all over myself?"

"You mean?"

Together they nodded. *That* was the stain.

Debbie Foster stood guard the day the other three tried out their smuggled goods. Zara Montgomery had a box of tampons she had stolen from the counselor's tent, of which all three of them coincidentally could make good use.

From outside the door of the unlit latrine, Debbie Foster read the instructions to them. "Instruction number one," she called out. " 'Place one foot on toilet or chair.' " Three feet went up onto the old-fashioned, single-holed board.

"Don't you think it's a little crowded this way?" Zara Montgomery asked.

Debbie Foster rapped on the door, and three voices called out of the dark: "What?"

Debbie Foster leaned against the outside wall in her cut-off jeans and shirt, reading loudly: " 'OR, sit on toilet seat with knees apart.' " Molly Van Horn sat down.

"Watch out, goofo," Sally Welke shouted. "You sat on my foot."

"My foot's fine," said Zara Montgomery. "I'm ready to shoot."

"Well, I'm not," Sally Welke said. "Van Horn broke my ankle, and I can't tell which end of this stick is up."

" 'OR!' " shouted Debbie Foster through the door. " 'Squat slightly with legs apart!' "

"Banzai!" Sally Welke yodeled, squatting over the narrow strip of cement.

Across the room, over the end of the bed, Michael O'Dea could see winter about to bloom on the window-panes. "Thanks for putting it so discreetly, Marilyn," he said. Michael pulled away from her.

"It's all right, Mike." Marilyn covered herself with the sheet. "You can't come on like King Kong all the time."

"Thanks, Marilyn."

"Oh, Mike." She ran her hand over his chest. "Really it doesn't matter." The light of the candle flickered across his eyes as he stared blindly toward the dark white pleats at the window's edge. "Really, Michael, it doesn't. I like to be with you, that's what counts."

"It happens to matter to me, Marilyn. And it matters to my wife. It's the whole ball game. Understand?"

"I hear you, Michael." She put her hand on his chest under the sheet. "And it doesn't make me love you one bit less."

Michael O'Dea pushed the sheet, her hand away from him and grabbed his clothes from the floor. "I don't need Marilyn Kleinliebelink's pity. Do you hear me? You're the one alone here, not me. Michael O'Dea has someone waiting at home for him. You're the wretched one, the lonely one, Marilyn, not Michael O'Dea." He took his clothes into the bathroom and shut the door completely.

Reaching into the bottom drawer of her desk, "Here," Ellen Whitney said. Zara received the bottle and raised it to her lips. "I used to have a recliner in here, before it fell apart," Ellen went on. "I've always been revolted by vinyl—especially red—but the junk-shop woman let me have it for ten bucks, delivered it for three on top of that. It shook the whole floor, and when you turned it off it was such a relief that everything, even this department, seemed the most perfect place." Ellen laughed and took another swig before she put the Scotch in the drawer again. "I got very attached to that object. When I first got this job, the only way I could get anyone in this college to listen to me was to sit them down and flick the switch. It turned out that the little chair was the vibrating kind. The Sidney Rodeo: grab your hats! And all that. After I turned the machine off, after the little surprise, every man in this department would speak to me. First there would be a little laughter, quiet laughter from the victim, and then a little spurt of real talk, and then a smile. I can't say I really understand why suddenly then each one would begin to talk seriously about his work, his problems with whatever he had undertaken. I believe, though, it was just plain easier for them to talk then about important matters than to acknowledge how embarrassed they had been."

Zara Montgomery smiled weakly, imagining her own father in the chair, imagining what Ellen had had to go through at the college.

"I guess you had to be there," Ellen said. "You had to see Horner *emeritus* in the red machine spouting his new oral tradition of Linear B to think it at all hilarious. Want one more slug of Scotch?"

They handed the bottle back and forth again, and then Ellen Whitney screwed on the cap, set the fifth at the back of the drawer, and pushed it closed. "I don't like to drink very often. I've had it out twice in two years. But, once in a while, on a good, cold day— Or I get it out for students who fail their comps and have absolutely nowhere to go. That relieves *my* tension at least." Ellen leaned toward her, resting her palms on the desk. "All right. Tell me, Zara."

"What? What do you mean?"

"I've never seen you silent like this. Well, once I did. But your mouth was wired shut, and that was seventh grade."

"Oh." Zara Montgomery's hand tracked through her hair.

"There's something going on," Ellen said. Back and forth the dark brown eyes followed the blue as they tried to fly around the room.

Zara Montgomery pressed her hands together in her lap. "I guess I don't know what to do with myself, that's all. I never thought it would happen to me."

"There are lots of things you do well, Zenith."

At home her desk was strewn with inconsequential notes scribbled in felt-tipped pen; books were jackknifed over the arms of chairs; her journal was spidered with ludicrous geometric forms: the configurations of cells. And in the attic: strange, multicolored, papier-mâché constructions of people and organs, pots of paint. At the bottom of her sweater drawer, beneath the least favorite of all her garments lay the trilateral worm, her stethoscope. "I don't know. I just don't know anymore."

"You must have some idea. Imagine yourself ten years from now. Where are you?"

With a crash the fist came down on the edge of the desk. "Certainly not in this town!"

Together they blinked; together they watched Ellen Whitney's pencil rolling back and forth across the blotter under Ellen's fingertip. "Well, that was a dead giveaway," Ellen Whitney laughed. Ellen opened the drawer and handed up the bottle again.

"Can you imagine how it would be, Ellen? To be somewhere entirely new, somewhere where no one knew you! To start all over again. I have no idea what I'd do there, but I know it would be right, right for me, not anyone else." Ellen Whitney was looking at her very seriously. Ellen Whitney in the neatly tailored jacket, the white blouse tucked beneath the hand-tooled leather belt, her perfect jeans. Her hair was cut neatly now at her shoulders, her arms set squarely on her desk. Ellen Whitney risen up out of poverty into this perfect room: every wall shelved with books. Ellen Whitney had married happily. Ed Anderson had not taken over her life. "But, Ellen. Ellen—what would Michael do," Zara Montgomery cried out, "if I left? Michael can't take change anymore, Ellen. He's been hurt and hurt. And my father—" Zara Montgomery wrung her hands in her lap. She watched them growing smaller, wringing each other back and forth. "It's worse than that— I've never even lived alone, Ellen." Zara Montgomery pressed her face with her palm.

"Don't you think it's odd," Ellen asked, "that you've

come around to questioning whether you could support yourself? I've never heard you say anything like that before. People have been twisting all your reasons around in you, Zara. People are fools, we both know that. And maybe your reasons have changed."

Zara Montgomery's eyes darted up into the dark eyes of her friend. She twisted her rings.

"You're one of the few people I know who could do just about anything and do it well," Ellen said.

"And won't."

"And can't," Ellen Whitney said.

And then Zara Montgomery's lip was trembling. "There's something else—" came the small voice, and then the smaller one: "Could you come over to the house, Ellen? Sometime soon?"

"Sure," Ellen Whitney said. "Of course. But why are you so meek about it, Zara?"

The small half-moons wavered in her lap.

"What is it, Zara?"

"You mustn't tell anyone! I don't want anyone to know about it. Oh, Ellen. It's all so pathetic. I tried to make something and no one has seen it. No one will look at it."

Her friend came over to put her arms around her then, and Zara was crying. "Come on," Ellen said. "We'll go see it today. What is it, Zara?"

"Oh, it's nothing," she sobbed. "I shouldn't have asked you. Michael won't even look at it."

"Is Michael home? Your father?" She crouched down beside Zara and pressed a tissue into her hand.

"Eight would be early for them. They're never home. Every day I'm all alone, except for Mrs. McGehry. And when they are at home, it's like it's dead, Ellen. It's dead there. Something is wrong with me! Something is wrong and I don't know what it is." Zara threw her head against Ellen Whitney's chest; and then she was sobbing as she hadn't since the afternoon when her mother had died in her strong hands. "I have strong hands!" she cried. "I have strong hands!"

Michael leaned back suddenly in the boat, adjusting the white handkerchief at his groin to protect himself from the remaining sunlight. All over the shore lay scattered remnants of his costume. "They see through their teats."

"What?"

He pointed toward the two forms floating in the distant dinghy, and Zara could see then the wild profusion. The two men's hair was entirely concealed beneath their painted bathing caps; two large dark eyes were painted on each chest.

"It must be the Johnson twins, the psychiatrists."

For a time they looked at them on the blue-green water, the great owl eyes staring back. She resumed then the conversation Michael had so suddenly disrupted. "I guess anyone who really thinks about it, Michael, is afraid to have a child. I'm afraid, too," she said. "But I want them."

"It is the shrinks," he cried. "Hey! Johnsons!" he called out. "Are those the eyes of depression?"

The brothers turned, their facial features flattened under yellow nylon stockings. "What's that you're screaming, O'Dea?" They rowed closer.

"I say—Johnsons! Are those the eyes of depression?"

Melvin Johnson set the oars in the locks and looked at his brother. Together the twins looked down at their chests. "We're Tibetan demons."

"The nipples are black, Zenith. Did you see that?" Michael O'Dea leapt then onto the gunwales, straddling the boat, waving his arms in the air and shouting. His handkerchief had fallen, fluttered like a downy feather between her feet. The boat went one way, then the other as she gripped the seat. "Keep your teats in your own boat, I say!" he shouted. The boat rocked. "The shrinks have titular vision!" Surprised, he turned around to hear Zara laughing. On and on she laughed until she was singing, joining in his temporary madness. He could not believe how lovely her voice was as it rippled out over the water:

> *"The virgin has a rosy hue,*
> *As does the bride of good fortune*
> *Until the second month after conception.*
> *'Areola, areola,' the women chanted."*

"Did you hear that?" he yelled across the water. "The woman's entirely wacko. Psychotic break. No concept of her surroundings."

Her voice rose up again, and he caught his breath at it.

> *"In the second month*
> *They grow and turn*
> *Much darker.*
> *'Areolae, areolae'—*
> *Darker, darker."*

O'Dea and the twin psychiatrists were staring at her. "Do you two mean something?" Marvin Johnson ventured.

"It's very simple," she shouted. "It's the only medical explanation for those black spots you call your nipples. Diagnosis. Prognosis. Get it?"

"Darker!" Michael O'Dea shouted with a burst of applause. "Darker! Darker!"

As the twins drew closer, a purple upper lip came into view—painted across the taut and straining belly of the brother with the oars. And then the identical lip appeared on the other. Across the thighs then: the lower lips, grimacing. "My God," Michael O'Dea said, and then he noticed them: two tongues like prongs, tongues of speech, two-tongued devils of raw desire. For there, between the multi-colored swirling psychiatrists' thighs, hung down the bright red paint of genitals. "Hail! Freudians!" O'Dea cried. "What's that you've got there? Cockatoooo!" he crowed. "Cock-cock-cockatrice!" The boat rocked wildly to and fro.

"That woman's nowhere near as mad as you, O'Dea," the brother laughed, rowing past them. "We can't stop now. Call tomorrow, we'll give you an appointment."

"Up your rosy Freudian asses," he shouted with elation. "I'll call a ventriloquist if I hear voices."

Merwin Johnson's patterned arm stretched out like an Indian print across the lake, pointing toward a dinghy in the distance. There the Knife and Spoon were streaking in their aluminum foils toward the shoreline. "Our wives," came the brothers' retreating voices, "refused to ride with us."

"Come on," Michael O'Dea said. "Give me the oars. We'll help curtail them."

On the far side of the pontoon the Pirate and the Nun were already attempting to shanghai the two escapees. Zara thought she heard the two utensils laughing. "Never mind, Michael," she said. "It doesn't sound like they want anyone catching them." She rummaged in the deep pocket of her caftan. "Here—" She handed him the whiskey. "Might as well sit down and have a hit off this bottle."

He took a long draft from the flask, looking out across the lake. "Shrinks. They're the real loonies." He sat down to face her.

"Never wanted to be one?" she asked.

"Never," he said. "Lunatics and weirdos."

"I have the poor kid on the phone," Marilyn said to him during her afternoon shift.

"How old is he?" Michael O'Dea took the receiver and punched the button.

"Sixteen."

"Your parents are dead," he said into the phone. Marilyn Kleinliebelink looked up, startled, from the desk beside him.

"My parents are dead?" The boy's voice wavered audibly. Hearing them, the secretary gripped her pen, punching a hole through the patients' records.

"Yes," Michael O'Dea said. "There's been an accident. But your sister is all right. You'll have to come down here."

"Mom and Dad are dead?"

"Yes," said Michael O'Dea. "Your sister is going to be all right. Can you come down here?"

O'Dea dropped the receiver into its cradle and jerked the blood-pressure cuff from off the scale. He thrust it at the orderly. "You forgot the pressure in four," he said. "How the hell am I supposed to deal with chest pain without a reading, Bassett? Answer me that one. Will you?"

The lights were hot overhead. How hot they had been! And all the little girls had declared that they were casting off their beanies and their neck scarves, too. With that, Mrs. Dormer had straightened her own neckerchief—rubber band beneath those serious double chins—and said, "Who ever heard of a Brownie Troop from Lake Marian, Iowa, sprinting in their cotton skivvies on Channel Six?" Up and down the scale Molly Van Horn, Sally Welke, the ragged little Ellen Whitney, and all the rest—Zara Montgomery, too—twittered at the vision of that: all of them in their undershirts and pants dashing and darting like an attack of brilliant white moths: circling in on the purple nose of the television Clown, circling the Clown himself in what would be seen everywhere. In black and white! It would be better than Jackie Gleason, better than anything they themselves had ever watched. The cameras turned in the studio, and the small green light went on. They were supposed to sing the song about the smile. The smile that hid in the pocket and no one could guess what it was.

Sometimes Tonto wore a handkerchief wrapped around his nose and mouth, Zara Montgomery thought as the

Clown took his place and all the girls threw up their arms to press their beanies down on top of their heads and tweak up the little stems at the crowns. When the Masked Man said "*Jump*," Tonto did—on this all the girls had agreed. Molly Van Horn had said that maybe Tonto had sewn a pocket in the scarf so he could keep the silver bullets tucked inside. There the Masked Man's ammunition would always be warm and moist.

At this, Debbie Foster had stuck her hands to her hips and declared that the reason for the bandana was nothing more than allergies. How could an actor with a red, runny nose keep his job, she said, if the illness were not concealed? "*Not true! Not true!*" all the rest of them had cried, naming off all the characters on television they had seen diseased. "But not Indians!" Debbie Foster said. And it was true. Not one of them had ever seen an Indian on television sneeze. Handing out the meeting treats, Mrs. Dormer had looked solemnly at them then and said, "Perhaps in the pocket of his scarf the Masked Man's Tonto has a *smile* hidden deep inside." And the corners of Mrs. Dormer's mouth had twitched. No one knew whether she was serious or not, and in confusion everyone had laughed.

"Ten minutes!" someone cried out again and again, and all the little girls let out one communal sigh and shifted their limbs. Mrs. Dormer's large brown regulation shoes stamped down on the dark wires that crawled all over the floor; Mrs. Dormer was now tapping her thick fingers absently on the silver microphone. Who would be so stupid as to believe that a smile could get into a pocket? Zara asked herself. She stuffed her small, indignant fists into the flounce of her skirt. In the corner the Clown was leaning against the wall, talking to a man in a short-sleeved shirt.

Mrs. Dormer had not been able to hold the question of Tonto and the smile-in-the-pocket down. Even when they were making paper animals it had flown around the long table again. No one knew for sure whether under the black bandana—some said it was blue, others red—whether Tonto wore a pleasant expression. Anything could have been happening under the scarf! Even a leer, a frown! When they had come to this revelation in the elementary-school dining hall, they had all looked down and munched quietly for a long time on the small melting panes of their chocolate bars.

At McNurty's that year they were selling bullets four for a dime with an actual silver coating and a see-through bag. Ellen Whitney had discovered them, and Zara had taken her allowance and bought a package for Ellen, too—Ellen Whitney who could not even afford a sock without a hole in the back. When the silver flaked off the bullet in the holster or the gun, it was a soft translucent pink inside. Then it wasn't a bullet anymore. It went straight into a mother's old lipstick tube; and when you screwed up the bottom, the bullet stuck right out covered with red.

The bullet made perfect Annie Oakley lips, like those on Sunday-afternoon movies on TV. Annie Oakley, in dark lips, shot straight. She always smiled, even when she was forced to gun the bad ones down. Perhaps Tonto some-times looked so glum that the Masked Man finally made him cover his mouth; that's what Sally Welke had said. But Indians were serious on TV; their faces were stark, if not serene. All the girls said that. All Indians, except for squaws who had married white men. When the squaw and the white man were alone—when no one else could see—the squaw smiled as much as anyone, or almost anyway. White women smiled all the time, that's the way it was. They rarely stopped—unless someone died or the women wanted something they couldn't get any other way. Then they cried. White women and a few black people smiling all the time, but not one of them ever took a smile out of a pocket and put it on, Zara Montgomery thought as the Brownies continued the song under the glaring lights of Channel 6 TV:

> *"And I'll bet you couldn't guess it,*
> *If you guessed a long, long while.*
> *I'll take it out and put it on.*
> *It's a great, big, Brownie smile."*

Maybe the song was an Indian song, thought Zara Montgomery, singing as loud as she could, swaying next to Debbie Foster in the heat.

Even though it had a brisk tune to it, it made her sad for all of them: the second-grade girls sweating and smiling in the hot studio with their lovely beanies on and their scarves around their necks. Out of the way of the cameras, the television Clown poked a cigarette in the orange rose they had painted for his mouth. He blew a smoke ring like a cloud of dust out one ear, and the rose turned into a crescent moon, and then a bud. Like the Clown, the Masked Man was a celebrity and a good guy, too; but he was afraid to take credit for anything he did. Perhaps it was because of the mask that he could never do anything by himself.

Now Annie Oakley wore her lipstick dark, Zara thought while she sang, then smiled. She wore her hair in pigtail braids. Her six-shooters were clean as Mrs. McGehry's kitchen drain. She went her way with no one to assist her but her horse. Zara had an Annie pistol and a holster, too; and she would not lend them out. Not to her favorite friend, the orphan Michael O'Dea who had told everyone that he'd burned up his parents and his own home too. Not even if he begged, which he would never do. *"Girls' guns,"* he said with disdain; he wouldn't be caught boots up, he said, with the six-gun of a wimp. Here Zara's smile faded from the song.

Boys were foolish, Zara Montgomery knew when she was eight. Boys didn't understand that they were small and insignificant in just the same way little girls were. Girls understood because everybody said it was so—*just girls.* Mrs. McGehry had warned her before she went to kindergarten three years ago that there was no use crying over a little cereal sloshed out on the tablecloth. Boys got one thing, Mrs. McGehry said, and girls got another.

What was that? Zara asked. What was it called exactly that boys got that girls did not?

Over the sink, Mrs. McGehry cocked her yellowish head like a finch studying a berry or a worm. "Well." Bridie McGehry stared harshly at her small charge. Her dishrag rummaged seriously in the places where the countertop met the lip of the porcelain sink. "Gender is assuredly divided in two lots," she considered, her arms up to the elbows now in the dishpan suds. "Even wee little persons like you can notice it. One falls to one side, one to the other. The die is cast from the start."

"But what is it?" Zara cried out. "What lots?"

"Ah, that's what it is!" Bridie breathed out in relief. "The stronger sex possesses one trait in common. An annoyance to be sure." Bridie thrust a plate into the drainer, and Zara watched the short and wiry arms diving again beneath the suds. "There's no use to be resisting facts, Zari Montgomery. They've a pugnacious nature, every one of them. But the weaker sex has been given something, too. A blessing, humility is. You'll be seeing soon enough that it's a mighty powerful tool."

"Tugnacious! Tugnacious!" the little girl cried out, jumping down off the chair, remembering all the powerful attitudes she had seen at the zoo. On lion paws, her haunches in the air, she growled across the linoleum. She was a grizzly then, and a wolf. In the passage beyond the sink, her howls yodeled through the canisters and pantry tins. "Tugnacious!" she cried. A snake wound down from the highlands of the refrigerator door. Annie Oakley shot him down. "We're the ones! Bridie and Mummie and me!"

Bridie McGehry turned, drying her hands on the apron at her waist. "No, no," she laughed. "You'll be getting it all wrong now; and then what will anybody do with you? The stronger sex means men and boys. They're the ones to take care of ladies and little girls."

"But they aren't stronger!" Zara cried.

"Ladies keep their strong points tucked away like underwear," Mrs. McGehry said. "That's their strength. Someday you'll be understanding it better, dear."

"I'm as strong as anybody on the block, except for Susie Franklin!" Zara Montgomery stamped her new red tennis shoes on the floor. "She's a girl and nobody's stronger than her! Her brother taught her how to fight and she taught me!"

"Leave off raising your hairs about it," Mrs. McGehry laughed. "It won't do you one bit of good. Now run along and play. When you go to school next year, you'll see how it is. You'll be finding yourself some little beaus; then you, and Susie Franklin, too, won't want to be so tough." Mrs. McGehry pinched her under the chin.

"Stop laughing," Zara yelled. "I'm not a weakling. I'm no such thing!"

In the Channel 6 TV studio, the second-grade Brownie Scouts were standing now before LuLu the Celebrity. The Clown was asking questions of each of the Brownie Scouts, and none of the questions were the same. There was no way of knowing what that Clown with the bushy orange eyebrows and the painted wrinkles would ask when it was your turn and he twisted his bubble nose your way.

In desperation, she strode out of the bathroom in the narrow black dress that ended below the knees and wrists, and Michael O'Dea's spirits took a leap. He looked in amazement at the elegant square of the shoulders. The neckline darted down in an arrow directly between her soft, almost translucent breasts. She turned in front of him. At the back of her head her long hair had been made over into a chignon. Was that what women called it? The dark lipstick edged in upon her lips. Nearly purple it was, and how it looked with her copper hair shining like a wide metal belt. In all this time, he had not seen the dress. She had refused to show him which one she had selected at the shop in the warehouse. That day when the saleswoman had come out of the curtained dressing room with his wife, there had been something concealed between them. The clerk's lips, he remembered, had pursed at the sight of him, her head nodding in absolute satisfaction. He had seen only these shoes before, the same shoes she had been wearing that day, the ones the saleswoman had unconvincingly remarked upon, saying that although they were·attractive everyone in the nineteen forties had worn the stiletto heel, of which she coincidentally had several that would fit Zara perfectly. "Size six," the woman had said, holding one up by the rod of the heel.

"No," Zara Montgomery had said very firmly. "Seduction is awful enough as it is, don't you think?" The woman's eyebrows had met in a line of graphite. "And if you think—even once—" Zara said, "that I'm going to cripple myself for his sake—"

"Of course not!" the clerk had cried, trying to hide her aching feet under the showcase.

Zara's shoes pressed into the red and blue of the Chinese rug now. Around the slender edge of each foot, the graceful line ran. And there was the sensible wedge of each heel. Yes, they looked as good as the ones named for a weapon. His eyes traveled over his wife. Yes, his wife was wearing stockings, and there were tender little beads strung at the hollow of her neck. She held out her ringed fingers to him and it was as if a ball of heat had socked him in the groin. As he rushed out of their bedroom without explanation, he saw her hand reach out and plummet.

He threw open the lid of one trunk, and then another and another, until *Here they are!* he nearly shouted. If he had not pictured her still standing almost directly below him in their room, he would have exclaimed at his discovery. He pulled on the baggy woolen trousers, yanked on the shirt, the vest, the jacket, and the cap with the blue-gray brim. But he'd forgotten to put on the arm garters. Off again came the jacket, and the bands went on like a political declaration. Carefully he removed one of his own cuff links from the shirt he had folded over the old chair in the corner. This he fastened through a hole in the broken leather of his belt. That belt, too, had belonged to his father-in-law; it had bisected the old man once around his young belly. How exactly equal Michael O'Dea felt to the elder surgeon.

Down the stairs he rushed, humming to himself a few bars of a song about a new day and other sentimental notions. His stocking feet went flap, flap, flap down the stairs and around the corridor as he settled the gray, moth-bitten cap jauntily on his freckled forehead. The door to the bedroom had swung shut; he pushed it open. Here he stood: his presentation.

How forlorn she looked now, how lovely, he thought, as if she had been neither seen nor heard from for centuries. The blue of her eyes floated toward the window, out among the maples, the Prussian-blue sky. Her arm was thrown back in the sleeve of the dress over the chair's needlepoint flowers; her hair glowed at the absolute Pre-Raphaelite center of his vision. *"Beata Beatrix!"* he cried. Her eyes turned toward him like two china platters. She was limp when he carried her to the bed, silent.

My God, he said to himself, why have I never felt like this with her? His hand slid up the silk sheen of the leg to where there were no panties. He felt the tight straps of the garter belt, the rubber nubs secured in the metal clasps like nipples. The tweed fell down around his thighs, the old metal zipper having given in to his furious insistence. The black skirt rode up and up like strata of night, like veils in a religious order, until he saw it: the source of everything. It came forward; it parted, opened, slid, encompassed. Deeper and deeper he drove into her, the dress hoisted like a rubber tire above her nipples. "My God," he cried out loud, plunging into her as if he could dive head forward, headstrong into the entire woman, as if he could be sucked up out of the present and buried in the fertile depth of something alien. And then for the first time in as long as he could remember, he shouted with joy at this woman lying so still beneath him. "Flower!" he shouted. "Orchid! Stamen! Pistil! Pistil! Pistil! Pistil!"

Tonight the Vincents will come to dinner.

I have seen Ellie Vincent only once, sitting in the lounge of the Bernhardt Dinner Theatre, flexing orange legs in the fluorescent lighting.

"You look like sisters," her husband, Gerald, said when Michael introduced us. He pointed to Ellie and then to me.

We surveyed each other, staring like purchasers viewing a horse. She was hipless; her breasts were small like an adolescent's. She was very tall. We shook our heads.

"Look at the faces," Gerald said. Michael looked intently

at this woman sitting on the settee by the grand piano. She brushed her hair up and away from her neck. It fell like the silk fringe on a coverlet.

"Yes," Michael said. "It's amazing."

One evening when Michael accompanied me to the pharmacy, he had said, "I don't see why you're always coming here."

"They make good sodas," I'd said. "Would you rather I went to the bar?"

He pointed at the college student who was looking at me over his French. "Who's that?" he asked.

"How should I know?"

Yesterday I watched Michael checking Mrs. McGehry's housecleaning, examining the corners for dust. "I want that table set up right," he told her, as if she'd never laid out forks before. He didn't tell her that we didn't know the Vincents well or that her cooking was part of his plan.

I told him I was going downtown; I asked him if he wanted anything. He was rearranging the magazines, placing the *New Yorkers* on top. "For Christ's sake," I said.

His mouth turned to a smirk. "An afternoon tryst with that kid again?"

"That's not my tactic. It's yours."

I came right back from town looking forward to a long soak in the tub.

On porcelain animal feet, the bath fills. The water rushes out the overflow drain; it foams around my neck. It is an hour until the Vincents will arrive. I soap the insides of my thighs. We are not alike, I tell myself. If Ellie Vincent and I were to walk together toward the square, skimming arm in arm, no one would mistake us for sisters. No one would say, "I see your sister was in town last week."

The Vincents have their own problems. I could see it in

the way Gerald looked at her, ready to grit his teeth or bite down on the insides of his sallow cheeks, each time she smiled at Michael.

I could hear him tapping gently at the door while the water ran hot around my feet. "Come in, Michael," I told him. He put the toilet cover down and straddled it, watching me. He pushed his moustache down as he always does, forefinger and thumb extended to each side. He shaped his whiskers with his fingertips and announced our guests' early arrival.

"No hurry," he said, putting out his hand. "Your father is doing the entertaining."

"Oh dear."

"Relax," he said. "They like him. Wait until you see what she's wearing. She has on someone's flapper dress."

I asked him what he thought of that. I watched for some indication of his plans for the evening.

"Ruffles. It has ruffles down the front." He hated ruffles and I smiled at him. "Lavender," he said and frowned. He hated that, too, and I felt a little better.

"You look pretty there," he said. "All bubbled." He pushed up his sleeves as he leaned over and kissed me on the mouth. He rubbed the soap onto a cloth, sudsing the terry nap, running it around each breast.

"Will you rinse me off?" I asked. "Nibble a little bit?"

"I have soap on my nose," he said. "Wipe it off." I took the towel from the ring beside the tub. I wiped his face, his temples, his cheekbones. "Stand up," he said. "I'll dry you."

"Suds in your navel, too," he said, using a corner of the towel. "Your tufts are matted down." I watched him gently rubbing me. He put his cheek up to my belly; he pulled me close to him. "Lovely, lovely one," he said.

"Do you want to get in the bath with me?" I asked. He looked up and I watched his eyes changing.

"I can't," he said and let go of me. He sat down again.

Slowly he dried his arms. "Zara—" He rubbed his arms up and down. "I'm attracted to that woman downstairs." He said it very quietly.

"Oh," I said. I put on my bathrobe; I covered myself.

"Gerald is very nice. You could like him." Michael moved only his eyes toward me as he talked, as if this lack of movement were an act of penitence.

"I might not want him."

"I know that," he said. "Why don't you get dressed and come downstairs." The door closed between us. In a moment I could hear his voice in the living room. Suddenly he was feeling very cheerful, but I could not make out what he said.

I can hear Ellie Vincent's sons calling to each other as I open the window onto the garden. Twigs snap as the boys bound through the leaves, leaping into the warm autumn air, sailing the red soccer ball over the little brown shingles of the summerhouse. The older boy hurls the ball as if it were a discus, extending his arm to one side and whirling his body to obtain momentum.

Ellie Vincent's laughter rises through the air vents as I put on my long green dress. That lady looks like a flapper, he said. I braid my hair into several plaits. I braid them like my mother wore them; I wind them around my head. Gerald Vincent plays the saxophone. Perhaps I have heard him in some club or restaurant. Perhaps I have seen the brass instrument resting against the dip near his hipbone. It balances on the thin white strap at his shoulders, the honeyed sound following behind the beat of the bass. I have watched men leaning into their music, taking their breath in from the belly, not forcing it, as if they were giving themselves to air. I can hear the screen door slamming. They are going down to the beach.

As I leave the house, I can see them. Their limbs are long and red in the sunset: Father building his round fires of driftwood, Michael holding the woman against him in water, Gerald looking up at the house from the beach. Her sons reach for the red woman in water. The woman they say looks like me. All I can remember about Gerald is that I do not like his eyes, or the thin way his skin shadows under the evening lights. I turn up the walk and go the other way.

I walk past the hedges unnoticed, past red-seeded bushes at corners, past the gardens uprooted and waiting for winter, past old women who sit on their peeling white porches, nodding behind the minuscule squares of their screens. I take off my sandals in the schoolyard and sit on the wooden seat of the swing, pressing my feet in the dust, thinking about Michael. I remember our first year together. I remember Seattle:

"The Coast Guard gives you twenty-eight minutes to survive in that water," Michael said. "It's forty degrees."

"How much time do I have out here in the air?" I asked.

The wind belled the mainsail out full above us. The jib was up, the boat heeling over so far I was nearly upright standing on the port railing with my back braced against the deck.

"I could never take anyone else out on a day like this," he said.

"Why not?"

"They're scared."

"What for?" I asked him. "There are worse things than drowning."

"They think I'm a lunatic taking the boat out in December."

"No," I said. "You're hardly that."

It was half an hour before we arrived at the cove on the other side of the Sound. He dropped anchor and I watched the chain spinning out while he secured the tiller and lowered the sails. Below in the cabin he apologized about the lack of a heater; he lit the cookstove to make coffee for me.

"A blanket?" I asked.

No, he always sailed alone in the winter; he didn't need one, he said.

"What's this?" I pushed at the tarpaulin roll lying on one of the bunks.

"Canvas top."

"Fine." I began to take off my clothes.

"My God. What are you doing?"

"Unroll that tarp. Don't just stand there." I took off everything.

"It's freezing out here."

"That's obvious to me."

The boat was rocking hard in the wake of a tug going up the channel. I could hear the churning of motors. "I refuse," he said, "to take off my T-shirt."

"Okay. Hurry."

"You have good ideas," he told me, drinking more coffee in the marina that evening, warming his hands on the cup. He looked out at his boat in its mooring, snapped tight at its edges, secured under its tarp.

At the drugstore the boy was murmuring his foreign phrases, biting the end of his cigarette. "I could help you with your French," I said and sat down beside him. I needed someone to talk with. A companion while Michael made love to a flapper, lifted her lavender dress.

He lived in a room with a fireplace, the mirror rising above it surrounded by wood to the ceiling. "Non-functional," he said, "but it appeals to me." He put his keys on the mantel beside a picture of his mother, her blond hair curling like his, curling like the soft white hairs on his knuckles.

He closed the door and sat down on the edge of his cot, spreading out mimeographed sheets on the Indian-print spread. I pulled the drapes open and sat in the window, my eyes falling on his books, Flaubert after Flaubert; I started to cry, startling him. "It's nothing," I said. "I'm just starting my period. Don't worry. I'm being silly, of course."

"It's all right if you cry." He pressed my face to his shoulder; he undressed me.

It was awkward, the boy rising above me, nothing quite working. "Roll onto your back," I finally said. I lowered myself onto him, touching the hairs on his chest, gripping his arms as I moved.

"I knew you were beautiful," he said. His eyes rolled back before we'd barely begun. He disappointed himself.

"Don't worry," I said. "It's always awkward the first time two people are together."

The boy held me on top of him, stroking my hair where it fell over my back onto his arms, stroking in this way both of us. My knees were pressed to his sides. He had comforted me; I told him that.

"I've never slept with a woman who was bleeding before." A small muscle twitched in his neck.

"There's nothing wrong with that," I said quietly. I called him lover and kissed him. I lifted myself away from him then. His penis and belly were covered with blood. I had almost never seen so much blood on a man before. He looked up at me. "I'll wipe you off," I said, not knowing what else to say. He swallowed and looked away.

The Vincents were gone when I came home, and Michael was in the den drinking. We spent the rest of the night going to the sideboard, pouring each other more, not wanting to speak. In the morning before Father was awake we took the rowboat onto the lake. The sun was beginning to rise as Michael rolled up his sleeves. He pushed his hat back onto the crown of his head, saying nothing. He dipped the oars into the crimson water, easing himself back and forth, pushing us through the reeds and mosses at the shoreline, steering us into open water.

Halfway across the lake I took the oars, marking our direction by centering the ruddermount just below the topmost peak of our house, stopping now and then to hand the bottle back and forth. The public bathhouse sat at the edge of our property and I could see where the children would soon be diving, their parents sunning on the great concrete stairs that ran the span of the cove and descended into the sand.

"I slept with the boy," I said. If I had not been drinking, I would never have told him. He took a small minnow from the bucket and hooked it. "I was lonely," I said, "and you were with her."

He reeled in a few inches of line, pulling the fish close to the tip of the pole. "No," he said, "I wasn't." He studied the fish a long while then, and I asked him what he was thinking.

"Ellie Vincent," he said, swinging the pole behind us and out to the side. He cast the line and we watched the little fish skimming out over the water. It was barely visible when it fell.

To the Montgomery house, he had moved very few of his former possessions. Among them were those photographs he had obtained of pilots and their wartime planes. All of these, except for one, he had packed away in a crate and secured in a remote corner of the attic. Goggles, helmet with dog-ears, the clean-shaven smiling face that had

caused him in college to take a razor to his own moustache
—that photograph now was framed and hung in the bathroom off their bedroom.

He couldn't say why he had insisted on keeping that
picture that had disappointed him so much, the grainy
newsprint copy of another man's father crouched on the
camouflaged wing of a P-38 Lightning, hand reaching out
as if for a document or orders for the night raid. "Why this
one?" she asked, coming up behind him as he washed his
hands. One shoulder went up and came down.

"Sentiment," he said, pushing her out, away from the
gleaming toilet bowl, the nozzles of the sink where he had
automatically turned to twist tighter the handles again, the
silver frame with the plexiglass pressing against machine
and pilot. With the heels of his hands he persuaded her out
of that room, the pads of his fingertips prodding at the
plateau of her belly, pressing under the crests of her hipbones as he urged from behind. "I'm very sentimental, you
know." He had not said that he still thought of that pilot as
his progenitor, if not of his bone and blood, then of his
spirit. He pushed her into the bedroom. "Don't worry.
When I leave this house behind, I'll put your picture in
just such a position." Lightly his palm held her breast now,
his other hand at the small of her back. "Imagine it—"

"Michael!" She boxed him on the shoulder.

"Me lighting a votive candle to you each night over the
toilet."

"You'd never leave me, you fool." She gave him another
jab. "Would you."

"Oh, no?" And then he had picked her up by the waist
and was holding her up over the edge of the bed like a doll.
"No?" He set her down and brushed the auburn waves
back behind her ears. "How can you be so sure?"

"Ha!" she laughed right out. With a jerk, her hair fell

into place again. "You're absolutely sick with love for me."

"I am?" He leaned down and touched his nose to hers, inspecting her blue eyes.

"Of course you are!" She shoved him back on his heels.

"Whoa!" he shouted catching his balance. His arms were out like wings and then the great weight of him fell forward on top of her. Immediately she had the tufts of his brown-black hair in her fists. "Orpheus never felt a thing compared with you, O'Dea." Impulsively she nipped him on the cheekbone. "You're just that possessive."

"Oh no—I'm a roving man; that's the way I like it." He kissed her severely on the lips.

"You aren't." He pressed his weight against her again, his white shirt against the light-blue sweater that made the eye he saw stand out like an ice storm in her pretty head. He pressed the tight knot of his corduroy pants against the seam of her jeans until, in a panic, he tried to jerk away from the arms she had wrapped around him, and in anger and frustration she bit him.

"Ouch!" he cried, sitting up. "That hurt!" He set his fingertips gingerly on his upper lip. "Well, that does it. Get out my bags. I'm packing up."

"Oh, Herr Doktor, you wouldn't do that." In the bed-stand drawer was the candy bar she had been saving. She stripped the corner of the brown paper off the end, and then it was exposed. She frowned into it. "Not just anyone could put up with the likes of you. Not just anyone would want to." She looked into the colored printing on the wrapper. "You've got bad habits," she said. She separated the creamy segments: each one a separate filling.

"I wanted to be all right for you," he said sullenly. He was standing beside her, pulling hard at his sleeve. She could see the cuff clasped tightly in his fist by her knee, his cuff link dangling. "Can't you understand!" he yelled. "I wanted to be good enough for you. How many times do I have to tell you?"

She gripped the corner of the waxed paper and looked up at him. "You know I didn't mean that. You started it, Michael—you were joking. You're turning everything around again. Don't do it." She reached out to touch his arm where the brown hairs curled out from under the stark-white shirt. But he thrust his wrists behind him.

It had been like this before—the sudden shouting and then this sound wrenching out of him. He had flung himself back and forth across a room, fighting down a rising shriek while she stood by helpless, frightened, trying to beat back her own words, reassurances that after a certain point would only intensify his anger. Slowly she had learned to be struck mute as if in a nightmare. When he had been afraid to present his cases on grand rounds, he had flown around the hospital chapel like a frantic butcher bird. When his impotence with her had become obvious, she had seen him throw his naked limbs against the walls. The tic had begun under his eye again as he stood beside the bedpost. The rosewood footboard spiraled up beside him, but he would not secure his hand on it. He fixed her with his stare until finally, in fear, she burst out from under it. "You couldn't; would you, Michael? I can't—"

"I could not." He threw his head back, laughing bitterly. "So the philosopher has told us. Again and again! It's evident."

She turned her head and stared after him as he paced away from her toward the far side of the room. He had neglected to unroll completely one of his sleeves, and part of his shirt tail had come untucked. It flapped over the back of his beige pants. She had no idea what he meant. Back and forth he paced when she asked him who the philosopher was and what it had to do with them. "What is it,

Michael? What is it?" she cried out when still he did not answer her. Now she caressed the rectangular segment of candy like a weight, a heavy melting box on her tongue. It slammed the lid down on what she might have said. He had said he might leave her. Seeing him there, even in that state, she said to herself: I have never seen him when he was not beautiful, when he did not need me.

But his freckles stood out like violence as if he had been shot from the inside out. He wrenched his hands. "There was a nun at the orphanage." His voice stumbled before her and halted. Here and there he went over the Chinese carpet, trying to collect himself. Here and there in the strip of light collapsing through the windows. Again he stopped at the side of the bed, but he was facing away from her. "No one could have asked for more perfect, delicate features," he said, "than the Little Nun had." His back swelled, and he cast out his breath again. "The Midget Nun taught biology at the orphanage. But she had an abnormality. She said she was very proud of it. Without it she would have been beautiful; with it, she was the only source of pride in the Home. It led to discussions—philosophy for wretched, orphaned Catholic youths.

"The Little Nun had a moustache. She was proud of it. But the meaner boys said she had become a nun because no man could bear two sets of lips with hair on them in one woman. They said this within her hearing. It was unintentional, but still she heard it. A hairless mouth, she heard them say, could be the only introduction to the other one. But she was proud of herself. And not one person, I tell you, ever saw her without thinking that she must have beautiful thighs." He was trembling.

I have been watching his back a long while now, Zara Montgomery thought, gripping the edge of the bedspread in her hand. Perhaps his shoulders are not shaking like that at all, she thought. Perhaps there is a small animal running from sleeve to sleeve under his shirt. It will be an amusing little story now that has nothing at all to do with his wanting to leave me here alone. In his silence she could almost imagine it: herself alone. Her hands rushed into the dead air between them. "Michael, you're so upset. I don't want you to leave me. Please understand—"

He turned abruptly. "Don't interrupt."

"Things have been better off and on, Michael. They're getting better, aren't they?"

His eyes were strangely frozen in front of her—so green were they, like oval flakes, so small the beads at the centers of them. His head snapped up. "Oh, Michael!" she cried out. "Won't you please let somebody help you once? Please stop now. You look like an apple stuck on a stick."

"Exactly! Exactly that! That's what I am." His strong chin lurched up; the hard cheek pounded. "It's a story about freaks. You know—cripples without legs and arms, the blind, the deaf, the institutionalized; weeping Gargantuas, runts; women with skin cancer like warts from head to foot; the hairless, homosexual, and hirsute; albinos like white rats. Orphans, children of child molesters and drunks, infants called bastards, mongoloids. Freaks—" He closed his eyes. Slowly his finger came out of his fist, traced up his arm and into the folds of his sleeve until it touched his cuff link. Deeply he breathed.

"Beyond the breadth of the Midget Nun's small, delicate nose, the fur did not extend. In this way, it paid a compliment to both her fragile nose and her upper lip. *Gentle* upper lip! Many of us! she warned, would never advance to an age when we would have sprouted even half so much or so glorious a growth. We were so sickly and irresolute a group that we had not even been able to keep our parents. Her hairs were not thin; they were not curly. This was good fortune—straight hairs being by nature much stronger than curly ones, though less attractive.

"Students!" Michael O'Dea shrieked, and Zara Montgomery twisted the white coverlet up over her sweater and pressed it against her shoulders. Back and forth he paced. The Midget Nun trod the length of the laboratory table. "Dear, dim students!" he cried. "What is imagery? You are correct to say it is the surface. We see something; we hear it. Few in this life will truly understand depth, innuendo, interiors. Wretched orphans—many of you will think of yourselves as being insightful; you will see everyone else as fools. You will spring about declaring your minute discoveries in life, collecting followers like family, like brittle little bugs. You will say: These are the facts; this is the life I have made from nothing. Orphans, I know this. I have seen it before and often. I tell you now, I pity you the day when you discover—and it is inevitable, students. Inescapable. You will discover that you are no more important to any human being than you are at this moment. You, sitting like a slug, a rejection in this classroom. That day you will realize that you have projected your own fears, desires, repulsions, and egocentric interpretations onto the personalities and works of others. You will know that you are nothing."

"Michael! Michael!" Zara Montgomery cried out.

Michael O'Dea whipped around to face her. "Ms. Montgomery has a question. Does Ms. Montgomery have a question so important that she would interrupt biology class? Would Ms. Montgomery care to stand then on the laboratory table and speak her insignificant piece?"

"Are you saying, Michael—"

"Someone was speaking of Michael O'Dea's dedication to his wife!" he shouted. "To the Zenith Montgomery!" She saw his back then, his face in the dressing-table mirror: lip twisted, his short trimmed moustache contorted in the wannest of smiles. "We—your orphans—watched the Midget Nun lowering her delicate, delicate face, pressing her palms together as she often did in chapel. Students. Assemble before the microscope." His hands gripped one another behind his thin back. Rigidly he crossed and re-crossed the red segment of the rug. His feet were thin as fins as he skimmed lightly over it, his shirttail a flounce behind him. With each perambulation his back stiffened, his white feet grew swifter.

"Advance, I said, to magnify and inspect specimens!" Zara drew her knees up; she silenced her mouth with the bedspread. "Just so, students. Just so," he crooned. "You will see before you the word irony. Perhaps you see no such thing? Perhaps you see two hairs under the lens? One the dark hue of your professor's moustache?

"*Point one!* Straight hairs invariably present on trans-verse section a cylindrical or oval outline. *Point two!*" He unclasped his hands and thrust them to his sides. "And well. Zara Montgomery? How will you find a home if you do not speak up?"

She felt the blood drain out of her face, and he began again, even more loudly, shriller. "The curly hair is *flat* when similarly examined. Is there no irony in that? Do you not see the word irony in every root and shaft? Orphans, orphans, little worms. Point three is this. Straight hairs are frequently faulty visions. These are the paths to disillusion-ment. The orphan's place in this world, little slugs, is a precarious one. All the world will give you what they no longer want. To give is to love, it is said. And yet we must ask ourselves, little men, whether this is love! Do these people even know your names? Do they know how you laugh and why? Do they comprehend what makes you so uncertain of yourselves, what makes you proud of what you are? They do not. Say thank you; do not call it love!

"You have been left without that natural connection to

the world, to affection, orphans. You will seek love in everything and everyone if you do not understand one thing. Though the world might make a monstrous pretense of caring for you, you—the lost and abandoned ones, you who will grow to be the dross drifting adults in their midst—you are no more loved than the common flea, though certainly more worthy. You must look to yourselves and others like you to raise yourselves up. You must love yourself.

"Until the day arrives when you can do that, you will be as straight as the mundane hair appears at first glance, but no one will understand you. Or you will take on affectations to cover up who you are. You will be the most spiraled individuals imaginable in your attempts to win the admiration of those you do not know; yet you will feel flat, deserted, hollow inside. Learn to love yourselves, little boys; learn to love yourself as your Savior alone has loved you. Then and only then will you see and be seen. Then you will find your place in this world, and the one that comes after this so often imaginary place."

Zara Montgomery lifted her face from her hands. Her husband was leaning toward the bureau, one arm drooping before the mirror. Slowly his eyes came into focus on himself, and she heard the laughter sputter out of his throat. He stepped back heavily, laughing.

"And have you done it?" she asked anxiously. "Have you done what the Midget Nun said?"

He swept his hand across his forehead, through the membrane of sweat on his brow. She saw the grimace on his mouth. "See? Don't you see?" he cried. "That's the way all us little orphans got our start in biochemistry. It's okey-dokey. Everything is absolutely all right here. The freak is the epitome of everything that is interesting and lovable. Isn't that right? I pass all the tests. The freak holds the whole world in his hands." He flung himself onto his side of the bed; he stared into the swirled plaster hanging over him. "Trust? What is trust to me? I can only *think* about caring, understand? I don't love anyone. There's no one but myself," he cried out. "And I don't give anything for him, not for that person who calls himself me. In the end he's useless!" He lay coiled up on his side, his ribs poking through his shirt like the end of a white fence rolled in on itself. "What good is he?" he wailed, his forehead, his mouth against her leg where her hip met the side of her thigh.

What will happen if I touch him? she asked herself. What will happen? She clutched at her hands. "It's hopeless, hopeless!" he cried. And it was as if she had heard a ball of sand coming apart in his throat. "I wish someone would put that person away, that man who is wearing that moustache. He is killing me, destroying everything I want to be! Why can't they get rid of him, Zara? Why can't they? Throw him under an outboard motor in the lake, run over him with something, anything. Bury him—he's putrid, he's dead! Do something, won't you, Zara? Do something."

Her fingers were clamped then over the sleeve of his shirt, as if she could resuscitate him with her belief in how far he had already dragged himself. She shook him hard. "Michael, Michael," she called as if he were at the end of a very long hall and could not distinguish her voice for all the echoing. His arm flopped limply back and forth. "You're not a freak, Michael. I care about you. And you care about me. You just don't know what to do with it yet. You're too afraid." If she could have she would have pressed his waxen face against her until, infused with the emotion she held for him—and surely he would feel it, it was so strong —he would bloom. She would have carried him to some brighter, happier place. She would have had the right words to pour into his wounds. He would not hurt himself any-more. She shook his arm.

He lurched bolt upright then, yelling straight into her astonished face. "Liar!" he yelled. Her head snapped back away from his clenched teeth, but then he gripped the hair at the back of her head. He set his face against hers. The line crept up at the corner of his mouth and moved toward his hair. "It's all a lie!" he hissed into the fear that was Zara Montgomery now. "I'm using you, don't you understand? I pretend to love, and you pretend to love me back. We fit together, see? We make a picture in the world, and they call it love, devotion, family. We're nothing together. We're no more than a hollow shaft of filament laid down among others in a wig. I've tried it, and *you* come the closest. You! This is the closest," he shouted in disgust, and his face went nearly lax in front of her. The knot of hair tightened again, but he held her away. "You're so real," he whis-pered, "that I can't stand it anymore. Your skin, your slob-bering mouth, your petty bones. Moisture," he hissed. "Moisture like phlegm—even in your eyes! But the others, the others—" he cried. "I would give anything for them! That succulence! Do you even know that with finger, cock, fist, and thumbs you could break apart those hemispheres?" He caressed the side of her face, pinning her with his arm.

She could see him out past the white arena of his shirt gawking at his hands. He held out the one, examining it: the long fingers, the broad stiff thumbs, the squared-off nails.

When she felt the pressure release at her back and side she did not move for a moment. His hand turned over; he was inspecting the other side. Slowly she tried to creep away from him, but he tightened his grip. "Do you want to know what I say to a woman when I'm through with her? Do you want to know?" His chest swelled up, fell down, and swelled again under her ear. "When I'm through with them, with her, I say: Scud, I will go home to someone real; I will go home to my wife."

She could not shut her eyes. "Sometimes," he sighed, staring at his hands. "Sometimes I look at you, and you're not a magazine photograph. Sometimes I'm not a fresh piece of plaster clinging to these walls. Sometimes I see you and I do not think money; I do not even consider the quality of your father's face. And then I understand it, Zara; I know it's real." He laid his hands on hers; and she knew the pressure of them, his hot palms. She cast herself away from him, propelling herself toward the side of the bed, toward the door. But he caught her wrist.

"Not me at all!" she sobbed over the length of their arms. But his voice was flying at her again, drowning her out.

"You don't understand," he shouted. "I am winning. I am winning now. I understand now. It's you I love."

He let go his grip then, and Zara stumbled over the haze toward the wall. She caught the edge of the door. "Like phlegm," she sobbed. "Phlegm," she wailed.

Michael O'Dea yelped then as if someone had hit him in the face with a board; and she, even in her weeping, turned to see the single bead of moisture falling down his stricken face. "Isn't it just like she said?" he whispered. "I'm a freak." Again and again her name rushed out across the sudden emptiness of that room. She heard the notes of it bawling up and down the hall, through all the lifeless rooms. Her strange name. "I *am* a freak. I didn't want to be a freak, Zara." And even her mother had never answered when she asked, why that name? "Zara, Zara." Once she had pressed her finger into his navel, and there she had felt the tiny ridges, the whorls of his identity, of the man he would be. As a girl she had left her own romantic fingerprint on those whorls. In quick succession, his singular drops, the flood rushing out of his beautiful eyes. "I've torn you," he cried. "I'll never hurt you again, Zara. Please believe in me." She saw his long lean legs, his thin emaciated arms. The spattered, feverish face that had been zany, zanier, zaniest. He had helped her through her own grief. On the bed he flung his head back and forth. And then she was sitting beside him on the bed. She pulled him against her breast. Again and again her hand went over his soft hair, his swollen cheeks.

"Michael." Her fingertip pressed the hair against his temple, around the smooth outer circuit of his ear. She had no idea how long they sat that way, how long they were contented before she talked to him. "I want you to be sure, Michael. We have to understand each other, Michael. Isn't that true for you?" His hand curled around hers. "There's a story in the Bestiary, Michael— When a monkey bears twins, immediately after parturition the mother takes a liking to only one. The other baby she despises—" Immediately he retracted his hand and she did not know whether to continue. "Don't we have to understand each other, Michael? Is that true for you?" The sun had fallen, pink and orange into the windows, into the mirrors. She stroked his forehead then. "Are you too tired, Michael? Do you want a drink of water?" His hand relaxed then and she felt him slowly shake his head against her breasts. Throughout the room the light called back and forth. Mirror to window to mirror again. She stroked his forehead, and he took her hand.

"The monkey mother does not, however, abandon the child she scorns, Michael. She feeds it as she feeds the other, doing a duty of sorts, keeping up a pretense. Now a tragic thing happens, Michael—" *Hemispheres.* The word beat at her as if she were hearing it for the first time. His hand in other women. In the early evening light, through her hair, she raked her red hand. *Hemispheres.* It beat at her. His left hand on her right hand. Hemispherical conditions, a sun mauve around the central crack in the silvering of her mother's mirror. His hands; hands that can break. She closed her eyes for a moment. "If the mother—" But her voice caught. She felt it: his hand tightening on hers. She cleared her throat, rushed on. "If the mother and her two babies are threatened—if they have to flee, the monkey runs away from her pursuer, carrying the one she loves in her arms. The one she scorns rides clinging to the back of her neck. Eventually the mother tires under the weight of the two babies. She is forced to abandon the one she loves and run on, saving the one she despises, which is clinging to her neck."

"Zara, tell me!" Michael O'Dea cried out, jerking his head up to look at her. "Tell me! Which one of the babies am I?"

"You're not a baby!" Zara Montgomery cried. She saw him clinging to her belly. "You're not the baby! You're not the baby! Why doesn't anybody want me? Why am I always left behind?" She could not control it any longer, and inexplicably her husband on hearing her cry took hold of her. He took his stance.

It was like being at school in the gymnasium, waiting for the polio vaccine: watching your father coming down the line of all your friends, making them cry one after the other as the school nurse said to you what a good man he was and how lucky you were to have a father like that just as he stuck the needle in and pushed the stopper down. It was just like that, she thought, when the Clown turned to her. There he was beside her with his big painted hand on her arm so she couldn't run away; there was the microphone. The large camera moved back, scanned the audience, and approached again.

"If you could see anything in the world, what would it be?" the Clown asked. His voice was like a car door—Mrs. Willoughby's, next door, when it needed grease. He reached up and squeezed his nose; it made a noise like a duck. "Anything in the whole world. What would it be?"

She lifted her head and said in a frightened voice as she tugged on her braids, "I'd like to see the Leaning Tower of Pisa, please."

"Oh," the Clown said, so surprised he honked on his horn. He turned toward the camera and winked. "And do you know where the Leaning Tower of Pisa is?" he asked.

Zara Montgomery was twisting her foot, examining shyly the Brownie insignia on her sock. Yes, she said; it was in a book she had at home. A large book and she would show it to him sometime if he wanted her to.

"In a book," he laughed. "Isn't that grand?" The audience was laughing, too, while Zara Montgomery was turning red. "Is it an Italian book?" the yellow-orange lips asked her now.

"I don't know," Zara said. "Mummie got it from a museum somewhere. It came in the mail." The audience was cooing at her as she looked down. There was the little Brownie on her sock; it was crawling into her shoe.

"And what do Mommy and Daddy do?" the Clown asked, holding the microphone again to her mouth.

She tugged at her braid, staring down. "Mummie was a singer once."

"And what does Daddy do?"

Zara Montgomery looked toward the green light where the director of photography was motioning now. She saw him smiling at her; she was reassured. She cast her eyes up at that cameraman, as if she were heaving her vision heavenward, away from the Clown, as if she had seen a long lost friend. "My Daddy is a saint."

"A saint?" the Clown asked.

"Yes," she said, casting her eyes toward the cameraman.

"Oh, my," apologized the Clown. "You mean your Daddy is an angel, not a saint."

"No," she said with petulance. "He's not an angel. He's a saint."

The Clown smoothed her kerchief down at the back of her neck with sympathy; he smiled seriously into the camera and the audience. "You mean Daddy's gone to heaven? Darling? Is that what you mean?"

"No, no!" Zara Montgomery cried out in defense, stomping her foot at the ridiculous man. "Angels are dead! Daddy's not dead!"

"There, there!" the Clown burst out. "There's no use getting so angry if Daddy's all right. Where's that pretty little smile you were singing about?"

Hot, indignant tears sprang down her face. "My Daddy's a saint! A SAIIIIIIIIIIINT!" she wailed as the Clown's boldly painted eyes searched frantically for help.

Heavily, Mrs. Dormer stepped forward; decisively she pulled the little girl toward the solace of her skirt. "She means, Mr. Clown—though she may not fully understand it—" Mrs. Dormer drew her breath in aggravation; she stroked the child. "Her father is a physician. To his patients and his family, he is, metaphorically speaking, a saint."

"Oh," the Clown said, patting the sobbing child on the head. "There there, little tike. It seems your father is a sort of modern day saint, just as you've said."

"I'm not a little tike!" Zara Montgomery screamed. She kicked him in the shins.

"Oh, Zara," he said, hurrying now to reassure her. "I didn't mean that about your father, about the money. You know I didn't mean it, don't you? It wasn't appearance, Zara." He held her. He saw her tears, and he felt love. "I would have married you if you'd been a penniless immigrant, Zara. I'd have married you if you'd been an orphan like myself."

"My mother was an immigrant," she sobbed bitterly, crying for herself, not knowing how to save what she had begun, not knowing where she had gone wrong, why she had become so undesirable, so lost in a life she could not understand to be her own—it was so far from what she believed in, from what she had dreamed for herself.

"Oh, yes," Michael said hastily, "but your mother was English, Zara. You know how people coo over an English accent here. She wasn't your standard immigrant." He tried to wipe her eyes.

"My mother was unhappy, Michael. She was always saying to me, 'He makes me tired, Zara. Just listen to him. All Forster says is *me, me, me, me*—until I want to lie down and die, Zara, just to feel a part of this place. I want to die, Zara,' she'd say to me. And when he went out of a room, and she knew he was far enough away so he couldn't hear, she would hiss, Michael. She would hiss: 'Me. Me. Me! Me! Mean!' And I felt sorry for *him*, Michael."

Michael O'Dea took up the corner of his shirt again and dabbed at her face. "That must have been so terrible for them both, Zara. Of course you'd feel bad for him."

"But why should I! Don't you see what he is? Do you think he was any help to her, any companion, or lover, or friend? Do you think he even hears or sees anybody else? He's never been worth a goddamned thing when anybody needs him for support. She lived her life entirely alone, Michael. She lived in a cell. And I didn't even know it until she was sick, until she was dying." She was crying again then, thinking only of her mother, driving out the thought of what had passed between herself and her husband, until Michael, regaining his composure, held her by the shoulders. Gently he shook her saying, "Zara, tell me why you've been moping around here for the last month."

Her fingers clutched that small insignificant button on his shirt.

"What have you been doing with your time?" he asked. "Whenever I ask you, you change the subject."

"Oh—" she said, her voice in a tremor. "I've been reading a lot." Phlegm. Succulence. These deaths moving against her. "Ellen's given me a reading list."

"Ellen Whitney's not good for you. No wonder you're down, Zara." He chucked her lightly under the chin.

"She is, Michael." His belly between the hipbones of someone else; her own little body a mucus; his soft hairs against the breasts of women he would torment. *I'll never hurt you again, Zara. I've torn you.* His arms around her. "Oh, Michael!" she cried. "I don't know where my guts have gone. I feel like a rag, a dreadful rag inside."

He tapped her on the back. "Let's forget about Ellen Whitney for a moment. What else have you been doing?"

"I made a series of papier-mâché heads in the attic. Ellen—"

"Likes them, I suppose."

"She does, Michael. She actually thinks they're very good. She's not just saying it, Michael. She's not that way. She's not a hypocrite."

Michael O'Dea leaned back against the headboard in disgust.

He had known Ellen Whitney nearly all his life. He had never liked her, though she was attractive—he could not deny that. She had grown up poor and had, rather than disavow her background, embraced it. She had a quick mind and was apparently doing well in her profession. Ed Anderson had mentioned that Ellen had recently published several articles. She had yet to finish her dissertation, though she was teaching at the college while she completed it, which Ed said would be very soon.

All that was good enough, Michael thought; it was her extreme political nature that irked him. It was as if she had one foot in respectability and the other back on the street of the old neighborhood. She had often confronted him on political matters in public, asking him: Had he really so little awareness as to support the American Medical Association? Would he mind terribly giving up a little of his own security so that medicine might be socialized in this country? Would he consider adjusting his rates, when he had finished his residency, to take into account the situation of the impoverished? All of this, they had argued vehemently until Ellen Whitney had looked him straight in the eye, for she was nearly as tall as he was, and said, "You would allow the disadvantaged—orphans, for instance—to fend for themselves. Is that it? Am I reading you right, O'Dea?"

With that Michael O'Dea raised an eyebrow and looked at her with the most severe of glares. "I have every sympathy for the underprivileged, Ellen," he said. "I have, however, come to understand one thing—water seeks its own level. I have no intention of lowering mine so that others may swim." With that he walked out of the room; that conversation had been squelched. Now here he was, annoyed at the mention of her name in this conversation with Zara after he had so definitely stuck his foot in his mouth about the Midget Nun. Here was his wife dropped out of medicine to make papier-mâché heads in the attic and going out only to see Ellen Whitney. Here was the woman he had married lying fully dressed in the bed, her head thrown back against the pillows, the tears streaming like accusations out of her face.

"Why haven't I been shown these heads?" he said. "Do you have any idea how angry it makes me to think I've been preempted by that radical Ellen Whitney?"

"But, Michael. You've been so wrapped up talking with Father whenever you come home. Or you were always reading, Michael. You didn't want to see them."

"Please don't bother trying to think for me, Zara. I can do that for myself. Sometimes I wonder if Ellen Whitney has any judgment at all. There now," he said stroking her leg. *Why does he only want me when I'm sad?* The hand went up and down her thigh. "What else have you been doing with your days?" he asked. She jerked away from him, and he looked up.

"I won't have you demeaning my relationship with Ellen Whitney," she declared, wiping her hand brusquely across her cheek. "I don't ridicule your friends, or the things you find important."

"Yes, Zara, but really, Ellen Whitney?"

"Ellen Whitney's the only person in this town who doesn't have three-quarters of herself rented to somebody else. I might never have come back here with you if it hadn't been for my friendship with her. She gives me some hope."

"Because of Ellen Whitney you left Washington with me?"

"To everybody else I'm just the daughter here. And now your wife. You said it yourself: that Montgomery girl again. Money! That's what you said."

Michael O'Dea stretched out his legs and crossed his ankles. "Even Ellen Whitney can't change that," he said coldly, brushing a piece of lint from his sleeve. "Face it.

You had to come back. What would you do anywhere else? You refuse to do anything related to medicine. The truth is: you can't take care of yourself. You can take care of everyone else, but you won't do that. You dropped a brilliant career so you could sit around and pine over your own inability to stick with it. And now I'm going to ask you, Zara. Who's stopping you from practicing medicine? You've got your degree. You can be a G.P. at the clinic any time you want. Or you could do your internship and residency. You could specialize. You've got privileges around here. You don't have to wait like all the rest of us low-life schmucks who have to work their butts off just to get into the hospital cafeteria for an interview. You could start in late. Your old man could pull it for you."

"What do you mean—" she burst out, "my old man could pull it? I don't need his help in *medicine*. And if I did do my residency, it wouldn't be in this town. I'm here because of you—"

"Did you really expect your father not to be disappointed in you, Zara? Did you think your father and I would sit there and applaud? I'm going to ask you again. I want you to get this straight in your head. Answer me. Say it out loud. *Who* is stopping you from practicing medicine?"

She looked at him with an anger that drained her face.

"Well," he sneered. "Don't just sit there glaring at me, Medusa. Tell me who it was took your identity away."

She spat the word out then. *"Mummie!"*

In exasperation he threw his hands out in front of him. "Your mother?!" He had her head in both hands. He was shouting; he was shaking her. "Your mother is dead, Zara. Your mother is dead!" He let go of her then as if he couldn't stand to touch her again. "Don't you get that?" he asked, incredulous. "Don't you understand that at all?"

"Do you think I don't know?" she screamed at him. "Do you think I don't realize she's dead after all I've been through? Do you think I'm some sort of psychotic who can't tell the living from the dead? She died in *these*." She smashed her palms against his chest, smashing them down the front of him again and again as if to wipe something off. He grabbed hold of her wrists but she yanked them away. "Listen to me!" she cried, screaming at him. "I said *Mummie* is keeping me from medicine." She was pounding her thighs with her fists. "Mummie with her shriveled-up body, shit, flatulence, sweat, acidosis, cigarette smoke so thick you could barely see. The huge running sores, urine on the sheets, the piles of diapers between her legs. Her breasts shriveling, the thigh bulging, the toes crusted and gnarled, the hips grown together. The blast of blood into the bedpan, spontaneous fractures, the times she stopped breathing and I thought she was gone—" And Zara Montgomery could not stop the weeping from starting again. "Her fevers, her chills. *'Turn the heat up, Zara. Turn the heat up, Zara.'* With me in my underwear and her smothered in quilts. Or the other way around in the winter, the windows thrown open with me under every blanket we had; and she was under the sheet naked in twenty-degree weather, enjoying 'that balmy spring breeze.' Her little face grown so old, so young like a baby's, her hair fallen out, turned gray what was left. Her body gone into parchment and sickness and stench, and all the time she was calling out—'Zari! Today'll be a party. We'll have a party! We'll enjoy ourselves!' "

Michael O'Dea shook his head. Slowly he moved it back and forth. "Zara, why did you do it? Why, honey? Why?"

"Because it was a party," she screamed at him. "Don't you understand that? Can't you understand one thing about me? Can't you even try? It was a party, I tell you! It was a party the whole fucking time! She *cared* about me!" she cried. "And some people *like* to live."

How sentimental we all were in the beginning. Michael was stretched out beside me on the blanket, his limbs long, cool, damp. The others were lying in couples, too; nostalgic songs showered around the campfire. Michael had given me presents that day: a woven silver bracelet; the yellow T-shirt with Lermontov on the front; the 1930s postcard he had found while he was away at school. It was this last that endeared him to me: the photograph taken from the inside of a cage of elephants, looking out past the wispy hairs that stood straight up on the rough-textured hides, their tails like jute. Elephants cocked their lily ears, sprayed water toward a Depression crowd behind bars, behind the grids of shadow in that natural light. I felt like that.

Across the lake I saw that night a window ignite in the upstairs corner of our house. In a moment it had gone dark again, and then there was the glow of a smaller, lower one through the slightly swaying leaves. It had been all right. Mummie preparing for bed and turning on the reading light. Downstairs, a row of rectangular flares—Father with his medical journals in the den. I ran my finger along Michael's face, past his cool ear, down along the quiet pulse of his neck. "What are you thinking about?" He turned his head into the light from the fire, and his green eyes went amber in the glow. "Are you dreaming?" I asked the boy who had gotten away, who had gone beyond the old Victorian houses clustered around the lake, the newer houses at the fringe of town, the yellow-tasseled fields. He had gone away to school; he had sent me shells from some remote stretch of beach that went on and on, that did not begin and stop at a light at the top of one large house.

When he returned, he stayed in one of the old towns-women's boarding rooms, collecting—he said—flowered wallpaper in his memory like a catalog. He rested his hand on the hip of my swimming suit. He had been so far away, but when he came back he saw only me. "Dreams?" he laughed. "Yes. My mind took a flight," he said quietly. He had made his own way in everything. He had earned it all himself, or won it through intelligence.

Beside the fire, Sally Welke laughed. Molly Van Horn sighed and leaned into the silhouette of the man she had known these last few months at the college in town. Michael's hand went up and down my side, caught for a moment at the edge of my suit, and settled again comfortably on my hip. I touched the soft brown hairs at his throat. "Dreams in color?" I asked. "Or black and white?"

He smoothed the blanket out between us with his hand. "It's like an old movie," he said. "In the dream, I'm a very large house with vines across the front. And I'm a field out back." I did not have to look across the lake to imagine it. "You're in this dream, too, you know. Do you want to hear about it?"

"Of course I do." Up beside the blaze, over the ring of stones and the stack of wood rattled the drunken voices of my friends as they competed in Everly Brothers' tunes we had learned as children. Male voices shouted along.

"All right," he said. "You're with a man called O'Dea, for reasons no one understands. You have a small plane, and the two of you laugh when you call it Spitfire, when you hear its name. You put on your goggles, dark ones, and the two of you buckle in and roar up and down over my field all day. You laugh so hard you don't even have to take off. You're just that satisfied."

"Could I add to your dream?" I asked him then. "Is that allowed? We could spin out over the lake once or twice?"

"If you like—I'm the lake, too."

"I'll wear my presents. We'll hang the postcard from the instrument panel. I'll sing arias to you."

"Yes," he said. "Michael O'Dea will wear the Earhart shirt."

"Earhart without catastrophe."

"Together the two of you will flee all this," he said.

I reached up and touched the hair that had grown so thick since I had last seen him. He was trimming it differently around the ears; his moustache had gone from down to manliness. It grew then, full and carefully trimmed, down around the sides of his mouth nearly to his chin. Yes, we are nineteen now, I said to myself. It has begun. This is what they mean when they say it, when they murmur "love."

I had trusted Michael since that first time when I spent the whole night in his room. I had made love to him a few times before that, but sleeping all night beside him had made me feel grown. After we had made love in his bed and kissed good night, that moment came when we turned, each toward a private restfulness. Then I felt him drawing his knees up and pointing his feet gently at the backs of my calves. Lightly his back, his buttocks, his feet rested against me—as if he were balancing himself there so delicately, as if he were as fragile as a bird. I had needed to trust him then; I always needed that.

Even then, on the beach that night, I knew that I would have to be very careful of him: this man who knew nothing of familial reassurances—of the loyalties that accompanied the passage of time, quarrels, and misfortunes. I said that to myself. He rolled away from me on the blanket then, turned onto his other side, looking out over the small scratchy bushes sticking out of the Iowa sand. And I lay down, too, studying the fire, my friends there. Yes, it would be difficult, I told myself, but Michael O'Dea had a determination that no one else had. He had developed a wit, an eloquence that I—even with my family, my financial situation, my intelligence, my home—had never believed I could have. Perhaps we will be comfortable, I said to myself; in time we will still be lively together, and we will be as homely with one another as we were that first night lying back to back without fear of separation, without expectations, with no fear at all in his bed.

Sitting beside Zara Montgomery, Michael O'Dea had watched the play being performed in the college theater; and there he had identified himself with the midget, a minor character relegated to a pair of shortened stilts, who beneath the grotesque mask and ballooning white pants had fallen in love with the lady of the singing-bird act. The soprano sang to the enormous bird, and the midget had taken it as a sign of love for him. And when the players had removed their masks on the stage, there had been other masks underneath. An even more involved story had begun.

Michael O'Dea washed his hands, scrubbing them unconsciously with the surgical brush. He had tried to watch this play, written by his wife, objectively. But then, too, he had found her notebook that week. Always he had imagined that the notes would contain some romanticized version of their relationship. Or memories of her mother. That, he had expected. He had not imagined that she would record in such a confessional manner her own emotions and distress over their marriage. He had not been prepared to find their sexual life—or lack of it—recorded in her long, flowing hand, which Forster, or anybody else coming across it, might read. Seeing that day described when she had put on the black dress, the old-fashioned undergarments, had hurt him unutterably.

"I can't stand it any longer. The black dress," she had

written. With pounding heart he had braced his knees against her open desk drawers and read from beginning to end her diary. He had read that passage several times and with each reading he had felt a fresh wound. "I had put on the black dress," it said. "I was embarrassed but I did it. He could not even come forward when he saw me. Immediately he fled the room without explanation. He left me standing there. As always he turned away. I thought terrible things about myself—sitting there in that getup, having lowered myself to that, having had to lower myself and then to have failed to interest him! He could not even let me have that much. He could not share it without having to initiate it. He left. And then suddenly he was back again, dressed as absurdly as I was. How could I then feel anything? I lay like a filet on the counter, and he did it to me. How else can I say it? There was nothing tender, or personal, or human about it. There I was, a slab of meat in garters."

And now her play had been a success. If curtain calls were any indication, it had been. She had been right to leave medicine. Perhaps he should have left it, too, he thought bitterly. Perhaps he should have taken a job playing violin in a dingy candle-lit restaurant; maybe that would have made him happier. The hospital had become for him, however, a sort of refuge.

Always now when he thought of making love to her, he thought of it while he was at the hospital. Always when he thought of her in that way, the thought was accompanied by an image. He saw it clearly: that blue sliver of eye staring directly at him from her mother's coffin. Sometimes he felt purified to lie alone on the narrow, physician's bunk in the emergency room and feel his pulse racing as he stared into that combination of visions. Sometimes he did not bother to turn off the flickering of the overhead light when he went to sleep.

He went into that room now to relieve himself during the

lull between patients. The yellow stream hit the back of the bowl, the bubbles forming at the water's edge. Forty-eight hours on call and twenty-four off to rest. That night they had called a Code Blue over the hospital intercom; the technicians had rushed in with their equipment to help shock a cardiac arrest back to life. Victims of automobile accidents had rolled in, one after another. Broken skulls and lacerations from barroom brawls. All tangentially connected to a victory of the college football team. There had been the usual influx of student complaints: the colds, the earaches and bladder infections, a case of pelvic inflammatory disease, an attempted pre-exam suicide. The last, an overdose of aspirin of all things, and the result: a gross hearing loss.

In the secretaries' cubicle across the hall, the red phone was ringing again. Michael O'Dea shook the few drops off the end of his penis and looked at it: vile slug that now had only one purpose—making foam at the bottom of a toilet bowl. Whatever the pain was, it was not enough to justify this worthlessness. He tucked himself back into his shorts and zipped his pants.

As he came around the corner of the second trauma room, he saw the cart come crashing through the ambulance entrance. The body swept past him clothed in a black char that had been epidermis. The nose, ears, lips, scalp all seared away. All distinguishing features gone, even fingerprints, even toes and fingers. The cart spun through the double doors, turned at an angle onto the corridor, headed directly for the burn unit where what remained would be coated with silver nitrate. In a few hours, the body—male or female, he could not tell which—would be in the morgue. As he walked into the secretarial suite to hear about his next case, he could hear echoing up the corridor from that cart a high-pitched animal wail, and he was not sure that he himself had not uttered it.

Ed Anderson swayed beside the sideboard. "More?" Michael put both hands around the bottle and poured his friend another. Liquor wafted in the firelight of the den.

"Got a story about cows," Ed said, sinking beside Ellen on the couch. "A farmer's story from a man with hem-roids. Man with hem-roids does two things. Right, O'Dea? Zara? Talks on the table and will not shut up. Or grits his teeth. Nary a word does the victim speak. Doesn't talk about crops, weather, hem-roids."

"Skip the shop talk, Anderson," Michael said, "and tell the story."

Anderson questioned his glass.

"Cows," Ellen Whitney reminded.

"Right," said O'Dea. "Moo moo, you know. With the dugs."

"Ah," said Anderson, as if he had just learned some-thing. "Cows. Old man told me cows eat apples. They've got all these stomachs."

"We know," Zara mumbled, peering into the side of her glass at the ice cubes. "They have four. Two cows—eight rumblers."

"Eight stomachs and they carry these apples around fermenting in their guts for a long hot while. Yup. All fall, they walk around drunk. Some die from it."

Michael O'Dea draped his leg over the arm of his chair and hissed.

"A true story. I wouldn't put you on about cows, O'Dea. Would I, Zara? I wouldn't put O'Dea on about cows, now would I?"

"Too insignificant," Zara said.

"That's right, O'Dea. Insignificance in cows is a major defect in farm country."

Michael scraped the edge of the clam dip with a cracker. "That's it, that's what Anderson has to say today on the stock market. Cows up eight stomachs and going higher."

"Nah!" said Anderson. "That's not it at all. You can die from it."

"Teriyaki steak?" Ellen Whitney asked.

"Nah!" said Anderson. "You never listen."

"Who dies from it?" Michael O'Dea asked.

"The cows drink themselves to death."

"Why don't they fence off the orchard if it's so dangerous to the herd?" Out the window Michael O'Dea could see the leaves wet and falling through the moonlight.

"I get it," Zara said. "I get the joke. The cows are eating horse apples. Admit it. If a cow ate a horse apple, he'd die right off."

Ellen Whitney tssked in Zara's direction. "She. Cows are she's."

"Right." Zara pulled at her drink. "I forgot."

Ellen Whitney pushed her hair out of her face as if it were a curtain. "Anderson?"

"Whitney?"

She looked at him very closely. "Knew it. Anderson's spoofing. Never was a cow. Never one hem-roid."

"Have not," said Anderson. "One cow in the herd wouldn't drink, the farmer said. Know why?"

Michael O'Dea stacked more wood onto the fire. "Why, for Christ's sake, Anderson?"

"This cow was an itty bitty cow wandering in the pasture—"

"Louis Pasteur: born in 1822 and he didn't even like cattle," Ellen said, "but don't let's let that interrupt you."

"This cow encountered big apples on south forty. Yummy yummy ate them all up. Got so drunk she nearly died of the hangover. Wouldn't ever touch the nasty stuff again." The three of them turned in silence to look at Anderson. "That's the end," Anderson said finally. "It's a drinking story, get it?"

"And that," sighed Zara Montgomery, "is the cow story from start to blasted finish."

"Yup," said Anderson.

"No more?" asked Ellen Whitney blowing the hair out of her face.

"No more, baby."

"Ohh," said Ellen Whitney. "And it was getting to be so much fun."

"Here, have another," Michael said, pouring liquor all around. "It'll help you get over Anderson's delectable anecdote."

"Cut up an apple and throw it in," Zara said.

"This one knows where the liquor is," Michael said, turning the bottle up at Zara's glass.

"Dish it out, O'Dea; I've got to catch up."

"You'll be pickled before the sun is up at this rate."

"Mummified. I'm leaving town, just going to pull up stakes."

"What?" Anderson asked. "Who's moving?"

"I am. Going to relocate in the new New Mexico."

Ed Anderson rubbed his hand along his neck, thinking. "I want to know what this New Mexico's got that Lake Marian hasn't got."

"What's it got!" Zara exclaimed. "Why, Edward, there's cities there so healthy you can leave dead bodies and they won't decay."

"I've heard of it," said Ellen Whitney. "San Atlantis. Sea salt, great medicament of restoration."

"Nah, Zara's not moving anywhere," Ed Anderson said. "She's going to stay right here and keep us company. Aren't you, Zara?"

"Yes," Zara sighed. "I guess you're right. I guess I probably will."

Michael leaned against the mantel, looking into the flames.

"Michael's sulking," Zara said. "Look. Michael's sulking."

"Cut it out, Zara," Michael O'Dea said. "Anyone for another drink?"

"You drinking, Mike?" Anderson asked. "Or you just getting us looped?"

Michael turned the bottom of his glass up and swallowed. "We're all out to pasture, Ed."

"Ooooh," said Zara. "Michael's getting morose. Want to watch Michael get morose?"

"Cut it out, Zara."

Zara watched the fire shadows fluttering against her husband's and her guests' faces. She took another drink. "Michael, do moths eat sheep?"

"You've never seen a sheep in your life," Michael said. "Zara lived in Iowa all her life and she's never even been on a farm."

"What? Never been on a farm?" asked Anderson. "Have to see about that. Line up a moonlight ride into the country. Hay and kissing."

"Don't be an idiot. Zara's been into the country," Ellen said.

"Name once, Zara."

"I used to go with Daddy into the country all the time."

"Get a load of that, the old man made house calls."

Zara turned to where Ellen Whitney was searching all her pockets for a match. "When I was sixteen, I helped deliver twins on a kitchen table."

"Christ," Michael O'Dea said. "Medical romance."

"Underestimate. Underestimate," Ellen Whitney said,

steering the match toward the candle. "Consistently under-estimate. Look at this woman, O'Dea." She was pointing directly at Zara's face. "Not only has Zari been on a farm, she was delivering babies when you were jerking off behind that brick garage on Johnson Street."

"That's right, Ellen," O'Dea said, smiling politely. "And still the ex-physician asks if moths eat sheep."

"Well, do they?"

"Do they?" Anderson asked, nuzzling into Ellen Whitney's side. "What garage?"

"How the hell should I know if moths eat sheep?" O'Dea snarled. "They eat processed sheep, isn't that enough?"

"Whooo boy. O'Dea's gotten tight and fallen off the cliff."

"Cheer up, Mikey," Ellen Whitney said. "Only the rich moths eat."

"Look out there, Ellen," Ed Anderson warned gently. He smiled at Zara. "Or I'll leave you for Miss Zara of the Montgomery Place."

Michael O'Dea pivoted toward the center of the room, his whiskey spilling out over the edge of the tumbler. "*You* watch out! Or Miss Zara will take you under her big swooping wing and smother you to death."

"Goddamn it!" Ellen Whitney slammed her glass down on the end table. "Sometimes I think you two don't know us at all. As if Zara would smother anything! As if you, Ed, could shut me up by threatening, even in jest, to move on. Don't pit me against my friend with your unconscious fantasies."

Michael ran his fingers along the piano. "*K-K-K-Katie, immortal Katie*," he sang with bitterness. "The mother will rise out of her grave on her angel wings," he droned. "Every night Zara exhumes the mother bird." Michael continued to play, humming along.

Zara set her glass at the edge of the table. "That is in pretty poor taste, Michael."

"Poor? A garçon couldn't pick out better tasting feathers than your mother's. It makes the little girl feel ethereal, important—munching away."

"O'Dea," Anderson said. "They've got a point. Don't be an ass."

"Ha!" O'Dea laughed, waving his glass around. "That's where the old lady got it! The utopian sarcoma. Primary site right on the ass. Do you know how rare that is? Not secondary, mind you, but primary. A bona fide pain in the butt."

Zara stood up and started for the hall. She stopped in the doorway. "He has a pretty sobering effect, doesn't he? Lots of cheer from the old boy every day, a regular epiphany of joy."

At the sideboard, Michael's hands moved along the bottles, flicking them crisply with his nails. "Anyone for another drink?" he asked. "Anyone for a little brightener?"

Ellen Whitney rose almost calmly from the sofa. "You don't have to be a misfit, O'Dea. You could learn from your own misfortunes. But then, that would take courage." Ellen Whitney followed Zara out of the room.

"That was a real shit thing to say to Zara," Ed Anderson said when Zara and Ellen had gone into the library. Michael was cracking open a tray of ice in the kitchen.

"You don't live here."

"And you aren't helping her get over anything by heaping guilt on top of mourning."

"Christ," Michael said. "Three years we've been married. When does it end? When do the dead get buried?"

"You aren't helping, are you? Bringing it up every time she's having a good time. It doesn't allow for much forgetting."

"Ed," he said. "Forget it."

"All right, O'Dea. I just don't think you're being fair to Zara. Zara's a lovely girl, I don't think you know that anymore. You knock yourself out at the hospital trying to be top dog every damn day. It's all right to be second once, or even third. There's other disciplines besides medicine."

"What are you suggesting, Edward."

"Your marriage, for instance. You could spread some sensitivity around. To your friends, your family."

"Ed," Michael O'Dea said.

"I know. I know. I should have kept my mouth shut."

"You don't understand."

"What don't I understand?"

"I'm in love with someone else."

"What?" Ed Anderson asked, thinking he had misunderstood.

Michael O'Dea released the ice cubes into the bucket. He was in love with no one, he thought, least of all his lonely self. Marriage was something he had done. That was the depth of it.

"Jesus," Anderson said, leaning against the cabinet. "And you won't say who it is?"

"You don't know her." Michael was determined now that he would find someone he could really love. He would set about it.

"This is terrible news," Ed Anderson said. "Dreadful."

Michael O'Dea shrugged, running water into the tin compartments of the ice-cube tray. "All right, Anderson, spread your great white sensitivity around. See if I care."

Anderson put his arm around his friend's shoulder. "You're just a little wigged out on the wine, O'Dea. Ten bucks it's just a little fling and you never thought it was serious before tonight. Am I right?"

Michael O'Dea drew his hand over his forehead and

back through his hair. "No. Yeah. Maybe you're right, Ed."

"Sure. That's what it was, drunken overreaction. You're just a little tight tonight, buddy. Everyone has a fling now and then. Take a shower. Make love to your lovely wife."

"Thanks," O'Dea said.

"Just too much liquor and work. Pressure."

"Yeah, pressure." Michael O'Dea started to laugh then. "You know, I always wanted to be a musician, and here I am sucking blood out of people and checking neurological response with a tuning fork."

"Take a shower."

"Right," O'Dea said grimly. "A shower and the lovely wife."

She turned down the covers, smoothing a crease out of the pillowcase, remembering how he had held her before they were married, how he would say, "Go ahead, tell me. You'll feel better if you can." Down the hall, the moonlight would be falling on Foxie's vacant bed. Foxie, who had suffered so much humiliation, so much agony. The little ruinous figure who had laughed bravely.

The door opened and Zara closed her eyes, breathing deeply as he came in. The lamp clicked beside her. "Zara." His hand groped under her nightgown—after he had hurt her, when she couldn't possibly want him. The hand groped under the sheet.

"Michael—I was asleep."

He rolled on top of her then, stopping her mouth with his. She turned her head. "Michael, don't." What did he know of grief? What did he know of what Foxie had been? As if she would use her mother against him. He was the one doing that: *Ethereal, important.* He knew none of it. Seeing a patient and walking away ten minutes later—he knew nothing at all. "Stop it." She twisted under him, trying to throw him off with the heels of her hands. He pinned her shoulders. He gave her no time. "Stop, Michael. Michael, you're hurting me."

"I thought that's what you thrived on," he said, going on. "Tell me. Am I blond enough for you now?"

"You're hurting me."

"Tell me. Am I your little daffodil?"

"You with her," she cried. "You with that woman."

"Admit it. I'm as good as that kid at the drugstore. I am." His face tightened then as he gripped the edges of the pillowcase. He groaned. "There," he said, pulling out of her. "Was that pain enough for you? Was it?" He put his knuckles to her forehead. "You didn't know I could make it, did you?"

She got up, pulling a blanket around herself, and went downstairs. What is he doing? she asked herself. Am I supposed to feel married, ethereal, important now? When she woke up, Mrs. McGehry was shaking her. She had fallen asleep on the kitchen floor.

Up through the last red of sumac she strolled toward the house in the park where she had begun that year her summer puppet plays for children. She was close enough to the children's acrobatics to hear the chains creaking around metal shafts as the children were lifted higher, rising with their shrieks and laughter and the expectations of first snow. Zara unlocked the door and threw the shutters back. Light entered the cabin, soft and gray as the color of bark on the poplar trees. Two at a time the children ran, stirring leaves with their feet as they plunged for the worn path, the wooden planks. A swoop like a bird, the feet lifted. Hair floated up beneath scarves, chains caught at themselves, feet descended. Zara pulled the glass pane over the window screen.

The heater never ignited the first time she tried it. She knelt down to investigate the source of the flame, striking the long match on the brick floor, holding it inside the metal tunnel as she turned the fuel on. There was something of comfort in the whoosh a stove made before the heat could possibly have helped, the smell of dust burning away.

She hung her coat on the nail by the door and filled the percolator, plugged it in, listening to it ping as the wedges of her chair rocked over stone and the leather of her boots bent at the ankles. They, too, creaked as she rocked toward the footstool, her head back against the oak, sifting the air for the smell of coffee and autumn and the scent of rusted metal in small sweaty palms. She went out to them.

"Miss Zara, Miss Zara," they called as they ran to grab on around her thighs and knees. In a circle, whirling together, they turned her as they ran, as if she, Zara Montgomery, were the center of their collective lives. She put her hands on their knitted red caps, the brown ones with synthetic-fur flaps for the ears, her fingers brushing against cold cheeks. "Miss Zara." Her skirt wound around her. They turned, twisting into the wind.

"What did you say?" she laughed.

"Could we see the puppets, please?" Under one palm a child's crown, the size of a melon in thick purple worsted, balanced her as they moved.

"See the puppets?" she laughed. "I can't see a thing."

"Promise," they whined now, growing ecstatic with each revolution. Branches, the joists of the swing whirled into gray sky, the grass gone gray with leaves.

"Of course you can." They stopped, waiting for the world to stabilize. On each side they supported her, asking now for kisses. "A minute, a minute," she pleaded. She bent toward them. Lips moved over her face like leaves.

"The puppets. The puppets," they called, their voices rising like the chatter of birds as they called out for their favorite performers.

"Shhh," she said. "Quiet now or you won't have anything." In a bunch they led the way, pulling her along, the wind catching at coats and scarves, at her dress and hair. They crowded against the door. "Move aside now. How will we all get in?" She put her hand on the knob and turned to them. "No talking and carrying on," she said.

Twelve Saturday playmates sprawled onto the floor in front of the heater. Arms and legs bent at angles, feet protruding onto the rug. Coats and mittens, piled in a heap, were propped behind the others against the wall. She watched for a moment the flames flickering beside them; shadows moved over their faces like raindrops rising on the windows of a speeding automobile.

From high shelves the puppets peered down, moving their motionless eyes. "Now I'm going to point to each of the players," she said, "and I want you to clap when I come to the one you want. That way it'll be fair." She moved from the satin knee of the king's pantaloons to the wooden peg of the sailor. She fluttered the countess's silk handkerchief, wound the black yarn of the witch around her long, garish nose. Reaching through the spine of the leprechaun, down through his legs into the brown velveteen boots, she curled his menacing feet.

"It's been decided," she said. "The King would like to speak today." The inevitable moans crept out. Always there would be dissenters, disappointments.

"I suppose someone wants to argue with me," the King said. "I suppose my kingdom has forgotten who's been chosen?"

"No," the children called out, for the monarch was speaking now, his head perched on Zara Montgomery's hand. His eyes, bright green sequins shining from the fingertips of white gloves, stared out from their wooden sockets above two mango cheekbones, above the dark brown yarn of a moustache.

"A King must look his subjects in the eyes," he said. The gloves turned corners, surveying them. His pointed boots dangled limply beneath his robe as the rod extended in his arm. "Once I lost my kingdom," he said in a voice that almost broke in half. "Once I had a tough time keeping this shack. Want to know what happened?"

"Yes," they hooted. "Please."

On and on went the emotional voice.

"We should have taken the dock in by now," Forster Montgomery said, sitting down on the edge of it next to his daughter. Zara buttoned the sleeves of Michael's wool jacket at her wrists and pulled the coat around the swell of her belly. She could see the thin layers of ice forming in the moonlight and cracking again. She could see a green bubble near the far beach rising and falling in the tide of the lake. The thin layer of ice broke, froze, and splintered again.

"It's nearly time for dinner."

"Yes," she said.

"The moon is almost full tonight."

She drew deeply on the crisp air. "Yes."

"How do you see it?" her father asked. "Do you see a lady or a man in the moon?"

"A woman," she said, swinging her feet slowly under the wooden planks of the dock and out again.

"Sometimes I see a woman, sometimes a man."

"I've never seen a man," she said, looking into the disk, watching its light cutting slow and silver across the black waves.

"On the right you can just see the brim of his hat," he said. "And halfway down he's wearing a moustache."

"Where?"

"Halfway down, it's probably what you call her nose."

"Ah," she said, imagining the baby hesitating inside her. "I see it now." On the other side of the lake, shadows moved. Fishermen late at night, late in the season, she thought. "It's lovely out here; I could stay forever." She listened to the last calling of the locusts before the freeze. She could hear the sound of cars pulling up the graveled roads.

Mrs. McGehry wiped a ring on the window seat of the landing where someone had left a sherry glass the night before. She clucked and shook her head, humming solemnly a tune she had heard Zara playing at the piano. It was a sad song. She would remember to ask Zara what it was, this pretty song, this sad one. All night Zara had been playing it until Bridie had come out of her room and put her hand on Zara's shoulder saying, "Would you like some hot milk and honey?"

Zara Montgomery had a knot of tears in her throat; that would be the reason she had only shaken her head and gone on playing in the dark. That would not be the reason, Mrs. McGehry thought, that Michael O'Dea had been on the phone talking to Ed Anderson, speaking in a normal voice, his tears streaming down his face. "Would you like to play tennis tomorrow, Ed?" he had asked. "So you've forgotten tomorrow is Sunday?" Michael asked, the tears running down his face. "Yes, yes. That's it, drinking. Didn't realize it was so late." Mrs. McGehry had gone back to bed, tucked the feather comforter around her bed stockings, and turned off the light. Zara was still playing in the dark when Mrs. McGehry finally fell asleep.

Bridie poured a spot of polish on her rag and folded the cloth. She curved it over the railing of the staircase, rubbing methodically as she ascended. When she came to the oak globe at the top, she bent over it, breathed a little cloud of moisture on its gold-streaked surface. As she did this, she saw a movement from out the corner of her eye. Through the door that had been left ajar, she saw Zara folding and refolding a long brown scarf, tying it around her neck and untying it again. Mrs. McGehry stepped quietly down the stairway again.

In the kitchen she put the coffee water on to boil. "Zara," she called from the bottom of the stairs. "We've got coffee." I'll cook up a fry, she said to herself pulling a rasher of bacon from the refrigerator. Today Zara Montgomery will be wanting a fry. She laid out the strips in the pan and set a plate on top to keep them from curling. She was stirring two lumps of sugar into her own cup when she heard Zara at the front-hall closet preparing to go out.

"I've got you a rasher all fixed," she cried. "Now come and eat it." Zara buttoned her coat around the muffler. She shook her head. "Take off your coat. It's almost ready. Come in here." Zara turned to the corner to take her muffler off.

Bridie cracked an egg into a bowl. "Got a song in your head you couldn't get rid of, was that it?" Zara nodded and the old woman's eyes rushed down from the center of Zara's face. Under Zara's chin, a vast purple bruise erupted from under the edge of the turtleneck sweater. Bridie pivoted suddenly toward the stove. My God, she thought, what's happened to her? Quickly she pried the plate up with a fork, grasped it with a pot holder. "I thought you might be hungry with all that music last night," she said.

Zara moved her head slowly back and forth.

"What was that song you were playing?"

In the den the clock was changing from one hour to the other. Mrs. McGehry drained the pan into the crockery pot. "Yes. A sad song."

Zara reversed her fork on the napkin, tracing a circle with the prongs on the flowered cloth.

"Want juice?"

Zara's hair swayed slowly left then right. The fork went back and forth. Bridie cut the toast at a diagonal and framed the bacon strips, the egg with it. "You'd better eat all this. It's not every day I fry you a rasher," the housekeeper said, not looking at the edge of Zara's sweater. "I sometimes wonder why I get stuck on one song." The old woman's fingers rubbed nervously at the embroidered ridge along the scallop of the tablecloth. "Why is it one song pops right into the head and won't go out?" Zara punctured the egg, the yellow juice running around the toast. Mrs. McGehry watched her bring a bite toward her mouth. Zara closed her eyes to swallow it.

"Oh, dolly," the old woman cried out finally. "Don't you think I can see that bruise? Don't I know you're in trouble?"

> *Mitten im Schimmer der spiegelnden Wellen*
> *Gleitet, wie Schwäne, der wankende Kahn;*
> *Ach, auf der Freude sanftschimmernden Wellen,*
> *Gleitet die Seele dahin wie der Kahn,*
> *Denn von dem Himmel herab auf die Wellen*
> *Tanzet das Abendroth rund um den Kahn.*

In the confessional, Michael put his hands on the railing. The door slid open, the dim light flowing through the small caned squares, the profile there, the gentle circuits of the priest's ear.

Michael closed his eyes and opened them again. "Bless

me, Father . . ." He closed his eyes. "I was married in a Protestant church. I haven't been to Mass or confession in almost five years."

"Five years?"

"Yes," Michael O'Dea said, swallowing. "I want to begin again. I don't know how."

"We'll have your confession first."

"I don't know how to love. I've committed adultery many times."

"Many?"

"Over and over again. But that's not the worst, Father. It's so much worse than that." Michael O'Dea stopped then, looking through the cane. The priest did not turn. Would no one reach out for him, for Michael O'Dea lost and unimportant in his world?

"The worst sin?"

"I want to die, Father. I want to die," he cried, rushing out of the booth, knocking through the line of penitents in their long gray autumn coats.

I remember in particular one patient on the ward when I was doing my psychiatric rotation in medical school. "You're not to be alone with him," my superiors warned. At night I sat with the head nurse and one of the resident psychiatrists playing cards; a fork lay on the table. When I looked up, that patient was staring at me, grinding the fist of one hand into the palm of the other. "We're about to have a crisis," I said, drawing a card from the deck.

Mary Andreason took another and arranged her hand. "If he'd broken Bloom's jaw last night instead of nicking it, he'd sure enough be in the White Room tonight."

The resident drew on his pipe. "I suppose Dr. Bloom had his reasons for keeping Granam on the ward."

Out the corner of my eye, I could see the fist striking. I glanced at him. "He's looking at something on the table." The fork lay prongs down on the tabletop beside the cards.

The resident rocked onto the back legs of his chair, studying his cards. "I suppose your orderlies, Mrs. Andreason, are in the kitchen eating sugar cookies again."

"No way to stop them," Mary Andreason said, putting down her hand. "Nothing short of a little Thorazine and a run through ECT."

"Well, I think you might just take a look in on them. Make sure they're on their feet."

Mary stood up slowly, pretending a weariness of games. She stretched her arms above her head. "While you're out," the resident said, ignoring the guttural sounds coming from the corner, "why don't you whip up a little Thorazine in a very thin glass. Twenty-five milligrams should feel about right."

Mary Andreason sighed, edging her chair back. "Two tablespoons and the spike."

The patient was on his feet. "Evening, Harold. Would you like me to bring you a glass of milk?"

"Do you think it's the fork?" I asked, seeing Granam's eyes fixed on the table, somewhere near my hands. Slowly I took hold of the stem. I could see now, looking obliquely at him, his eyebrows going up. "It's the fork," I said. "I'll bet anything it is." Slowly I turned it over; the resident drew on his pipe. Mary Andreason was part way to the door when the patient sank back into his chair, completely relaxed.

"There you have it," the resident said, almost in affectation, lifting up his pipe. "Now you understand how intricate insanity is and how little control we have over it."

Now I could see in from the hall through the metal latticework of the window as I pressed the button above the light switch. The head psychiatric nurse was carrying a tray of paper cups and yellow capsules around the ward. With a heavy rubberized step, Mary Andreason passed a dark crest at the back of a chair. "Dr. O'Dea," Mary was sure to be saying gently as she fingered her coal-black hair under an outdated cap, "you haven't showered or spruced up one bit, and your wife will be arriving soon." Again I pressed the buzzer; I watched the nurse turn. Mary searched her pocket for the key chain.

"Sorry to keep you out here so long, Dr. Montgomery."

"Someday I'll give up wincing, Mary, when you call me that."

"I'm not an amnesiac yet, Zara Montgomery," Mary Andreason scowled. "And I don't plan to be one soon." The door swung shut, and the middle-aged nurse secured the bolt in the lock with her key. Her hand was on my arm.

"We've got news for you today." Mary motioned toward a corner of the room.

I looked toward Michael. "Good news, Mary?" Still he looked out that window.

Mary Andreason rested the tray on the small round of her belly, speaking enthusiastically. "Yes, good news. Michael asked for butter today at breakfast. How do you like that?"

"Michael said something?" In the green armchair, Michael's hands dangled like two white birds. "Did he say anything else? Did he ask for me? Or anyone?"

"Patience, darling. You of all people should know that." The tray shifted as we watched the light filtering through the dust-coated pane in stripes over his rumpled white shirt and gray flannel pants, over his unshaved face. "He asked for butter is all. That's a beginning, isn't it?"

"Oh, Mary, it is good news. I didn't mean that."

"Two months is no short time, girl, to wait for the margarine to be passed."

On the front walk Cary Stephenson looked up at the large white-curtained second-story windows, dreaming of cornice work and gables on her own house, if ever she would have one. Baby Stephenson bounced along. Cluck cluck coo, he sang with the squeak of the wheels and the exotic catapult of the carriage over the sidewalk. Baby tuckoo, Zara Montgomery thought under the influence of her recent reading. She had pulled the curtains aside to view these small dramas on the street and driveway. There went Mrs. Willoughby in her stout new autumn hat, a zinnia pinned to the bosom of her sweater, her arm wrapped around Mrs. McGehry's latest copy of *Family Circle*. Followed by a pack of yellow dogs, the mailman stepped up the leafy walk; and Cary Stephenson bumped the stroller up the opposite curb talking dreamily as she repeated her surveillance.

Wearily Zara Montgomery leaned against the window watching, until the young woman's hand fluttered up in embarrassment from the depth of the window. Up her hand fluttered from the dented aluminum handle of the stroller. Zara watched the heavy green-and-white wool coat rapidly retreating. Baby tuckoo has gone away in his frayed knit cap and sweater suit, kicking out his feet in indifference. Baby tuckoo overdressed and jolting all the way across town to have a look at the Montgomery household. And all this so early in the morning.

Zara Montgomery dropped the curtain and went back to her reading. After a moment, she looked up, her eyes resting on a small spot on the carpet. Why did people without money always burden themselves with so much clothing?

Most small molecules move across a membrane because of chemical or electrochemical gradients. When these gradients cease to exist, then the rate of exchange across the membrane becomes equal in both directions. The quantity of solute transferred by simple diffusion is described by the Fick diffusion equation:

$$\frac{Q}{t} = \frac{KA(C_1-C_2)}{L}$$

Mrs. McGehry threw on her coat with the rhinestone circle brooch at her breast. "How do I look, Forster? How do I?" Back and forth she rushed between the hall mirror and the doorway. "Imagine it! Can you imagine it? My little Teddy getting married? And old! Old? Why, he's fifty-four! Forster, do you suppose he got that girl into a bad way?"

Forster Montgomery pulled on his gloves and his wool dress scarf. "That's preposterous, Bridie. Your new daughter's way past forty; I guess she can look out for herself. Are you ready?"

"Why, no older than you, Forster! You and Kathryn could have one practically in nappies."

Together their heads jerked toward the staircase and up —toward the room where the doctor's dying wife lay like a stalk of wilting celery in her bed, where the doctor's only daughter sat with a college English text in one hand, a washbasin for the mother's illness at her side. "Oh!" Mrs. McGehry's hands fluttered at the dyed rabbit-fur collar of her coat. "Oh my," she sighed, her head down, eyes tracing the flagstone entrance.

"It's all right, Bridie," Forster said, his hand on the doorknob.

"You won't be holding that against me now, will you, Forster? Do you want to go up and speak a word to her before we go? If it weren't Teddy's wedding, Forster—"

Kathryn Montgomery's voice swept out of her bedroom and down the staircase. "Are you going now, dear? You'll be late if you don't hurry."

"We're headed out the door, sweetheart."

"Throw a little rice on Teddy for me."

"A whole pilaf."

Zara's auburn head popped out of the bedroom. "Some for me, too," she said. "Have a good time, Bridie."

Mrs. McGehry's hands flew up to readjust her hat again. "Zari! Tell me the truth now, Zari! Do I look all right for Teddy's wedding? Do I?"

"Who is that down there?" Zara called.

"What?" Bridie McGehry craned her neck up the stairs. "Why, it's me, Zari. Can't you see me clear from there?"

"My goodness! I thought you were the bride herself for a moment."

"Pooh!" Bridie said. "Pooh on you! You'll get yours. Teaser, tormenter!" She jerked her yellow head through the door and into the cold February afternoon. "Forster," she said. "I do look significant, now don't I? Won't Teddy be proud when he sees the new permanent wave on his own old mother?" Bridie McGehry took hold of Forster's arm as they went down the walk. He guided her over the icy spots. "I never thought I'd see it. Never thought that Teddy Bear would take a shine to anyone."

In the first upstairs bedroom, a mother and a daughter were waiting. They heard the car engine turn over. It sputtered out and died; they heard Forster trying to start it again. Then the car revved under the insistence of his foot; they heard the ice crackling under the tires as he pulled out under the snow-laden trees.

Zara jumped from the chair beside her mother's stark white bed. "Let's celebrate! What'll it be?"

"Is the sun shining?" her mother asked. "Is that the sun shining out there in the sky?"

"Happy Bridie McGehry—" Zara held up the mirror for her mother to see the crisp blue sky so stable, so stationary beyond the leafless trees. "Bright as anyone could hope for. Negative ten degrees. Want champagne?"

"No—" her mother said, her dark hair tied back in a pony tail, the slightest film of sweat on her forehead like an exotic cream, "not if the sun is shining. The sun is shining, isn't it? I didn't go imagining, did I?"

"Bright as your eyes, Foxie, no less." Zara tied the curtain back and held the mirror up again.

"Mint juleps?" Kathryn cried out. "For a sunny day."

In the kitchen Zara took out the tall glasses. She crushed the brittle dark leaves of mint into the sugar. She crushed the ice, humming a little song. The glasses frosted as the whiskey slipped down the sides. She took a small sip. Yes, she said. A celebration. She got out the corrugated straws. Upstairs she could hear the television on. It was almost time for the afternoon movie. She put the glasses on a silver tray and dropped a sprig of mint on the top of each.

"Here are Laurel and Hardy!" her mother shouted as she came into the room.

"Great news!" Zara set the glass down with a flourish on the chest beside the bed. "And which one are you?"

"I'm the fat one," Kathryn said, reaching out her lean arm. Zara put the glass in her hand and adjusted the straw.

Already the unlikely team had begun moving the piano up the stairs. "To crazy Teddy," Kathryn said, raising her glass. The straw spun around. She drew a long, clean draft into her mouth.

"To the Crazy Ted," Zara saluted, cross-legged on the bed.

"A great julep, Zari. A really good one. Another toast! To Flory, the fool who married him."

"One for the absurd."

"To Bridie's new permanent."

"To Bridie's curly hair!"

They smiled at one another in the mirror. "To us."

"To me and you, little fox."

Kathryn took up her stick and adjusted the television antenna. "Next commercial," she said, "make some more."

Zara curled up behind her mother on the bed.

"Ha!" her mother laughed. "Look at them with this piano. This is my favorite one." Laurel blinked his eyes and squinted at the piano, and then up at the stairs. Long, narrow stairs: up and up they went. He squinted after them.

Shouts echoed up the corridor. Somewhere chairs were hitting the floor, feet scuffled, then moved as if in regiment. "Listen to that," Mary Andreason said. "B Wing's got themselves into a riot again. You go over, Zara, and see if Michael might say hello to you this morning. I'll be back soon as I corral the coyotes."

The tray and the white dress moved beyond the nursing station. "Zara—" she called over her shoulder, "I tried to get her out of the way, but it wasn't any use." She waved her hand in helpless circles. I turned to see a woman approaching from Michael's corner of the sunroom.

In the muslin house dress, Madeline introduced herself, as if I could have forgotten this daily ritual or the red pastelike cross lipsticked on the woman's forehead. Brown eyes fluttered above the woman's frenzied veins. The woman thrust out her hand. "Madeline," she said.

"I believe we've met, Madeline." I took her hand. "I'm Zara, remember?"

Madeline extended her lower lip and blew abruptly into the slate-gray strands of her bangs. "Don't disturb the doctor." She drew back and pointed, depicting Michael's motionless form by the window. "Mustn't disturb," she said. "He's thinking."

"That's right, Madeline. I'll just sit alone with him for a moment." Gently I began to pry the woman's grip from my arm.

"We've got rifle practice. Tat a tat tat," Madeline said, shooting down a man where he sat staring into the freshly painted fireplace.

"You told me that one yesterday, Madeline. About

shooting the man in your garden." My skirt brushed between my knee and Michael's pantleg.

"Who told you about the man who sold flowers?"

"A despicable profession, you said—selling flowers. I'd like to talk to Michael, Madeline."

Madeline pressed my hand between the damp layers of her palms. "I've gotten so depressed here. I need anemones, country. I'd feel better if I could see anemones."

"I feel that way myself," I said. "Depressed, depressing."

Madeline sighed and the cross smoothed out on her forehead. She made a coiling motion with her finger at her temple. "Yes, dear. Crazy." She patted me on the shoulder.

On the sofa a woman wound the hem of her hospital gown in her hands, telling a small group of people how she had been assaulted. A nurse turned to the new medical student beside her. "No," the nurse said. "The phobia is unnatural." The student went on writing. He recorded numbers on an index card; he nodded.

"Poor lady," Madeline said. "They raped her in her garden."

From across the television room a California voice gave away home furnishings, automobiles, trips to tropical islands. Song broke from a patient: "Mad mad Madeline," the tenor crooned, "the sweetheart of my dreams." At round Formica tables patients looked up from the small squares of Aztec-rug kits. From beside the row of iron beds patients applauded.

"Maybe you'll like it here. . . . It isn't long until everybody knows your name. P and Q," Madeline said, collapsing into the vinyl chair beside Michael. She thrust her feet straight out. "Peace and Quiet."

There are four common mechanisms of transport across the placenta: diffusion, facilitated diffusion, active transport and pinocytosis.

Along the bluish stubble of Michael's cheek my hand brushed, then stopped at the soft skin of his hairline. I stepped into his view, watching for movement—a nod of his head, the drop of eyelashes.

It was a tour de force the way the brown canvas wings swept out from the proscenium of the Lake Marian Theater, passing up the orchestra pit and swooping to a halt in the side aisles. "This way the audience will feel they're sitting in the tent," I said, showing Michael the set for my play. I explained the way the puppet ropes attached to the actors would be rigged to movable bars above the stage.

"I didn't realize you could make such a big deal out of puppets," he said. He fit the grotesque mask onto his head and, looking out, tried to mount a pair of the stilts. "The whole cast wears these things?"

"You're only about nine feet tall. The rest of the cast tops you by another three or four feet. Everyone, that is, except for the puppeteer. She sits on a stool up front."

"Does the puppeteer look like you?" he asked, trying to get up on the hoists.

"Hardly," I laughed, assisting him in his ascent. "She's one of the largest women I've ever seen. Her voice could almost knock the seats out of the balcony."

The stilts struck the floor as Michael moved unsteadily away from me, across the stage. Jerkily he turned around. "Hello, midget!" he shouted, looking down at me from out of the mask.

That night she watched him scowling into the curtained window of the door as he rang the bell again. "Why is it they're holding a Greek Easter dinner a week after Easter? That's what I'd like to know." Rainwater gushed down the eaves. Together they watched it pouring out the pipe and soaking into the ground.

"Easter, Schweitzer's birthday—who cares, Michael? You'll meet some of my new friends. You'll have a good time."

"*Pièce de résistance*," Ellen Whitney was shouting over her shoulder as she opened the door. She swept around again and kissed Zara on the cheek. "The lamb is in; and the retsina is on the way, if Winters actually finds it." She cocked one hand behind her ear. "You can hear the dithyramb revving up right now."

Zara glanced around the corner into the living room. "My word, Ellen. Look how many people you've already got in there."

"Quite literally—" Ellen laughed, "the caretaker was run off her feet. And then, Ed had to go out on call. He may not get back at all tonight." Michael groaned audibly. "I know," Ellen said turning to him. "I had hoped that they— Well, why don't you throw your rain gear into the closet, you two. I've got to baste the lambkins."

Zara hung up her coat. "Stop fretting," she said. "You'll like them all right."

Michael secured his beige raincoat on the hanger next to her green one; and they turned to see Don Winters, tall and blond, at the front door waving a bottle, a shopping bag under his other arm. "Zara—guess which god I am?" Don Winters kissed her on the mouth. "Hey, is this the husband?"

Zara introduced them and the men shook hands with a great deal of solemnity. "Well," she said nervously, seeing Michael's sternness, "we could all use a fire to cheer us up on such a cold, rainy night." She took the bottle from Winters and held it up to the light. "Unless, that is, you've been watering it down again, Donald."

Winters laid his hand on Michael's back. "It was this way, Mike. I took a drive into the little pond one night."

"The little pond?" Michael asked with reserve.

"The lake, after a get-together something like this. Everything was bloated that night."

"You should watch that," Michael said. "It's bad for the health. To say nothing of the reputation."

"Right." Winters set the bag on the table in the hallway and pulled his plastic poncho over his head. "Don't give a damn about the reputation though."

"Winters hasn't got one," Zara said. "At least not that anyone could mention in public."

"Right," Winters said, winking at her. "My renown is like one of those diseases only you doctors know about." Winters picked up his bag of groceries and directed them toward the living room. "Zara, reach into my coat pocket," he said. "I've got some great weed we can wind up with."

"Nothing like a good inhalant," Michael smiled half-heartedly, following them into the group.

Zara took a sip of her wine. Together they watched Don Winters across the room in his denim sport jacket and jeans, his blue shirt open at the collar, a gold earring at his earlobe.

"A mechanic," O'Dea said, studying the short, thick arms, the hair that spilled like an avalanche from Winters' throat into the V of his collar.

"Guess again," said Zara Montgomery.

O'Dea cocked the side of his mouth in condescension. "Amateur wrestler, race-car driver, a pilot—small craft only."

"Wrong species."

"I've got it. The guy's a stockbroker. I should have known it."

Zara Montgomery laughed out loud, glad Michael's humor was improving. "I thought you wouldn't guess it," she said. "He's a painter, and he's actually got quite a reputation. That's what he was joking about earlier."

Michael O'Dea turned quietly to accept a joint being passed around the room. He took a long hit and handed it to Zara. "Right," he said, suddenly bitter, speaking through the smoke. "I've seen him in the U-district. Sells self-portraits for a dollar, himself for a dime."

"Know something, O'Dea?" she said when she had passed the joint on. "You're a lousy judge of character."

"Is that so?" Michael said haughtily.

"I don't like it very much. You get intimidated and turn it on everyone around you."

He draped his arm about her. "Oh, sweetmeat, you make me ecstatic when you're angry."

"Don't ignore my anger like that," she snapped in a whisper. "Respond to me or shut up, but don't patronize me."

"Ah," he said, lifting his glass from the bookcase and staring down at her over it, "so it is the two-penny painter."

"It's no such thing. He's married to Rachel."

"That shouldn't stop him. It wouldn't stop you." He fingered the coins in his pockets. "Tell me about it."

"You're a lousy judge of character, O'Dea."

"You're wrong. There's me and them. I know the difference. Besides, if the dude's so good, then what's he doing out here in Sun City?"

"Same thing you are, making a living. Same thing as everyone, O'Dea."

"Same as everyone but you, you mean."

Zara Montgomery bit down on her lower lip. Suddenly she pivoted, spoke to the woman next to her. Michael O'Dea merely nodded as Zara introduced him to her friends in their jeans, embroidered shirts, and sweaters. Self-consciously he jiggled coins in his pockets, removing his hands only to take part in the smoking of the marijuana or to lift his glass from the top of a shelf and raise it to his mouth.

All through dinner he was silent, answering questions people asked him and saying no more than that.

After dinner, he carried his silence back into the living room, where eyes followed him and dismissed him almost in the same moment. Not until he noticed the violin did he attempt to interrupt Zara's conversations. He motioned toward the dusty leather case in the corner.

"She's just had it restrung—maybe a month ago," Zara offered, putting her arm through his as if nothing had happened. "I'm sure she wouldn't mind if you looked at it. Why don't you ask her?"

Michael—having gone to the dining area and then returned—took the case from beside the sofa and opened it. He ran his hands over the aged spruce surface; he took the bow and rubbed the hairs methodically with rosin. Zara was on the windowed side of the room now, a wineglass in her hand. He could hear her talking about the use of stilts and papier-mâché masks. They would attach thin yet visible ropes to the actors to give them the appearance of marionettes.

Michael rested the instrument under his chin, drawing the bow across it, turning the pegs. Faces turned, conversation ceased as the first sour notes of his tunings began, and then he was in the middle of it. It was as if he were alone in Bach's partita. He did not notice Zara's friends leaning in from the distance of other rooms to hear him. He did not notice their admiration even when he had finished the last passage and lifted the bow. He put the instrument in its case and then, before anyone knew it, he slipped outside without a word to his wife or anyone.

Zara tied the scarf around her neck and hoisted the strap of the handbag onto her shoulder. Slender lines formed and fell together again as she ran the comb through her hair, waiting. "You're worried about something, Michael; I can see that. So I'll go without you. It won't be a better time alone, but you can sit here and think that if you want. I told you I'd be glad to listen, but you don't seem to want that." She hesitated then, her hand on the door, waiting for his reply. In the living room she could hear him breathing heavily, as if he were angry. "All right, Michael. I'm going then—" The door was halfway open when he broke his silence.

"I wish we'd never gotten married."

She closed the door in front of her and turned, almost relieved, to listen. He was sharpening a pencil with a steak knife.

"When I was making love to you, it was like it wasn't you there."

"You mean you were thinking about someone else?" She sat down beside him, startled.

"No!" he cried. "It's you, not me. I couldn't do anything that would be enough. I knew it."

"I was always more than satisfied with you, Michael." She touched his arm, but his hand fled through the shavings on his lap. He brushed them into a pile on his thigh. "It was good, Michael."

Shavings were falling into his lap like confetti. "How can I do enough for you," he demanded, "if you're thinking of something else?"

"I guess mostly I wasn't thinking at all when we made love," she said, trying to see his point. She remembered his arm around her; he kissed down the inside of her arm. The light from the street fell across his shoulder.

"And when you do, what is it?" The blade went up and down, nicking the painted yellow surface. He hovered over it.

"Besides you, you mean?"

"Yes, Zara, besides me, I mean."

"Sometimes I notice the way the light looks in the room, but I don't really think about it. You must do the same thing, Michael."

"What else do you think?"

"Sometimes I think about what the future will be like with you. Or the past."

"How do you like that?" Michael O'Dea said, addressing no one at all. The lead was nearly stripped of wood now as he held it up to inspect it. He snapped it off with vehemence. "She thinks about her past when I make love to her. And she calls that a satisfactory relationship."

"This is absolutely absurd, Michael. You *are* part of my past. I'm talking about *us*. Can't you understand the difference between a fleeting thought and preoccupation, Michael?"

"Certainly," he said, whittling neatly at the eraser. "Whenever we go out, your eyes nearly fall out of your head looking at everyone."

"Perhaps—" She stood up and pulled on her jacket. "Perhaps I should wear a habit!"

Michael picked a piece of pencil off his lap and skewered it. "Something happened on intensive care," he said quietly. "It was terrible."

"For Christ's sake, Michael," Zara said, sitting down beside him again. She put her hand on his knee and looked at him: his head drooping over the flakes of yellow paint and wood, over his unhappy self. "Why don't you just say you've had a terrible day at the hospital, and we can talk about it? Don't you think that would be better than all this crazy paranoia of yours? My God! You're driving us both to distraction."

"A kid came in one night last week," Michael O'Dea said, fingering the particles in his lap. "He had multiple fractures, skull and c-spine. Davidson's team put him on curare to stop his seizing. About a week later I went in and said to the kid, 'You know, don't you, that you're being given a drug that paralyzes you temporarily until your body has a chance to heal? Did anyone tell you that you're not actually paralyzed?' I don't know why I thought to ask him that. I wanted to cry. He's been lying there for six days unable to move or ask and thinking he was going to be that way for the rest of his life. I could see it in his eyes, Zara."

"My God, Michael. How could they have neglected telling him?"

"For a moment I thought I was that kid," he said, pricking viciously at the upholstery of the sofa. "For a moment I wanted to change places." Almost automatically he ran the blade of the knife down the sofa arm. She watched in astonishment as he slipped his fingers carefully into the stuffing.

I center your chair before the window and pull another up beside you. "Did you have breakfast, Michael?" I ask you softly. I hold your cold, motionless fingers. In your eyes—gone pale with . . . what are your emotions? How could I know them?

I remember the day they took you. Cornered in our room, swinging a statue like a censer, crying out for a tiny nun who taught you piano, crying out one word: "Mama!" And again. Your word without a face, with all faces, as you smashed terror through the windows, as the attendants—

men in white, in blue with badges—pursued. You flew around the room like a bird trapped behind a pane. "Mama!" I cry it, too. We all cry it. You smashed out all the windows; you would have fallen several stories with your plaster statue, too, if we had let you.

"We've got him now. Don't worry, Dr. Montgomery; we've got him." Father threw his bulk around the room, standing in the doorway. You did not see him, your eyes gone remote even then, while I stood weeping, watching your long limbs pinned to the floor. Sweetheart. Spider.

Now I sit. I hold your hands, your memories—what I know of them. Pale, unfocused, sad eyes; you look like metal. I wonder what you, Michael Francis O'Dea, Named and Unnamed, can be thinking. We started out so differently. Why have you hurt me, when once I knew you? I say words to you; I say what comes to mind; I ask you questions. Perhaps beyond the bars of this window a bird is fluttering, a moving object that only you can see. I press your arm. I say, perhaps foolishly, as if you could want to hear such things: "Father says Jeffrey Kinsey came in yesterday." There is an odor about you, Michael, an odor once that moved me, now gone strong and rancid. They cannot make you shower. "You know how Jeff Kinsey is. He refused to see Father. You're his doctor, Michael. Not Father."

A whisper in Aztec ripples from the corner of the ward. Words are woven. "Commercializing nature. Red Cross sisters. Crocus."

I take the box out of my pocket. All this time you have not looked at me, perhaps all the time I've known you. "I've brought you something, Michael." I take out the cufflinks, little relief of bones. I lay them in your hands. Along one side of your face a nerve, a movement; your lips curl as if to speak. Your mouth opens.

"Time to eat the grub, Doctor." Madeline has grabbed you by the shoulder.

In the experimental animal, the rate of umbilical blood flow and the rate of uterine blood flow can be determined simultaneously by the infusion of antipyrine into a fetal vein. Under these circumstances, the quantity of a solute utilized by the fetus can be determined by multiplying the rate of flow by the concentration difference between the umbilical vein and the umbilical artery.

We make our way to the dining hall through the surge of inmates, you slowly dragging your feet along, Madeline on your right arm. I hold the other. We sit at the center table facing those patients the nurses feed. Between each bite, a row of jaws blooms open. You grasp a utensil in your fist and spoon up your potatoes.

"That's the spirit," Madeline says. "Shovel those spuds right down your gullet, Doctor."

Your eyes shift left, then right, surveying the patients lined before you. You plunge your fingers into your salad. You smear two orange circles on your cheekbones.

"Whooooeee!" Madeline cries, waving her paper napkin. "This one's putting back the roses!"

Michael didn't know I was following him that night after Ellen Whitney's party. When I came to the clearing, when I found him, he was sitting underneath a tree, drawing in the mud with a stick. The rain had stopped and I could see him clearly in the moonlight—crouched there, his hair in agitation, his eyes remote as I approached. Again and again he dug the stick into the mud, entrenching the design: the moustached face with the grotesque large ears and lopsided grin.

"Michael, are you all right?" His eyes closed, and he thrust an arm over his face. "Do you want to be alone?"

His arms reached up toward a low-hanging limb of the tree behind him. Hesitating, he grasped it, dangling there like a dead sparrow. Or a possum.

"I can leave if you want, Michael," I said. "I could stay if you need me." There was mud all over his hands, his knees, the hem of his new raincoat.

"Stay." He stood up in front of me.

"All right," I said, concerned and waiting. "You played beautifully tonight; everyone thought so. I don't understand why you left so abruptly."

He averted his eyes as I looked up at him. I put my hand on his arm. "I wish you wouldn't touch me." I said nothing; I could see that he'd been crying. I'd never seen that before. He sat down on a large rock, and I sat down beside him.

"The only thing I have as a child is a little dog. At first it sleeps at the end of the bed. Then it starts sleeping on my chest. We are together all the time, and everything is better, see? General anesthesia." He laughed suddenly, digging the ground with the stick. "It has small ears soft as a deer's ears, I think—though I have never seen a real deer. Its eyes are amber, and when I look under its rust-colored brow into them all my pity comes out: Who could have abandoned you? I ask him.

"Theresa Walling, my first real mother after the orphanage, gave the dog to me. But, 'It sleeps on the sheets!' she screams. Yet, when I cry she holds my head and tucks the sheets up around my neck. In the mornings I creep downstairs and there are cinnamon buns rolled tightly in a pan just for me. The kind from the supermarket that come in a cardboard tube and go on sale for ten cents. She has an old violin that belonged to her father, and she insists that I squeak away on it every day when she is ironing other people's clothes for them. Late at night at the chipped table with the one wobbly leg, a man sits with her sometimes. Those nights I sleep with my little dog on my chest; his hot warm breath is like a baby's on my neck, I think. For a few nights after the man visits she will not come in and make a scene. When the man is staying late, Theresa Walling does not force my dog to sleep on the floor; she does not yell in a rage: 'Your dog. Your animal.'"

Michael's hands were on his knees; he was staring straight ahead. "When the dog is out with us and I am walking it on its leash, she is proud to call it her own. 'The orphan dog,' she says. 'It walks very smartly, doesn't it, little Michelangelo?' When the man does not appear on his usual night, I have to play the violin while she folds the stiff white arms of men's shirts. He almost always comes to see us on the night before we go to confession. I spend most of every Thursday after I've gone to bed in terror, trying to contrive sins and praying that the priest will think them good enough to forgive me for being who I am.

"Eventually Theresa changes when the man comes to visit. Her eyes are hard as she stares at him. The two of them do not look at me when I come into the room. They glare red-faced at one another. He doesn't pick me up and set me on his lap, laughing, 'How goes it, lucky little orphan boy?' My dog and I avoid them.

"During the day we have taken up a great interest in birds in the backyard. The little dog runs after young robins on the ground, barking furiously as he sails along, his white rear and tail up, his yellow head scooting along the ground; and I tear after him, thinking: Look at my dog! He's teaching birds to fly! There is a nest of newly hatched sparrows in a branch just under the eaves of the old shed out back. Often I climb up that tree and watch them sprouting fuzz on their pink wings and bellies. It is a box elder tree, and it's filled with box elder bugs—bright orange, like little flames. I toss them down to him where he sits begging on his hind feet, and he snatches them up. I watch the white curls of his yellow tail bounce in the grass as I applaud him.

"One week the man doesn't visit at all. 'What will you do about this dog?' my mother cries. 'Your orphan dog has dug up my garden. All my zinnias and petunias, too.' Her eyes are red, her face puffs, and I think perhaps she has grown fatter, but I can see that the rest of her has not. My dog and I go outside as fast as we can get away from her. My dog and I investigate our territory, looking in on the development of sparrows, their beaks flying in the air; I've come to identify with them in some vague way—they are so naked.

"I fall asleep that night on her lap, her little fingers, nearly as small as mine, whisking back the hairs around my ears. When I wake up on my cot, my dog's heart is pounding on my chest. I hear a man's voice, and hers, yelling back and forth. 'I cannot,' he yells.

" 'Not off and on, not ever knowing,' " she cries.

"My dog and I are clenched tightly in our bed until we hear the back door slam. 'Not ever again,' she yells. I hear her crying then.

"In the morning we go down. Her hair is freshly done up; and for the first time she has makeup on her face, her lips red, her red eyes fringed with lashes we have never seen. There is Orange Crush for breakfast. The rolls are on the table, but her hand shakes as she brings down the knife to break them. She spreads the last of the stick of butter on my roll, laughing suddenly: 'We're all orphans now.' She bursts into tears.

"I put my arms around her, and the little dog laps at her shoes. I think now of showing her our animals; I take her hand and we go out, the three of us. She dabs her cheeks with the hem of her sleeve. But the wind has shaken the little birds loose. But there the nest is! It has somehow landed upright after all: the birds are suspended in a low-lying bush. Their heads bob frantically up and down. I cry out at first in fear, then in wild delight.

"She comes closer then to look at them. She wipes her beautiful hands on her dress. 'Why, look at the little ugly things!' she cries. 'The naked vulnerabilities!' I stare up at her. I understand only that there is an angry tone in her voice. 'You and your dog—' she screams. I do not understand why she is calling my dog to that low-lying bush. Then she tempts him, crying—'Here, little orphan dog. Here, dog—who will make your breakfast now after you've eaten all there is?' "

Michael O'Dea rolled the muddy stick across his knee. "What happened to the dog?" I asked. He was gazing off into the woods.

"Oh—" he said. "I moved to another house not long after that. They didn't want dogs; they gave him away."

"Oh, Michael, what a hard, hard life you've had," I said gently. "What a hard life."

"You don't understand one bit of it!" he exploded. "Not one fragment of my life."

"But, Michael—" I said.

"It's all lies, don't you see! I've had to invent my life. There never was a dog. There never was a bird. It's all a story."

He slammed the branch against the tree, but he did not release it. I sat quietly for a moment waiting. I waited until his hands had lost their tension. "You know, Michael, I see how hard you've worked. What you've made of yourself. That's no story."

"Give me a short life!" he yelled, slapping the branch against his leg as he sprang away from me. "Hercules!" he wailed. "A short death!" The features of the face he had drawn disappeared beneath his feet. He ground it under until, when he finally moved away, there was nothing but a circle there. It was as if all the energy had gone out of him then, he spoke so softly. "Pretend that circle is your life." He motioned with the branch.

I wanted to go home then. I would have left him if he hadn't looked so terribly pathetic, if I hadn't always loved something in him. I placed my feet in his circle, uncertain what he was trying to tell, or ask—if he was asking.

"Do you believe in death?" he asked. "Will you die?"

Turning around, I stared at my feet, the small shadows from the trees across them. "I'll die at some point in the circle. Is that what you mean?"

"If I were standing there, I would step on that line. I would step on that line, I would trample it under like an insect."

I stared at him for a moment, grasping what he'd said. "I don't want to end my life, Michael."

"You don't?"

He wishes me dead, I thought. He wishes I were gone away. Or dead! I thought. "I'm going home," I said, but he took hold of my arm.

"You can go home later. You don't understand me yet."

"I understand," I said. "This is the end of it."

"I want you to know how I feel," he said. His body pressed against me like a lover's, my back against the tree. I could feel the bark like a rod fused to my spine as he leaned his weight into me. I felt the stick against my neck; he rolled it roughly up and down.

"Stop it," I said. "I understand. It's over between us."

"It's not."

"I want to go home," I said, seeing his face like a stone, his hands tightening at the ends of the branch. "You can have all of it, you can have the other women. Take what you want."

"No," he said.

"You can have the house, stay here with Father."

He moved the stick lightly into the hollow between my larynx and chin.

"I'll leave, Michael."

"No."

"Please let go of me." Tears, sweat ran between us as I tried to push him away. His arms straightened.

I hadn't expected him to go so far; I hadn't expected him to thrust his strength into the stick. My muscles constricted like stones in my chest; air clogged. My nails gouged through his shirt. This is the way it is, I thought. His blood on my hands, the blood in my throat. I could feel his lips in my hair; I could feel them moving. His whisper came again and again: "I am suffocating!" Perhaps I slid to the ground before he flung the stick into the glen, I don't know. Perhaps his weeping was louder than my gasping.

I wish I could say that evening ended there, that it ended so simply. When I saw him, he was on the ground beside me. He sits here waiting for me to live or die, I thought. He is hovering. A madman, he waits to bind wounds. I did not notice for what seemed a long time, though it must have been short, that he had slit the cuffs of his raincoat nearly to the elbow in order to get at his arms. With the scalpel he always carried in the pocket of his shirt, he had slashed his wrists again and again. He could not have meant to kill himself, I think now, or he would not have cut them that way. Or perhaps he was so deranged that evening that all his medical knowledge had left him. I don't know. I only know that there we stood, falling against one another, his wrists bound in the pieces I cut from my blouse. On the embankment I leaned against him, holding his flowing arms above his head. It was as if we were nailed to a board as I stared into our green shadow as it feigned along the ground, rose up, and cut the trees in half. I sutured him. Like an idiot, or a saint, I patched him again and again.

Madeline is waving her sneakers like fans. "I have hyacinth and marigolds in the spring. Before the snow is gone, the crocuses stick their little heads up."

Today I have brought his violin. It rests on his lap. Down the hall someone pounds the piano in the sun room.

Madeline shifts one eye. "The doctor doesn't want to talk to you."

"I need the doctor's advice on a very personal matter. Can you understand that? Personal. Very serious, Madeline."

"Well, excuse me," she says, snapping her gray head against the cushion. The cross springs crimson into a shaft of broken light from the window. "You're one of Dr. O'Dea's patients. Why didn't you say so?"

"That's right, Madeline."

"Well," she says in a huff. "You could at least go into the proper exam room." Madeline extends her arms, like a child pretending to sleepwalk, and proceeds across the lounge. I hear the woman introducing herself.

> *Rootworm. Werewolf. Wrench. The story goes.*
> *And for those who sit*
> *And wait,*
> *What can they do?*
> *Sneaking in this way to*
> *A void, trying to play both parts.*
> *Life is reciprocal. Without the ear,*
> *What good the voice? Words spring*
> *Unchecked,*

Turn,
Implode our hearts.

"She'll burn this house down, Zara," Mrs. Mc-Gehry said, "dropping those cigarettes when she falls asleep."

"Don't, Bridie. I'll watch her." But Zara could not watch her mother every moment. Could she? And the house had not burned during the time when Foxie was dying. But still the marks were there where Zara could see them five years later as she lay across the bed, waiting for Michael to come home early on her birthday.

Already he was three hours late, and she remembered other birthdays: her mother asking from her bed that baby roses be sent, conspiring with Mrs. McGehry on just the kind she wanted. And when they came, Kathryn had wept. Chrysanthemums for this special bouquet, this last present she would give her daughter. "I told you roses," Kathryn sobbed to Bridie.

"They were out of roses, I had to get something."

"You waited too late," she cried. "Get out of my room. You've ruined it."

Overhearing this, Zara had not known what to say to stop her mother's weeping. Now Zara could see her husband coming up the street, strolling home in the afternoon. A white carnation in his lapel, roses a bloody stain at the elbow. Flowers that would have pleased if he had come earlier.

He tipped his hat to the neighbors on their lawns, moving a tricycle off the sidewalk. As the front door opened, she heard his usual exchange of pleasantries, Mrs. Mc-Gehry pointing out the frosting on the cake, the picnic basket. Zara stared at the smooth white walls of her mother's bedroom, the windows painted blue with sky, the change of a light pattern on the floor where the burns were. He opened the door. His foot fell where the warmth was, where the sunlight filtered in.

"I'm sorry," he said. "I got tied up."

She was dressed to go with him on the boat. Her back to him, Zara arranged his roses in a cut-glass vase.

"Do you mind if we don't go?" he asked, sitting on the bed and taking off his shoes.

"We could still make it to the other side, Michael, if we leave right now."

"I'm awfully tired," he said, "but I'll go if you really want to."

"I'm not in the mood now."

"I'm sorry, Zara."

In stocking feet he came across the room to touch the small of her back. "I'll just take a little nap, and then we'll go out to the movies. Is that all right?"

She said it was, although she went downstairs and threw the candles into the garbage. When several hours had passed and her father was not home from the clinic, she went upstairs and woke Michael.

"Zara," he said. "I have to tell you something. I did leave the clinic early. I meant to come right home, but something happened."

She watched him tensing as he stood to say this. I don't want to know what it is, she thought. She said, "Well, what is it?"

"I ran into Marilyn Kleinliebelink in front of the post office. She needed a ride home she was carrying so many packages."

"So you carried Miss Klink home with all her parcels and that took you three hours? You left Father alone at the clinic for that?"

"Zara, I didn't mean to get involved with her."

"Involved?"

"You know how difficult it's been for me lately, Zara."

"After all these months, you slept with Miss Klink, that blond-haired imbecile. You slept with her on my birthday?"

"Zara, I did it for us. I wanted to help our relationship. We could go to bed now if you want. I know I can do it. I know it."

"You think roses will fix this up?" she asked. She opened the window and flung the roses, the vase away from the house. "I'm going out. And don't you follow me." In the garden she saw the flowers scattered in the shrubbery as if they had grown there. She found her mother's broken vase. She ran her fingers gently along its edges.

Higher and higher, room to room her ascent: trying to be rid of him, trying to get back to him. Even in migration, finches and moths have no understanding of the journey's end or the return if there is to be one. Lingering like a flock, she floods the dining room. The kitchen, then the den. Sensing disaster, she veers into the upper guest rooms, pulls in her dreams, tucks her head before the next discouragement. Driven as if by fear, compelled as if this were desire, she lifts her head like mist, charted by the stars, pheromones, unhappiness, counting on these alone to carry her. Up and up she rises with her few belongings until in the attic there are no more encroachments, until she is only a shimmering of uneasiness and solitude in the farthest reaches of the house. From the uppermost window, tucked beneath the eaves, she looks out: half the town is sliced in gray and leafless squares, the lake a smudge beneath descending winter skies. And from here, she would try at once to fly and stay. She would try to guide her mother's house home again.

Forster Montgomery, returning from a visit to Michael, turned off the radio in his car to shut out the sound of neighbors calling in to the talk show. He shook his head and came in along the path he had shoveled that morning.

"How did it go?" Zara asked, looking up from her embroidery.

"Same. Do you want some coffee?" He retreated to the kitchen. She heard him lifting the lid to the soup, examining the roast, peering into the icebox.

"Mousse," he said. "Mousse for dinner." He handed her the coffee cup and sat in his chair across from her on the sofa. She is beautiful, he thought, wrapped in that afghan like her mother, sewing puppet costumes for the town children.

"Let me see what you're doing," he said. She held the tiny satin dress out to him. "Lovely, even better than the last." The needle wound through fabric again, then rested while she waited for an answer to her question.

"All right," he said. "It wasn't the same. It wasn't even that good. It's not that Michael did anything; he was completely non-responsive. I lost control. I've never done that before, not since medical school."

"What do you mean, Daddy?" She held the material in her lap, waiting.

"I told him about the new examining table he had ordered. Then I asked him how he was feeling. It's a typical case. No eye movement, nothing. I made a mistake, Zara. I told him how sad you are. Maybe it was good for him to hear it."

"I wish you hadn't said that to Michael."

"I told him he should stop thinking about himself, Zara. I said: 'Get off your ass, Doctor.' I said it like that. I might as well have been someone off the street, a layman. Then Michael said something."

"He did?"

"He said: 'Whimper.' "

"Whimper?"

"Just like that. I didn't know whether he meant me or himself. Hell, I'm no psychiatrist. I don't even like psychiatry. 'Yes, that's right, Michael,' I said. 'You've made a choice, haven't you? Here you sit: Lake Marian's finest whimper. Stand on your feet, for Christ's sake. You're an excellent doctor. You've got obligations.' Then I regretted it. I told him how, when your mother died, I wept, sitting in the chair day after day, until you told me to get out and put in a full day at the clinic."

"I'm sorry," she said, stitching slowly again.

"No, no, it was what I needed."

"And then you came home? Today, I mean."

"Naturally I didn't stop there. I told him he should come back to work. It was ridiculous, saying that to Michael when obviously this is a different matter."

Zara pricked the needle into the cloth, sewing the brown eye of a bird onto the puppet collar. He has done exactly what I trusted him not to do, she thought, what I have fought so hard against. He's hurting Michael with his own self-pity. And now he asks for my sympathy, how could he? But she could not hold it back. She lied for her father's benefit: "I do the same thing, Dad. I can't help myself."

"But that's wrong, Zara."

"I know it is," she said.

He took his coffee cup from the table then and watched Zara sewing costumes for children. I've had thirty years of experience, he thought, and yet I've done no better than this daughter. "I told him about your mother," he said. "All the times I disappointed her, how many regrets I had." Forster wanted his daughter to say she was sorry. He was asking much more: he wanted her to say his wife had needed him. They sat staring at one another. The cup on the old man's knee, the dress in her lap. Now Father will start again, Zara thought. She pitied Michael for having heard him.

"When I stood up to go, I offered him my hand. I thought for a minute he might take it. I stood there babbling about how much we care about him, how he's a son to me. I used every last guilt-generating relative-of-the-patient line. Hell, I sounded like he could just make the decision and it would all be over. Some doctor you have for a father."

Each year his shoulders slumped a little more in the chair, his hairs grew thinner, whiter where they feathered around his forehead. She saw his pale form against the white nasturtiums of the chair and suddenly she felt sorry for him. "Daddy," she said. "Michael probably didn't even hear you. You couldn't possibly have remained objective with him. His silence does it. You'll do anything to fill it."

"I couldn't be objective with your mother either. I wasn't good to her." She always wanted *you*, he thought. Even at the end, even then.

Don't whine, she wanted to tell him. Please don't whine again. Why must everyone always lean on me? Why isn't there ever anyone to bolster me? Zara told him he had done the best he could, the best any human being could have. Slowly Zara's stitches became stems, the eyes and beaks of birds secured to cloth. How much do you have to sacrifice? she asked herself. How much?

"I remember when you and Michael first came home to live here, how you both radiated with the little gifts and favors you gave each other. You were happy, Zara—"

"It was bad before that."

"Difficult maybe. It's always difficult at first."

"Michael slept with Ellie Vincent, Father. He slept with

Marilyn Kleinliebelink. He's probably loved up every woman in this town while I've been thinking of ways to cure his problem."

"Zara, Michael wouldn't sleep with Miss Kleinliebelink. Who told you such an awful rumor?"

"*Michael* told me! He told me on my birthday. He probably planned it that way, to tell me when it would hurt the most."

"Oh, Zara, Michael hasn't been responsible for a long time now. You mustn't hate him for it."

"Not responsible? Why is Michael *never* accountable when he's hurting me? What about me for once?" She could not hold back the tears then, and the old man rushed across the room and pulled her close to him, as he had done so many times, thinking: Zara is like her mother, Zara is a dear child.

"I've come to take you home for the weekend, Michael." He stood and followed her to the car. He didn't ask to drive; he didn't comment on the scenery, the habits and actions of the people on the street, as he customarily had before his illness. He didn't acknowledge her presence. His eyes were fixed on the windshield wiper, its rubber wedged tight against the glass.

"We're home," Zara said, pulling up the lane. "Bridie has prepared a dinner with all your favorites. Rock Cornish hen, just the way you like it. She's been planning dessert for days." Michael nodded his head as if he were barely tipping his hat, as if he were lowering the top of his skull into his lower mandible.

They played cards: three kings, two queens.

"My God, you've got the luck. You're trouncing me."

They played for an hour, Michael winning nearly every hand and winning without comment. Zara was not trying to lose to him, although she had considered it. "Do you want to quit and have a drink before dinner in the den? One glass of wine won't hurt; it might be good for us."

Michael shuffled the cards and dealt them. He won again. She talked about the new play she was writing. She said everything she could to fill the silence. Then she won the hand, and after that she could not stop winning.

Fifteen minutes later Michael folded up the deck. In the dining room he sat down at his usual place. He spread his napkin on his lap; he poised his fork above the empty plate.

"It'll be a while, Michael," Mrs. McGehry called from the kitchen, seeing him as she mashed the potatoes.

"Michael doesn't want to miss anything," Zara shouted to her, shutting the door to the kitchen. "He knows how good a cook you are."

"Let's go have a glass of wine before dinner, Michael." Michael watched the flowers in the center of the table, surveying their golden tones.

"All right," she said. "I'll pour you a little in here." Opposite him, she sat down, watching the fork suspended above his napkin. Michael's wine was untouched, his face unchanged, when Forster took his place, and when Mrs. McGehry brought in dinner ten minutes after that.

"Good evening, Michael," Forster said, unfolding his napkin. "It's good to have you home."

Michael gave no reply.

Resigning himself to this situation, Doctor Montgomery pointed at the trees, the oaks and maples in the valley covered with snow. He nearly forgot his dinner.

"When I was young," he said, "and we had just come here, Zara's mother started an arboretum. I thought it was frivolous. You see the large trees there. She told me if I didn't want to help her dig, she'd dig the holes and plant the trees herself. Well, she started in with the shovel, and I

came down to watch her, feeling more guilty all the time."
Forster Montgomery took a sip of wine and looked at Zara.
He continued:

"I told her I'd rather have tennis courts. I remember
exactly what she said then. 'That is bloomin' folly, Forster.'
That was how she said it.

" 'Maybe it is,' I said, 'and maybe it isn't. All the same I
want one.'

" 'Forget it,' she said, 'and get a shovel.' So I did. And
there they are, beautiful trees. I bought a new hammock for
the summer, Michael. You'll have to try it."

Michael sighed through his nostrils, lips sealed. "Those
beeches, too?" Zara quickly interjected.

"Yes, of course, that whole area. She had the entire living room filled with them when we started. I had to help
her just to get some walking space in the house. And when
we finished she said I'd done it all for myself and I should
be glad of it. 'Of course not,' I told her. 'I did it all for you,
Katie. I'd do anything for you.'

" 'Sure thing, Forster,' she said. 'Now let's have dinner.'
Three weeks later was my birthday. 'Let's go for a walk in
the arboretum,' she said. And so we walked through all
those sticks she called trees."

As Zara looked toward the window where her father was
pointing, she caught sight of a cold, hard face staring at
her. "Michael, would you like the salt and pepper? I didn't
mean to hoard them."

She held the shakers out to him, but he lowered his attention, pushing his fork around his plate. "Go on now,
Daddy. You were walking in Mummie's woods."

Briefly Forster glanced at Michael. "Is everything all
right, Michael?" Michael would not look up from his potatoes. "So anyway," Forster said, slicing quietly through the
butter, "there were hardly any leaves at all; I thought it was

quite unimpressive. Then she was proposing pine trees. 'Jesus, Katie,' I said. 'We already have pines, we have every conceivable kind of tree. What do you want to plant pines for?' " Forster Montgomery's eyes shifted toward his son-in-law. "I'll never forget her sitting on that rock. She was already in her fourth month and she had on some sort of yellow frock."

"Fourth month?" Zara asked.

"No! But that's the point. The bigger she got with you, the more plants she had to start. She was obsessed. Seeds and sproutlings." Forster pulled some tender white meat from the hen and chewed awhile, smiling out onto the terraces that swept down the wooded land toward the lake. He took a few bites, recalled himself then, and continued. " 'Now don't just walk over there without thinking about pines,' she said to me. 'You have to imagine pines all the way over to the far lot and back. Think you can do that?'

" 'I guess I probably can,' I said. 'I guess I won't like it much though.'

" 'You'll like it all right,' she said. 'Just think pines. Listen for the needles crunching under your feet; they'll feel like cushions.'

"An impossible woman, I thought. All these crazy projects. But when we reached the top of the hill over there and looked down onto the meadow, I saw it. She had our tennis court laid. Clay, just like I wanted. She was coming over the hill behind me carrying the net and the rackets. And I'll be damned if she didn't insist on playing. She beat me worse than I've ever been beaten in my life."

Michael had eaten everything but his mashed potatoes. He put down his fork at the conclusion of Dr. Montgomery's recollections, brushing the wineglass with his sleeve. Together they watched it spill. They watched the pool grow wider, creeping like a flood of embarrassment, running under his plate. Michael pressed his thumb into the center of it, the wine circling like a meniscus at the top of a test tube. He licked the droplet from his finger, smiling, obviously pleased.

"I'll get a cloth," Zara said. She came back to wipe the area around him. His forearm rested against the table edge. "Michael, could you please move your arm?"

Forster watched his son-in-law sitting there. He waited. "Michael, it would be nice if you would move your arm for Zara." Zara picked up his arm, wiping under it; she sponged his shirt and set his arm onto its place. When she sat down again, Forster Montgomery was glaring at his son by marriage, Michael staring back.

"There's applecake, Father," she said.

"Yes," he said. "I suppose there is."

Michael sank his fork into the potatoes on his plate. Swiftly he raised them with his utensil, flicking them like an insect across the room, hitting his wife on the cheek.

That evening Zara found him sitting on the edge of the bed, holding his hardened self in his hands, tears running down his face. She sang to him:

> "Gute Nacht, gute Nacht, bis alles wacht,
> Gute Nacht, gute Nacht, bis alles wacht.
> Schlaf' aus deine Freude, schlaf' aus dein Leid.
> Der Vollmond steigt, der Nebel weicht,
> Der Vollmond steigt, der Nebel weicht,
> Und der Himmel da oben, wie ist erso weit.
> Und der Himmel da oben, wie ist erso weit."

"You'll be better soon, Michael," she said, wrapping her legs around him in sympathy. *Nothing will happen.* "You'll see, darling. You'll see."

Zara watched her father's nurse rush by with a large syringe. "Alfred Minter broke his wrist. Hear him scream?" Alice cocked her ear toward the door as she went in. The child, yelping his apprehension when he saw the needle, forgot his pain.

Zara felt she didn't need to make the test to know, but she took the bottle and the blue plastic testing plate from the laboratory shelf. In the women's room she added her urine to the solutions. Two times Michael had come home from the hospital on passes. Two times Zara had felt his warmth, the signs of his improvement. Slowly she moved the plate back and forth. Always there had been the joke of the baby born juggling an IUD in its hands and a great deal of laughter in its throat. She hadn't planned this. How could she have come to believe that nothing between them could happen?

The control remained the same as she swirled the plate. The other turned white, coagulated to confirm her suspicions, to confirm the opposite irrepressible hope.

Just after she had replaced the bottle, Alice popped out again. "Hey, Zara," she said, "will you help us with this kid? I can't ask his father, he's already passed out once." Alice gestured toward the waiting room. "Sedated."

Forster Montgomery checked the X rays on the viewer again and told Alfred to be quiet. The boy wasn't feeling anything—he had made sure of that. Zara and Alice took the elbow while Forster pulled at the wrist. "Quite a break you've got there, Alfred. Tell Zara how you fell off your new electric motor scooter." Alice rolled her eyes; the child was only eight.

Alfred was pouting while they tried to align his bones. His arm was red from their manipulations, rubbery from the anesthetic. Dark hair fringed his sullen face. To Zara, his eyes resembled Michael's.

Zara smoothed the boy's cowlick down and gripped his arm again. "So you're a motorcycle man?"

He chewed on his lip, watching the workings with his arm.

"Your father's in the other room waiting for you to get patched up," she said. "Who gave you your motor scooter? It must be hard, driving one on the ice."

They stepped behind the screen while Forster X-rayed the arm again. "Hate wrists," he said. "Of all the bones, it must be wrists I despise the most." He offered Alfred a choice of colors for his cast. "Be careful," he advised. "This is an important decision in a young man's life."

"I've got news for you," Zara said.

Forster went to the basket and pulled out the next patient's chart.

"You'll have to tell me later. The gall-and-spleen crew is out there again."

Zara picked up her car keys. "When do you think you'll be home?"

"Doctor," Alice said, fetching the restrainers, "you'd better check out the room at the end."

Forster Montgomery shrugged. "See what I mean? It might be hours."

Zara asked if they wanted her help, but the medical students were coming in. She took the car home again, thinking about Michael. It would only be a week until he had another pass. Once he had wanted children, now she didn't know what his reaction would be. She didn't know whether she could subject a child of hers to Michael. Her hands on her belly, she waited for a light to change.

Bridie's car was gone when Zara pulled into the drive. There was no one to tell. Zara sat in the garage a long while listening to the radio: "Baby, baby, I need your love," they sang. Every day she drove over to see Michael sitting in a white sunroom in the same sunken chair, watching the daylight rise and fall through the metal grating at his window sill.

She wrapped her coat around her, each step sinking through the crusted snow. She followed a path through the trees down to the shore.

"When I learned I was going to have you, Zara," her mother had said, several years before she died, "my heart swelled like a balloon. But no one had to tell me I was pregnant really. It may come as a surprise to your father, but sometimes the body is connected to the mind."

Electrolytes are also freely exchanged across the placenta, each at its own specific rate. Although a "sodium pump" may be operating in the placental membrane, the concentrations of electrolytes in maternal and fetal plasma are essentially identical.

Her mother told her how she used to sit on the porch and rock, singing to Zara in the womb. She said, "When you have your first baby, let me know and I'll come. A woman always wants her mother there when she has her first child. My mama was in England when you were born."

At dinner Forster expounded on his day; he had forgotten his daughter's excitement. "What a kid!" he said. "Littlest Murphy had a laceration that ran across the forehead and split the brow. That boy didn't cry out once. He insisted Alice hold the mirror so he could watch me suturing. Wanted to know if fishing line would work."

Forster poured her a little wine. "I like a kid like that, curious. He'll be smart." Her father wanted a child in the house, she was certain of that. Zara watched him cut his steak along the grain. "Why are you smiling so much?"

She waited, watching him eat, watching him looking at her after every bite.

"Tell me."

"Do you think Art Kleman will take his vacation by the end of June or will he take an extra month?"

"He said he might go next month, for Christmas. Why?"

Perhaps, she thought, I shouldn't tell him. Perhaps I should decide this myself first. Suddenly then, she was blurting it out: "I want him to deliver my baby in July if he's around."

"Zara. Zara." Forster nearly whisked the tablecloth from under his plate as he pulled his daughter toward him. "Wait. Sit down. You barely ate." He called to the kitchen for Mrs. McGehry to bring back the last piece of meat. "This will be a happy homecoming for Michael. This will bring him out of his slump."

"Do you think it will?"

"Don't be foolish, daughter."

"*Kinder, Kinder,*" he said as he went to bed.

Friday Michael wanted to take the old road home after the papers were signed and he had been released for another weekend. She drove so he could watch as they passed through each village. "Everything is so white," he said. "I never want to see that place again."

"It won't be much longer."

The boughs were weighted with snow—the western sides streaked with white to the smallest twigs. The edges of banks along the road were sharp and high at the sides from the plowing crew that morning.

"I don't know how they stand it," he said.

"What?" She thought he meant the psychiatric ward, the walls staring white at him, the coats of all his keepers.

"The cattle," he said. "Look at them out there in the cold, pawing for grain until someone remembers to get in the truck with the radio playing and pitch them a little hay."

"You'd think they'd huddle together," Zara said.

"Yes. Huddle." Each one stood alone, brown against the snow, barely moving.

"It'll be spring soon. There will be grass. And little calves."

"Yes," he said. "Winter meat."

They passed through Applington looking at the clap-board fronts on Main Street, following the road into the country again. Suddenly Michael turned to the side window and shouted at her to stop.

"What's the matter?" she asked, pulling over.

He got out and shut the door. She followed him into the ditch where a small spruce jutted from a snowbank. Cranberries were strung around it. Oranges hung from the limbs.

"We can decorate our tree when we get home if you want," she said. He put his arms around her, and she told him about the baby then.

Michael went back to the car, got in, and slammed the door, eyes glazed. When they were halfway home, he spoke. "I suppose you did this to patch things up," he said.

All night he sat in the den while she imagined the two of them, specters walking hand in hand. Conceived in the dark of illness, the child might learn this depression, too; the child might learn the small perversions, the erratic wrath of father to child, of a father to a mother. She asked herself, is it fair to the child to do this? She dozed and woke and dozed again. A shutter that did not bang haunted her in the night. A rush of wind, a claw of tangled brush at the windowpane. She reached across the bed. *Old man, old man, the shutters are loose again. They bang; they pound against the house, old man.* The sheet was cold under her hand. All were gone. Michael, Mother, all the rest, gone to death or indifference or insanity.

Her father came peeking to see why that night Michael sat alone in the den, why Zara was in bed, why Michael and Zara were not with him at his midnight ritual of nog and crackers. "Zee," he said. "Would you like to talk?"

"No." The answer was clipped in her throat; she rephrased and softened it in her mind.

Forster pulled the quilt up an inch to cover her shoulders; he tucked the blanket at the mattress edge. "If you change your mind, you roust me out. No—" he said, "lean on the buzzer. You know me, this old character revs much better by remote control." Awkwardly he chuckled and shifted his weight under his nightshirt, looking at wires that had crept across the floor since his wife was ill.

Zara reassured him; she forced a smile. She told him half of it: "Michael can't sleep and he won't talk to me."

"Have you told him about the baby?"

Zara lied to him again.

"Well, you tell him about the baby. That will make him happy. He'll sleep fine."

"I want to wait."

"Don't wait too long. If you need to talk, just wake me up."

When he was gone, she reconsidered, called his name. In the room two doors down, he snored—a whispered current, followed by a puff of wind.

The Montgomerys' tree stood ten feet high in the living room between two chairs. Their backs were wrapped into arms where wooden faces were carved. Above Zara, a woman's face, the hair flowing down around her. Across the room Michael stared at the Christmas pine and then at his wife. He gripped his chair. Two fingers of each hand covered the wooden lions' eyes; he would have gouged them if they had been softer.

Every year they made new ornaments, carving them from balsa wood, painting them with bright acrylics. Each year she thought about the winters when she was small and she lay with her mother on her bed, watching a boy with a long green scarf skating on the lake below.

Michael's feet were laced up then in new black shoe skates, green corduroy pants tucked into orphan socks that old women knit for him. He was the youngest ever to cut the ice. "Little brave one," they crooned from the home for the aged. "Look how he falls on his bottom and jumps up again." When Michael went home to his latest foster home, they sat down to knit for him. In the morning when his ice etching flamed in the early sun, the women stood and read his message:

LOVE—

TO THE LADIES OF THE SHORE

FROM MICHAEL O'DEA

"Michael," the women said, "is a priceless child."

During one holiday season, Zara got a fleck of paint on the carpet; there was still a streak of blue at the carpet edge. "Don't hang that ornament," Michael said before it happened. "It's still wet."

"I'll be careful," she said, and then the bough bent and the bell dropped of its own accord.

"Let's start on the tree," she was saying to him now.

"Go ahead," he said. "While you're at it, hang up the little fetus."

Zara's voice came rasping out of her throat as Mrs. McGehry rounded the table. "That's right," Bridie said.

"You cry. Can't even talk, poor sparrow." She helped Zara off with the sweater and placed her fingertips at the collarbone, touching gently the bottom of the swelling. "Has Forster seen this?"

No, Zara motioned, waving her hands frantically. No. He must not see it.

"Of course not. Let's put something cool on it. Would that feel better?"

The old woman retrieved a clean dish towel from the drawer and wet it under the faucet. What kind of instrument could have made such an injury? She cracked ice into the center of the towel. I would kill that man, she thought. She pounded ice with a hammer. "Hold this on your throat now, and hold this dry one under it. Who did this, Zara Montgomery? Did Michael do this to you?"

Zara moved her head. Yes, then no, then yes again. Tears exploded over her hands onto the compress.

A creeping worm, Mrs. McGehry thought. "Do you want to tell me about it? Do you want to write it down to tell me?"

Against the breasts of her old governess, Zara buried her face. No, she motioned, holding the old woman tighter. In the kitchen, Bridie held her, the compress cold and comforting between them.

The stables were made of wood when her mother was young, when the flames went up around the horses. This her mother had told her. Young boys rushed in to save them; they led the frightened animals out to the pasture, out to the sky and fields where they could run. But horses are like people when they are afraid, her mother said. They run back to where they feel the safest. They run home. They bound burning walls to return. In the morning Kathryn had found them: flesh turned toward the walls in each stall, toward their last source of air.

Ach, es entschwindet mit thauigem Flügel
Mir auf den wiegenden Wellen die Zeit;
Morgen entschwindet mit schimmerndem Flügel
Wieder wie gestern und heute die Zeit,
Bis ich auf höherem strahlenden Flügel
Selber entschwinde der wechselnden Zeit.

After the initial lag period, which lasts until the appearance of the primitive streak (which also corresponds to the time when placental function becomes established), the rate of fetal growth in both mammals and birds conforms to a cubic law as related to time.

The Women's Clinic was in an old house and Zara sat waiting. Three other women were in the room. They were young; they held hands with friends and lovers, chatting as if they had not noticed the house trembling around them. "What's that vibration?" Zara asked when she first came in the door.

"Vacuum aspirator," the woman said as she took her money. The floors did not quake at the hospital; they were made of concrete and steel beams. Then she could hear the whirring.

"I'd like to go first," Zara said, afraid she would change her mind. "If no one cares, that is." But the others had their friends waiting. My husband is waiting, too, she thought. He sits in a hospital and stares into a fire that no longer burns.

The others were very young. One of them was fourteen years old; her parents had signed her papers. Her long thin hair falling across her face, she leaned forward as one of her friends selected a record. The music drowned the sound of the aspirator. It cushioned nerves while the house trembled and rested awhile. Their talk was as it was in a hospital room, superficial, high-strung with unspoken emotion.

An hour passed before they were ushered upstairs into a bedroom. The walls slanted warm and yellow beside the ruffled curtains. It was the room, the woman said, where they would rest.

It was a room that spoke of grandmothers, of women collected together. Here comfort had been the easing of generations. Skirts had been lifted in this room and thighs had been touched. Here the moist hair of infants had pushed past women's pubic bones. Stillness had filled this room.

When the first woman left for her procedure, Zara asked for an extra blanket. The attendant covered her; she was brushing the hair from Zara's face when Zara fell asleep.

The women of the town were seated at ice-cream tables under a glass dome in the sand, fluttering linen napkins, holding a parasol each. Zara found a table toward the center and ordered coffee. "Hello," she said, but no one answered. They were speaking as if a child were sitting with them, but she couldn't see one.

"Poor child," someone said. "Nowhere to go, no one."

"If someone doesn't find out who she is, they'll send her to the orphanage."

Bridie McGehry tssked. "A shame," she said. "Pretty child like that turning into a ragamuffin at the county home."

"Yes," Mrs. Willoughby said. "She'll run with that Applington crowd by the time she's wearing stockings."

"Motorcycle gangs," Mrs. McGehry said. "That's what happens to those girls out there. And you know what goes with that."

The whole room nodded in unison.

"Where's the child?" Zara asked, but no one looked.

"People shouldn't have children they can't take care of,"

Mrs. McGehry said. "Shouldn't even do the act that makes them."

"Where's the child?" she asked.

"Little bit of a thing," McGehry said.

Zara stood up. "Where are you keeping the child?" she demanded.

The waitress came across the sand with her coffee then. Behind her followed a little girl with auburn hair curling down her back and around her forehead. "She's mine," Zara said. She looked like photographs Zara had studied in the family album, but so much smaller. She came only to the waitress's knee.

"My daughter," Zara said and reached for her.

Mrs. McGehry swept the child onto her lap. "How can you be her mother?" Mrs. McGehry said. "You have a lunatic for a husband."

"But she's mine," Zara said. "Her blood is the same." In the dream Zara watched herself as if from a great distance.

"Are you still cold?" the nurse was asking as she woke.

Zara put her sweater over the dressing gown they had given her. "Yes," she said. "Is it colder in there?"

"No, we keep it just a little warmer there. You might even be too hot with that sweater on."

The woman across the room rolled over to face the wall; she rested.

"I have to go to the bathroom," Zara said. In the small room it was warmer. Why have I been in the wrong room, she wondered, when I could have been in here? She sat on the edge of the tub staring at runs in the paint. She realized then that the face in the dream, the child's face, had been her own. How many times had she heard her own mother say: "When you were born, Zara, I said to myself: Here is my own child, born to me as a second chance. Can you imagine my glee, Zara! A second chance in this wretched world."

As she lay on the table, she thought of Michael's story. She draped her knees over the metal leg rests as she thought of villages beside a long path, leaves that brush a belly extended for life, a body encasing a tomb.

The attendant stood beside her.

"I'm going to touch you now," the doctor said. He entered her body with his instruments.

There are four common mechanisms of transport across the placenta. She would carry this baby all her life, rather than cut her away like a growth.

"There will be a little sticking now as I give you these injections," the doctor said. With the stabbing in her abdomen, perspiration beaded on her forehead and the nausea began.

"You were right about the sweater," Zara said. The woman wiped her forehead with a cloth; she held her hands.

"Now this is the dilation," he said. "You'll feel pain. Some cramping now."

The pain came in a solid thrust. It did not stop.

"And now the curette."

"Don't move, dear," he said. "You mustn't raise up like that. A few minutes more and it'll be over."

The woman gripped her hands. "I'm sorry," she said, wiping Zara's tears. As the woman squeezed her fingers, Zara thought, This woman would kiss me if he were not here; she would place her lips on my forehead.

Zara could hear a machine; she could not feel its vibrations. Somewhere a woman walked with a child in her belly. She heard the villagers gathering around her. Flesh mother, they whispered. Immortal one, they wept. Stone child.

I look down the long, narrow corridor where once I completed my psychiatric rotation as a student. I will not be coming back to this ward. Today I will leave him here. I will begin, for the first time, my own life. Mary Andreason's hand tightens on my shoulder. "You can be thankful, Zara, that Michael's not like her." The nurse nods toward Madeline in the television lounge. "No good at all."

We can hear the soap opera going on, a show about a medical clinic. "Hey, doc," a patient is asking Michael, "is that the way it is?"

"The doctor doesn't want to talk to lunatics," Madeline sneers. "Can't you see that?"

The man hangs his head. A farmer, his chin on the bib of his overalls.

"That's not true," I say to him. "Michael is busy thinking."

"Yes," Madeline says. "That's right—thinking." Mary Andreason shrugs as the lipsticked cross passes abruptly by her. A white pillowcase is fastened to Madeline's hair. I can see the flowered housecoat in front of the fireplace as she leans toward a chair. She lifts the cushion, retrieving a plastic object.

We watch her return. She stands between Michael and the television screen. "For you," Madeline says. "Take it."

Michael stands, slowly wrapping his fingers around the dish. He looks down at the top of her head, at her face tilted and grinning. Gently she removes the cover for him, as the other patients gather. They look to see her gift: two egg yolks floating in a white plastic bowl.

"That's very nice of you, Madeline," I tell her. Michael is staring at them.

"Shhhh," Madeline says. "Listen. Do you know what these are?" Michael rocks them slowly back and forth, yellow circles floating in a mucus of egg white. Madeline takes hold of his arm: "These are the balls of a monk."

The room is silent, an echo chamber with nothing to echo. Michael lifts his eyes to me, to Madeline. He points toward the center of the bowl. A sound comes from his throat: "For me?" His fingers tap his chest. "Monk," he laughs. "Monk." Before I, or anyone, can answer, he is in his chair, sunken, as if he had never spoken, as if he has never known meaning or words.

"No, they aren't, Michael. No, they aren't. Don't ever think that."

I lean down to where he is cradling the bowl in his hands and kiss him on the forehead. Who is to know how fate is chosen? Or what gives one person a longer life or the will to live? Perhaps Michael will never recover. I only know that there are things that have become important to me now and to others like me. I brush the hair back gently from his face. "You know, I think I loved you because you needed me." His eyes stare out blankly over my shoulder. "We were all vulnerable, Michael. We all were."

Mrs. Willoughby looks away from her living-room window, the vacuum cleaner strung out all over the room. She turns it on, gathering dust, velocity, noise. A lice-ridden bird has, just this morning, nearly careened into the plate glass of Mr. Willoughby's reading room. Tree hydrangea lean toward the house turning purple, dirty brown. Paint peels at Montgomery's next door where, before, paint did not peel. Something is going on.

Mabel Willoughby is scouring the floor for particles, for lint, with a cold steel hose. Around corners, into cracks and stuffed appendages of chairs, along floorboards and bookshelves, the back of the TV, in and along and under. Around and beneath. Each with its own attachment. With the long plastic hose, she will investigate the dark, subtle folds of her drapes. She throws the front door open, props it with a chair on the porch. "Airing out, airing out," she hums, keeping the words discreetly to herself.

The room is immaculate now, the air clean. She would shut the front door, put away her vacuum machine, but there on the door jamb lurks something not dust, not fur, an extra line in the painting, in the sentence an extra word. Before the hose the dust kitty flees, and Mrs. Willoughby is after it. A sail full-blown in her gray corduroy. Caught between the currents of nature and machinations, that soft curling of lint rises and falls, deigns toward the carpet, flies toward the porch.

The nozzle is out again, hooked up. In a moment the source of Mabel Willoughby's agitation is gone, but still she is there: a regular frenzy, unpacified—her vacuum cleaner traveling into territories previously unknown. Dirt has slept for years in the refuge of front-step cracks. The base of each of those redwood planters: a society for the dead. Marigold petals, stray leaves have infiltrated everything.

The nozzle devours, skims, prods, sucks. Mabel Willoughby is smiling: triumphant. The cobwebs are down, the railing swept pure. And the stoop: each pore is being treated again. With the hose it is cured until, at the bottom, standing on the walk, Mabel Willoughby looks. Down the walk there are leaves. Like a lover she looks on them, leaning on her hose, committed, intrigued.

MABEL WILLOUGHBY VACUUMS HER YARD!

And what if she had? Mabel Willoughby is lying on her immaculate couch, smelling salts in her hands. This time she has done it, she knows. She's brushed it. She's come close. A serious affair, dirt, the real thing. I can hardly believe it, she says.

It is hard to say when one story leaves off in this town and another sticks its feet in, as I have often said to Mrs. Willoughby: we lean together between the roses over the clean white fence. I have been like a cat myself—in and out of everything, though I, unlike Mabel Willoughby, have rarely said a word—for the past fifty years. And they have always called us that—as soon as we got old: cats. About this I have understood less than one jig on a fishing rig: as I age, this surprises me more and more. A powerful indignation has risen up late in my time: about women, about four-legged animals with fur, with tails in the air and all their private parts displayed. Animals who are significant in their speed and intelligence, who leave no emotion undisplayed and for all of that seem covert. The use of words breaks both ways. When I was first a married woman, my husband said to me, "Kitten, kitten," as he laid me up on the counterpane, all my yellow hair spread softly out. Not one hair he touched remains: grown through years he's never seen, it has fallen out or been lost to shears. Kathryn Montgomery had a pretty story she used to tell about such things: *Atropos* and the other two of similar name. No part he touched is the same. Skinny, skinny limbs and the softer parts gone to wrinkles like a luscious cloth mislaid. Every cell he knew has been shed like petals off a tulip tree to lie on the ground in a funeral heap that after the winter disappears. I have looked at myself that close: looking again for him in the convolutions of my skin.

That is who I am more and more these days: a woman, young and old, who stands in the middle of the street watching all the old cobblestones stretching through the center of everything, through the town, toward fields, toward something beyond—that no one knows. When I look down these roads, I can't tell which way they go:

The Great War had begun: up and down the streets of Lake Marian the military caps bobbed up and down, boots clattering along the streets like the sound of horses raging against new automobiles. And we were all afraid. Even in a casual glance out your window you could see the young men turning toward a sharpness—like that of small, clipped birds—in their finer gestures; the youngest women in their hourglass clothes stood on the brick streets in front of their spindled, porched homes. With their palms they shaded their foreheads as if to flatten the vision out: watching the morning departures cut the row of elms in two. "Kitten," he said, and it was as if two pieces of the softest crepe had touched. It was the only time when we did not think as a part of the rest. It was the only time when we did not think our legs, too, would become pairs of sticks that marched; that someone could lay them out and set fire to all or some of them: the ones we loved. And there was nothing to be done. In modern times, there has been an upsurgence of the public voice, but then—it seemed—we had none at all, or what we had had was gone. If I could only write it down the way it was, then maybe something of it would not be lost. As it is, the good times rise up and fall before the bad. Life is all memory, and memory is a series of little stones set up on the ground to say: *It was.* That is what I am each day as I go around the house: bones grinding, as in a mill, against the past. That is what everyone is: painted monuments, carefully arranged, that a little thing —like rain—can wear away. One day the light strikes some in different ways. Teddy I did not come home from the war; Teddy II burgeoned into thirty years. Everyone saw things they could not have imagined for themselves, things everyone now knows. But no one knows what it was—for anyone else personally; and in the end no one cares. In the end we are all like a little dust on the sofa arm; we are all swept away into what we were.

I went to the Montgomerys' nearly a middle-aged woman. It is this time I remember most clearly in my life, this and when I was young. At the Montgomery house, I was and was not a part of them. It was like moving from seat to seat at the bandshell in the park, watching a story being told in actors' words. But before each act I laid out the knives and forks, made up their beds, set straight—as in a ritual—every button, every hem. Sometimes I said: If I had put fresh flowers on the table it would not have turned out this way. I carried out their leavings. My own life was a birthday unobserved.

There is a certain sadness in all of it. All my life I have fled from strife—from the moment when the clean white boat carried me out of Ireland to another place. I have been a failure in the smaller things, too, that might have set things right if I had only spoken out when they first emerged. "Bridie," Zara once said to me, "you always know what to say." She wanted to be like me. She was a child; she didn't see that I acted only when it mattered not so much to me, and that was nearly every time. If I had said, "Teddy, no," perhaps he would not have gone. Only in my old age did it come to me that I had had a way, and lost it. Perhaps somewhere in my early days women had done it, had not been paralyzed, had not lived to a sad end when they cried out in an arthritic sleep.

And those were the only times I had the comfort—those few times when I was practically a child—of a man between my legs. Once I said to Zara Montgomery with tears rolling down my cheeks: "How have the students done it? Could we have stopped them from going then?"

"I don't know," she said. "These days the power is in the voice." And I cried, an old woman, because we had never thought of it.

I am convinced that what Teddy and I had that one year was good. When I first moved to the Montgomerys', Forster would put it to Kathryn so long that I would shiver under all the blankets and percale. It's good for them, I said. And then there would be nothing for weeks and weeks. She would lay her hand on his neck as he came in for dinner: women's signs; but it was as if he could not read. Now—I would say—Teddy would have turned to me, we would go upstairs. But there was nothing until she actually had to ask him for it. Then he would put it aside, considering, for perhaps an hour or a day. In all the asking and waiting, Katie lost her own propulsion. She was like a vase waiting for a strange hand to stick the flowers in. Teddy would not, I said. And then Forster would put it to her hard—when he wanted it. I would lie in my single cot and cry how a man like that could live to take a woman's sparkle right out of her voice for the sake of his own control and a man like gentle Teddy could be taken to a foreign country and shot through the head by people he had never seen. How could it be right? And Forster Montgomery so jolly to everybody else! so affectionate to her when people stopped by to take a word with them. How can he keep up this act? I would ask myself. But he kept it up; it was Katie who could not pretend, who responded with abrogation, and for that was considered slightly mad: a woman to be shunned. And with the daughter: much the same. She drove Michael to the madhouse, the townspeople say: She did not stick around to see him get out, to see this fine thing he has made of himself. Though Mabel Willoughby has been my friend, I will say that she—like them —has a streak like a mean gruel boiling up her pulse. She will not see a thing straight even though the facts are laid before her on a plate. She will not see the confusion of things. But she has been kind to me. It has been a friendship of information—about the way to plant asparagus, trim the hedges back, make a soufflé rise up, the slight change in color at a petal's edge: all my life has become. There has been much to accept.

Today an old woman digs up carrots and plants them in the flat bed dirt to be taken into the cellar bins. My, how the veins stick out on my dirty hands. Like little creeks among the carrot greens. I have not done this since the Depression. I have found hobbies for myself. This afternoon that very young man from down the street will come to carry them. He has great dark eyes: the kind that, if he's not careful, will lead him into sorrow. Today he will stoop down beside me and admire the perfect rows. He does this not so much out of politeness as out of a curiosity in something like myself that has grown so old. He will quiz me about the events that he has discovered in books. When I don't remember, I will make up things to please him. He will throw back his sandy hair and laugh. He has long firm arms; soon he will go away to college. Though he is one of the smart ones, he does not suspect that a young girl kneels beside him. A young girl with soft blonde hair on her shoulders and breasts with tips as pink as petals. He hears the young girl's laugh; he follows me around the garden, the house for hours. He gives me a buss on the cheek when he goes home for supper.

Tomorrow I go to see Zara Montgomery at her clinic. She has written it down for me on my calendar. *Check-up.* 4:15. It has been a long time since she moved to another part of town. "Will you get one load of that?" Mabel said. "Moving out of your nice house, Bridie. And into what, I ask you."

I tried to explain it to her, but then I just nodded. "Yes," I said, "I think I am using peat moss this year around my new camellias." She thinks I am slightly dotty.

"Peat moss of what brand?" she asks.

Zara Montgomery's clinic is the first floor of the old house she bought at the edge of town. It's true that in comparison with this one, it looks an element on the side of ragged. The porch rambles out along an unrolled ground, and in the summer patients sit there in plastic chairs beating out the heat with pieces of paper she gives them. They can write down their complaints before she looks at them. "If you write it down first," she has often told me, "you won't forget the important things when I've got you trapped in here flapping around in a skimpy sheet." Some days when I have hobbled past, I have thought it looked more like a pleasant seaside resort: everyone there scribbling letters or snoozing in the sun with the stubs of yellow pencils stuck behind their ears.

Bones is what she fixes. When I broke my hip three winters ago, she said, "Think of a pin cushion, Bridie." I carry around a needle of steel that Zara Montgomery pounded into me, and everyone is amazed how good it works. Even Forster Montgomery will say it in the relaxation of his retirement. Sometimes he stares after me when I'm on my way from the downstairs to the upstairs. "She's done you right, by God," he shouts after me.

"I will hide the scar in this wrinkle," Zara said when she came to the hospital, and I thought: How touching that a young woman can understand that such a thing still matters.

"Who knew you had such beautiful skin, Bridie!" she said to me with that nightgown hoisted up around my bird waist, my hip split in half by way of a dash against the sidewalk. It was the way she said it made me smile. I was yowling, and then she said it. I smiled up at her.

Zara Montgomery has not had an easy time of it in this town; still the words go around about her: how she lives in a little house when she could stay in the big one; how in the early evenings she stands out back under the summer trees throwing punches at the air, scaring men when she has forgot to swing the gate shut; how in the evenings they can hear the sound of the upright piano ringing out its notes so cheerfully that it sounds like death to them. At night, they say, she has small groups of friends gathered in the back yard behind the tall fence—too tall, they say, for anything good to be going on behind it. Their laughter, and their singing, sets the neighbors' teeth on edge. Later, they can hear her through the open window where the curtains drift out for the breeze. They swear they hear her sobbing names. They do not sometimes know whether to call it wanton or to call it grief. And her father would not have retired, they say—though he was past the age of retirement —if not for all the talk about her. He cannot hold his head up, they say, for all the clacking.

In all of it, perhaps there is some truth. Over the years I have noticed in Lake Marian that the people here are not keen enough for invention. Distortion is the above and beyond. If I were younger, if I could travel more around this town, I would stand out on her corner and listen myself on a summer evening. I would hope to hear, flung out through the sounds of crickets, the cries of love. Out it would float like reassurance—or resurrection—toward the street lamp hanging over my head. I am afraid, however, that it would be the latter: a name, a face, wrenched out unexpectedly from the softness of a dream. And then the terrible voice, unanswered, winding its way along a dark Midwestern street. Every morning she is downstairs, cheerful, working. Why do they complain?

I am eighty-five; I am still walking.

I have asked no one for the names they hear. There are many Michaels in the world—though they would know who I meant. He has become a sort of legend. Still, it is best to keep quiet. I would not add to their rapid conjecture. Perhaps some patient named Michael would be brought up then with her name. Lives are delicate things. Anything could happen.

Zara cannot have forgotten him: Michael O'Dea has lurched up straight out of every obscure mind in this lake-side town. His handsome face is on all the counters at the drugstore and sometimes in the early evening he is on a talk show. And I have never heard a man talk with such lucidity about the small-town life. When he went to the hospital, I said to myself, He is a madman, but there is a nugget of something inviolate in that insanity. Still, I was glad he was gone, I can't say that wasn't true. It is a terrible thing to have a top spinning and spinning crazily in the path that leads from the house out into the world. People fall. When he was committed, his photograph was on the front page of the *Lake Marian Tribune*. Several write-ups followed, and then a flurry of stories creeping toward the back page, smaller and smaller, like something disintegrating. Then there was nothing until several years after she had left him and gone back to medical school. He had been released, an article said; and a little ruffle went through everyone's conversation for a week or two. I thought then, perhaps that madhouse is not unlike an orphanage. He had to go back in his life before he could go on. He had disappeared then; she had her clinic. Certain people came to her: those with less money who did not care whether their doctor had committed a husband, her own; those who knew her from the hospital and the patients they referred—who did not object. Her practice grew a little. He was gone. I think often that that long silence—not knowing where or how he was, or the part she'd played in it—must have been nearly the worst, although their life had been a re-creation of silences from the start. Yes, that part must have been a little like putting on the mourning veil for someone lost at sea: how—and had they?—gone down? Hope and sorrow at each other's throats. And then it was as if he had sent an emissary—one who could neither see nor hear, one who could not be touched or harmed by the people he had known. It was one of those surprises for which everyone lives. He had done it; he had knitted something out of his very flaws and made it good.

"Out! Out!" Mrs. Willoughby cried that day, bursting through the back door. "Out of the house! We're leaving."

"Where are we going?" I said. "I'm fixing up some ice tea for the doctor. Put your frenzy on a chair."

"The doctor can bother for himself this once," she cried; and I knew it was unusual. I got my handbag and we went out: two old women creeping hurriedly toward the drugstore. "There it is!" she burst out when we had arrived at the window. She had her arm linked through mine, leaning me toward the far right corner.

"What is it?" I said. There were the usual little rubber hoses, the pink douching boxes, the rows of brown-capped vitamins, the plastic squeeze toys.

"The magazines!"

I saw it on the cover. *Down Home: A Novel of Insanity.*
And there was Michael O'Dea's extraordinary face staring
right out of the printing, in color. There were his very own
green eyes. Now that is something not even Mabel Willoughby could have predicted in my life. We stood there for
a very long time, leaning against the dusty window. It was
as if whole episodes had flown up in our face. And then the
two of us were banging into one another trying to get inside, calling for the new man to retrieve us a copy—a good
one, not earmarked by an adolescent crowd.

Since that time there has been a lot of it: photographs
and articles. In every shop in town—anywhere an owner
can possibly sell such things—I have seen his novels: the
first one that everyone says is Lake Marian, and now the
other two. Even in the furniture store, on one of their walnut coffee tables, are three copies carefully wrapped in
cellophane. Even though I know Zara Montgomery is
happy for him—and there would be a great jot of relief in
that for her—I wonder how she stands it: everywhere his
green eyes risen up, the boyish look, her husband come
alive again. I have tried to imagine it; I have tried to put
myself in her place.

For years I have heard Lake Marian stirring itself up
into a batter about it. At the courthouse, in the Red Owl, at
McNurty's Five and Dime, beside the boathouse, among
the greasy automobiles that they raise up on metal posts in
the garage:

"Main Street doesn't have a median strip. Why, it's wide
and clean as a Texas smile."

"It says Oklahoma; how would Oklahoma get a lake like
that?"

"That Flory with the red hair, that waitress, does not
seem one iota like the Zara Montgomery I've met. Dr.
Montgomery would never be a waitress who writes up

travelogues—imaginary travelogues they are. What good is imaginary? Where would anybody go?"

"Zara Montgomery is the wife in disguise."

"Of course."

Even Judge Henderson's nephew is twisting still over his chess board. "His father was *not* a lawyer; there was never one mother of his on the P.T.A. Lawyers do not talk like that."

Arm in arm, secretaries walk along the street. "I sat with him just that way. I remember the light streaming in on my face the way he says. He pressed all his fingers into my palm." Perhaps it is just as well that Michael O'Dea is not here to see it, to hear them say: "And what is this? *And speech and wind-swift thought, and all the moods that mold a state, hath he taught himself; and how to flee . . .* Why is that in there all over the place?"

"That is his insanity," they say.

And I wonder if he is happy where he is now. We carry our pasts like heavy shells on our backs wherever we go. Tonight I will try to read the book again, lying under my bed lamp with the thick glass magnifier tilting one way and another over each page. I have tried to read it before; but the story is so lovely that it is too sad for me. The sadness makes my eyes tire, and soon I have closed them. Little scenes come back to me from all over my life; the way the band was set up in the back yard on the day they were married, with all the pretty little cakes laid out like flowers across the white tablecloths. Yellow birds dipped in and out among the fancy dresses of the guests. I remember the day when I was married; and the courthouse seemed no less a moving place.

I close my eyes, and I can remember almost everything that has been my life—from that first childhood memory—so small, so small—in that Dublin room. Even now I can press my small white lips against the inside of that window. I see the church across the narrow street and the men and women clustered in their dark clothes. White lace moves up under a veil. And then they all go in. A man stands in front of the door again, and there is no one else but a woman in a gypsy scarf sitting on the stone stairs. And then they are calling me: "Tea time, tea time, Bridget. Come downstairs, lightly—on your eyebrows."

Once I knew very little, and then I knew more and less —until I thought I knew everything. In all my life I have forgotten only one moment. For seventy years I have lain down, drawn up my white coverlets, and crossed my arms over my breasts waiting for it to come back: a white narcissus out of snow. I remember the day we were married, standing in the courthouse with his palm around my shoulder. I remember him that afternoon in the bedroom without his clothes on, looking at me with his soft eyes. I remember his hand on my knee later that night. Every moment comes back but one. That first afternoon after we were married we lay down and something happened to me for the first time: I know that. Something changed. But I have tried and tried. A whole lifetime I have spent. He took it from me, and I don't even remember what it was. If he were here now, I would ask him: *Did I cry, Teddy. Was it all right, young Teddy Bear?* If only I could remember that one thing, I might understand how it's all been for me and why. But, "Tea time, tea time," Forster Montgomery is calling. These days we sit at the same table, leaning together like two old crows.